SIX BONE
ANTHOLOGY 6

SIX BONE ANTHOLOGY 6

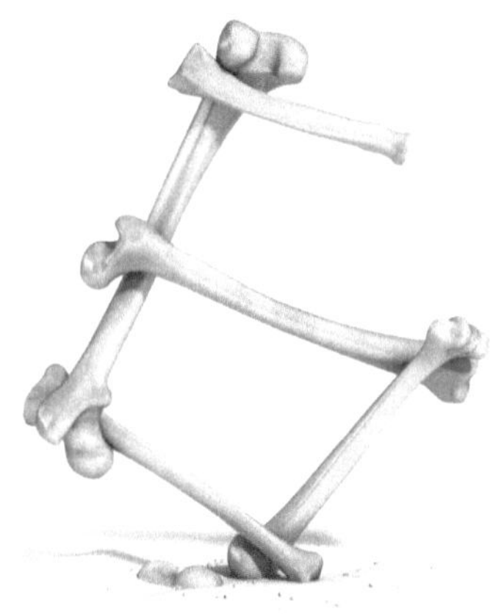

T.K. WRATHBONE

☠ Royal Star Publishing ☠

Skull & Bone is an imprint of Royal Star Publishing
www.royalstarpublishing.com.au

First edition paperback published in 2022
All Rights Reserved, Copyright ©T.K. Wrathbone 2022

Trade Paperback ISBN: 978-1-922307-55-2
Large Print Paperback ISBN: 978-1-922307-56-9
Dust Jacket Hardcover ISBN: 978-1-922307-58-3
Case Laminate Hardcover ISBN: 978-1-922307-57-6
All Clowns Must Die! e-book ISBN: 978-1-922307-49-1
The Demon Resides e-book ISBN: 978-1-922307-50-7
Infestation e-book ISBN: 978-1-922307-51-4
The Bones of Wrath: Terrors e-book ISBN: 978-1-922307-52-1
A catalogue record for this book is available from the National Library
of Australia.

Cover design: Royal Star Publishing and Sleeping Cat Books
Cover photos: istock.com/Koya79
Typesetting in Minion Pro by Royal Star Publishing

CONTENTS

ALL CLOWNS MUST DIE!

CHAPTER ONE

The man picked up the left shoe, inspected it for dust, and then whipped out a handkerchief from the breast pocket of the shirt and dabbed it to the shoe. There was no dust. But he dusted it anyway. Once he was satisfied with its cleanliness, he placed it on the floor at the end of the bed and picked up the right shoe. He inspected it, and dabbed at the imaginary dust. Of course, there was no dust. He'd made sure of that the night before when he'd polished the shoes until they shone. He'd then covered them in wax and polished them again. Plus, he kept the room immaculately clean with all the latest accoutrements from the cleaning aisle in the supermarket.

His work was precise work, and he needed to look good doing it.

He picked up the perfectly folded pair of black socks, unrolled them, and chose the left one. Left always came first. Left leg into left pant leg. Left foot into left sock. Left arm into left shirt arm. He daintily lifted his left leg and expertly pulled the sock onto his foot. His toenails were perfectly pedicured, just as his fingernails were perfectly manicured, and the skin on his feet was just as white as the skin on his hands.

He wasn't a sun person. He slathered himself in sunscreen before dressing, never worked outdoors during the hottest part of the day, or any part of the day, and preferred to do his work indoors. Hence, no suntan and lily-white skin.

After sliding his socked-enclosed left foot into the left shoe, he lifted his right foot and rolled on his right sock. He knew it was his right sock as he labelled *all* of his socks the moment he opened the packet. It was so much easier that way, knowing which sock went on which foot. It saved so much time and money. And he always pinned each pair together before washing them, so they were never lost, or separated from one another. That's how he liked things. Simple, easy, and never lost or separated from each other.

He stuck his right foot into the right shoe and stood, smoothing down the legs of his tan pants. They were the type that never crumpled, no matter how long he sat for, or what cramped position he was in. There were never any creases in his pants.

With a flick at imaginary lint, he picked up the matching suit jacket and carefully laid it over his left arm. As he was right-handed, it always went over his left arm so he could do everything else with his right hand. The suit was always tan. That was the only colour he had suits in. Tan suits and white shirts. No matter what. That's all he wore. Black accessories accompanied them. Shoes, socks, belt, and tie, when he wore one. But that was rare and never during the day.

He picked up his black wallet from the nightstand and slid it into his pants pocket. Next, he picked up a case and opened it to reveal his black, thick-framed glasses. He hated them. But at least they were black. He slid them onto his face, picked up his black sunglasses and hooked them into his shirt pocket. He couldn't see well without the magnification, nor could he see well in the sun without the dark over-lenses. Snapping the case shut, he put it into the small black bag he carried to work and made sure his other items were already in it.

He couldn't leave without those. They were his most prized possessions. A set of such finely handcrafted tools that were almost impossible to find on the black market. The *black* market. His favourite neutral. He'd acquired the tools ten years ago for a small fortune from the descendant of the maker. The man needed money and was selling off the family heirlooms, and he'd offered to buy them. A deal was cut, and he'd become the proud new owner of the most beautifully crafted surgical tools in the entire world.

According to him.

He carefully lifted out the small black pouch, unrolled it, and stood marvelling at the magnificence. Pure silver, ornately designed, expertly crafted. They were the most beautiful tools he'd ever laid eyes on. And he'd been the proud owner of them for ten years. Of course, he cleaned them after every use. He had to;

otherwise little bits of flesh would find their way under the ornate handles. And he couldn't have that.

A small smile etched itself onto his face as he gazed down lovingly. But only for a few moments. The smile disappeared and he rolled up the pouch and placed it carefully back into his small black bag. He had to treat them well for they had served him well.

The keys were the last item he picked up. Three keys on three rings, hanging from one small black key pouch. The house, the car, the office. Three keys, that's all that was needed.

Ever.

He placed them into his left hand, hung his small case over his left wrist by the strap, and carefully lifted his tan jacket to glance at his black leather banded watch.

It was almost time.

He walked into the room and over to the bureau under the window and contemplated what to do next. The plan was always the same. The note was already written, so he didn't need to sit down and write one. He already had it in his jacket pocket. But still, it was a nice bureau. It matched the rest of the furniture in the room and there was a nice view of the small back garden. He stared out the window at that garden. All kinds of flowers were in bloom for the very early summer, and the scent wafted over the place like his grandmother's cheap, smothering perfume. His mother had worn the same perfume. So had her two sisters. His aunts. Four women in his family had worn the same thick, suffocatingly hateful perfume year after year. It had smothered him whenever he saw all of them. They'd go to his grandmother's house and his aunts would be there. Or his grandmother and aunts would come over, and that scent would waft after them time after time, covering the house in a blanket of suffocatingly thick flowers. A scent he'd come to hate.

A sigh left him, and a small pounding at the back of his right eye told him he'd been frowning at the thought. His eye always throbbed when he frowned. It throbbed when he thought. It throbbed when he remembered. Remembered memories he didn't want. Remembered things he hadn't done. Or, at least, *claimed* he hadn't done.

His past wasn't completely horrible. Not by any means. But certain things triggered certain memories that triggered the pounding behind his right eye. Always the right eye. Never the left. Always the right.

He gazed out the window at the early summer day. The flowers spread their cheerful blooms across the garden. It was very pretty, and something he could sometimes enjoy, but besides the memories their scent evoked, they also evoked hay fever which he could feel coming on.

Hay fever was not something he enjoyed having. Did anyone? And, like every other sufferer, he could tell when it was coming. A stuffiness in the nose that dried him out, or, in turn, a bout of sneezing that made his nose run. Itchy eyes and a pain in the right ear. Again, never his left. A pain that often travelled to his right sinus and down his right throat.

God, he hated hay fever!

Breathing slowly, in through his nose, he exhaled through his mouth. The stuffy nose was getting worse. Turning from the bureau, he walked past the bed into the bathroom to recheck it for his belongings. He didn't like to leave items behind; he liked to double and triple check every room before he left just in case he'd forgotten something.

His gaze darted from corner to corner, counter top to counter top, and saw nothing. Nothing of *his* that was. He walked over to the sink and saw the small black speck scuttle sideways, unsure of what the large beast looming over it was going to do. He gazed down at it, pondering its life, whether it had plans for the day. What it had done with its life, whether it had a mate and children. Something he didn't have. All because of the women in his family and that damn suffocating perfume. He squashed the speck with his right forefinger, lifted the tap handle and washed his finger. He didn't care about some God-forsaken bug.

Watching the water flow into the drain reminded him of times long gone. Times spent under a pouring tap. A pouring trail of water colder than ice in often freezing times. All for things he hadn't done.

Sort of.

The throbbing behind his right eye started again. He snapped off the tap, strode out of the bathroom, and across the hall into the small kitchenette slash living room. He came to a stop smack bang in the middle of it, and his head swivelled to give his eyes the chance to look for anything he may have left.

Drab, boring, and dismally tan, the kitchenette living room was monochrome at its finest. Whoever had designed and styled it had managed to find the same shade of tan and decorate it in all its '70s style blandness.

His gaze roamed the walls to the floor to the counters and couches. He'd left nothing. Never did. At least, not physically. But places like this always left an imprint on him and so a part of him imprinted on the place. Always memories, always bad, always dragged up from the past.

His right eye twitched.

That was the other part of it. It always twitched to let him know it was starting. And then it throbbed when he frowned and when he remembered, and he remembered often. Remembered all the things that had happened to him as a child, as an adolescent, as an adult. But…didn't everyone? He'd often wished for memory loss. So desperately he wanted to forget some memories. If not all. There weren't any he wanted to remember. Well…*one* in particular.

One memory of one night when he was fourteen. That's the memory he wanted to have for the rest of his life, and one he'd so happily trade for the others, wishing they'd leave his mind and never come back. Just that one memory of the most beautiful, satisfying, illuminatingly perfect moment of his life. No others. Just that one night when he was fourteen.

He breathed deeply, allowing the bliss of the emotions to wash over him. A simple moment of pure joy and happiness. The one and only in his life… There had been no other moments. No other moments of such pure joy and happiness and he'd never felt them again. Not in person, not physically or emotionally. Just in memories. And when he needed to relax, to calm down from something that had gone wrong, he went back to the night in his mind and it brought him right down and relaxed him into a peaceful state. Sometimes…he'd even go into a deep slumber. How he longed to relive that night from forty years ago. The night he became a man and did what he had to do. It always gave him such a thrill down his spine and butterflies in his stomach.

Gazing around one last time, he checked the clock on the wall with his watch and found it correct. It was time to leave. Music sounded from his jacket pocket, and he pulled out his phone. "Hello, Marcia, I know what time it is. I'll be in shortly…yes…no, I'll be in shortly." Ending the call, he sighed and placed the phone back in his jacket pocket and removed the tri-folded piece of paper. He always left it. He had to. How else would they ever know? How else would he ever be famous?

Unfolding the paper, he looked at the words then let it flutter to the floor while he disappeared out the door. The letter landed on the crumpled clown costume that the man lying on the floor wore. Eyes wide, red nose crooked, mouth gaping open, wig akimbo.

He wasn't alive.

CHAPTER TWO

Oliver Nash was making breakfast for his friends when his dad came barrelling into the kitchen.

"Can't stop, I gotta call, I gotta go. You'll have to amuse yourselves all day and the station is off." Roland Nash grabbed a couple of breakfast bars from the box on the kitchen counter and shoved them into his lunch bag along with multiple pieces of fruit from the fruit bowl.

Oliver handed a freshly poured glass of juice to his father. "What? At all? We can't come to the police station for a tour at all?"

"Not today." Roland downed the juice and exchanged it for his large thermos of coffee that Oliver had filled. "You know there's a big case going on and it needs our constant attention. Your mum's on call and you have the neighbours if you need anything. I'll see you when I see you. Behave! You too, boys." He gave his son's friends a pointed look. "Behave."

"Yes, Mr Nash," came the chorus.

It's hardly as if they were going to disobey a

police detective. He had a gun.

Roland Nash was a decorated, dedicated twenty-year veteran of the Australian police force. He'd earned his way up the ladder before turning to homicide and becoming a detective. And having him as a father was intimidating as hell.

"Your father freaks me out when he gives us that look." Chase Emerson shivered. "It's like he's gonna skin us alive."

"Probably would if you did something wrong." Oliver snickered and scooped out the scrambled eggs he'd made his friends. Besides Chase, there were Trent Ryker and Scott Wylie. And every Saturday one of the boys made breakfast for the others. This week was Oliver's turn. "Here." He shoved three plates of toast and scrambled bacon and eggs across the island bench. "Enjoy!"

The boys sat around the island scarfing down their food, emptying a couple of cartons of juice, and saying nothing until Oliver used the remote to change the channel on the TV bolted to the wall.

"*In breaking news, there's been another body found in The Clown Killer Case. The man was found wearing a clown costume in his small one-bedroom apartment at the back of Dingles' factory. Police don't yet know the man's identity, or, if they do, they aren't releasing the information. But I'm sure the name will come out soon, especially since we have a location. No word on whether a note was found as with the other dead clowns. Once we find out we'll bring it to you.*"

"Hey! There's your dad," Trent managed around

a mouthful of food.

Oliver watched his dad walk up the driveway to the small apartment and through the door. It was barely an apartment, more like an attachment to the factory. "Maybe it's someone who worked in the factory."

"Why? Coz he lived in the flat behind it?" Scott finished off his breakfast and knocked it back with his juice. "Or did you mean the killer?"

"Huh?" Oliver tore his gaze from the TV to glance at Scott. "I meant the dead man. He probably worked for Dingles since he was living in the attached flat. It won't be hard to find his name. It will be in the press soon."

"Yeah, poor sod. You gotta feel for the families when they see the addresses blazing across the screen because those leeches want their stories." Chase shook his head. "I *hate that*. But kinda get a kick out of the murders." The others turned their heads to stare at him. "What?" He shrugged. "I'm intrigued by someone killing clowns. When was the last time *that* happened in this town?"

They thought about it while Oliver changed the channel. All he found was morning TV shows and advertorials with over-tanned presenters.

"True." Trent thoughtfully scratched his chin. "I don't think there's been one, so this is the first time." He was a crime buff and watched all the real-life crime shows, listened to all the podcasts, and read all the books. He wanted to be in law when he grew up, either as a detective, or a lawyer. It was going to depend on which was the easiest to be.

"Either way…" Oliver started collecting the plates. "It's kinda crazy to think someone's killing clowns and leaving notes."

"And not one bit of DNA or evidence," Trent added. "They can't find anything on who might've done it. Does your dad have any ideas?"

Oliver added their glasses to the dishwasher and closed the door. "No, he doesn't." He clicked a few buttons and listened to the machine start. "But someone leaked info about that note because *he* certainly didn't." He thought about his father and the stress he must be under.

*****

"What do you mean no DNA?" Roland Nash barked at the forensic specialist at the crime scene. "Again? Nothing?" He was sick and tired of having multiple crime scenes with no forensic evidence of the perp.

"No." Jessie Jo Robinson raised a brow at her colleague. They'd known each other ten years and she knew how to deal with Roland. "And you should've known full well we wouldn't find any. We never have."

Roland sighed from the pit of his stomach and stared at the letter in the Ziploc bag in his hand. "Do I even need to ask…?"

"No DNA, fingerprints, samples of any kind," Jessie Jo told him. She was sympathetic to his pain. She felt it too, as they weren't any closer to knowing who was committing the crimes.

"How…? Why…? Just…" Roland's hand lowered and he stared at his colleagues. "*How* the hell does he do it?"

Dt Andrew Dalton shook his head. "Don't know, Ro, but we gotta find something. We just gotta pray something turns up."

"You know full well I'm not religious, Drew, and won't rely on something that doesn't technically exist whereas science does. *So*…that's what I'm going to rely on, except it's not coming out to play." He handed the bagged letter to Jessie Jo. "Log it in and do what you can back at the lab. There *has* to be something." His voice came out in an almost pleading tone.

Sighing behind her mask, Jessie Jo took the letter. "Sure, Ro. See you in five hours." Knowing that was the amount of time he gave her to find something, she collected her kit and left.

"Ro, we *will* get this guy," Drew said. "I'm frustrated just like you."

"Are you?" Roland snapped at his partner. "You've been a detective for ten years. I've been in the force for twenty. It's not a good track record for me, having a serial killer on my hands."

Andrew placated him. "Roland, calm down. We don't know it's a serial killer, yet, it could be copycats, it could be anything."

"This is *the fifth, Andrew*," Roland used his full name, something they only did when they got tetchy with each other.

"And clearly we now need to back off," Andrew replied. "Let's wrap this up and go back to the station. Cartland and Gibson are off interviewing the owner of Dingles to find out more about our vic, and they'll meet us back at the station. There's not much else we can do."

Roland glared at Andrew and walked over to the body of a middle-aged man about 5'10, with short, dark, greying hair under a green curly wig, a face full of make-up, lying spread-eagled on the floor. The black with lime green polka dots clown onesie had lime frills at the neck, wrists and ankles. Large black clown shoes were still tied to the man's feet. "No DNA, no fingerprints, and no physical sign of the cause of death. How the hell does the perp do it? How does he not leave any evidence that he was even here? Or of how he kills his victims?"

"Well, at first look, it's poison, as there are no visible signs or wounds. At second look, you might think he was killed elsewhere and then dumped here. But, once the bodies are on the slab at the morgue, it's all on the inside. And *no one's* been able to explain that." Andrew stood beside him, looking down at the deceased.

"No physical wounds, even under black light, but once you cut them open, the wounds are all there. How in God's name does the perp do it?" Roland rubbed his eyes and sighed. "Let's get out of here. I'm done with this." Leaving the techs behind, he walked out of the flat and stopped at his car, eyeing off the small crowd gathered around them. Press, networks, news, and neighbours from across the street. Both streets, as the apartment was on a corner. So, if any of the neighbours heard or saw anything, it would be a long list to go through. A crossroads of eyewitnesses or a crossroads of perpetrators. "Have the constables collected witness reports?"

"They have, and still are, I think." Andrew casually glanced along the road to see if he could pick anyone out. But no one stood out except for those in day clothes, as most of the residents were still in their bedwear.

"Ah, God dammit, let's go." Roland swung open the door and got in behind the wheel, slamming the door shut. He sat in the warm quiet and breathed evenly while trying to collect his thoughts. This was the fifth dead clown in as many weeks and he knew if they didn't get a break soon, they'd have a sixth, seventh and maybe an eighth. God help them if they got to double digits. Breathing calmly, he slid the key into the ignition and started the car.

✶✶✶✶✶

"How does your dad feel about this case? This is like the fifth or sixth clown in as many weeks." Trent lazily bounced a tennis ball off the back wall of the house as he lay back on a patio lounge chair.

Being a Saturday, they didn't do too much, and early summer meant school was nearly out for the holidays and they couldn't wait.

"He hates it." Oliver swung back and forth on the

hammock attached to the corner of the patio. "It's the one and only serial killer case he's had and it's stressing him out. Which is understandable."

"Maybe we should look into it," Trent suggested. "We're nearly out of school, so we're not doing much in the next couple of weeks, except for wrapping up the year. It would give us something to do for the holidays."

Oliver hooked his foot over the back of Trent's chair and came to a halt. "What do you mean *we* should look into it?"

"Just that." Trent sat up. "It would keep us entertained over the holiday and give us something to do. We could use Google and the library for research on serial killers; learn about clowns, and here's an interesting tidbit I bet you haven't realised. The clowns have only been killed since Halloween. Before that...*nothing*. So, either someone hates Halloween, or someone hates clowns."

"No, I didn't realise that." Oliver frowned at the information. "Still, doesn't mean *we* need to look into it."

"But it *would* be cool," Trent argued. "And when we go back to school next year and they ask us what we did over the holidays, we can say we became junior detectives and helped crack *The Clown Killer Case*."

"Isn't it being called *The Red Nose Killer Case*?" Chase asked. "That's what I read."

"I heard it was *The Killer Clown Case*," Scott piped up from his seat on the patio railing. "How many names does this thing have?"

"Who cares," Trent went on. "We could look into it, go looking for clowns, maybe do some interviews, and be junior reporters as well as crime-solving junior detectives."

Oliver stared hard at Trent and then at Scott and Chase before reverting his gaze to Trent. "You're nuts, you know that?"

Trent shrugged. "I'm gonna be a detective or a lawyer one day. I better get the practice in now."

"So you wanna be a Hardy Boy," Oliver joked. "And who are we supposed to be? Your faithful sidekicks?"

"Who the hell are the Hardy Boys?" Trent demanded. "And *no*, I don't need sidekicks when I have my best friends. What'd'ya say? Y'up for the challenge? Maybe we can help your dad crack the case."

"That would make my dad Fenton Hardy and I'd be Frank. Which would make you Joe, and Scott and Chase would be Biff and Chet because neither of you look like Tony." Oliver chuckled. He knew none of them had any idea what he was talking about. His elder sister, Jean, had been a devoted Nancy Drew fanatic and he'd found the Hardy Boys via sneaking a few of her Nancy books. "Either way, I'm not about to get into trouble with my dad by digging where I shouldn't be, or I'll end up in the emergency room being treated by my mum." His mother was a paediatric doctor at the local hospital.

"You wouldn't, you wuss. All we're doing is

research." Trent stood up, excitement coursing through his veins. "We'll hit up Google, hit up the library, and if we have to, read the newspapers—"

"We have a *tonne* of those," Oliver told him. "Mum and Dad bring home multiples every day. They haven't been thrown out yet—"

"Great! What are we sitting around here for? Where are they, let's get started." Trent clapped his hands and ushered everyone inside.

CHAPTER THREE

The man carefully washed his ornate silver tool in the bathroom sink, making sure to delicately scrub around the hilt and the inlay so no speck of blood or flesh was left. He didn't want anyone finding them. Didn't want anyone finding *him*, and he certainly didn't want anyone finding any evidence of his having been there. Not that they would ever find that.

He turned off the tap and gently laid the tool on the triple folded white towel. It wasn't black, but it was fluffy and soft and perfect for seeing what might be left behind on the tools. He dabbed at them until they were dry and then placed them back into their pouch. They would be safe there, all rolled up and snug as a bug in a rug. Rolling up the pouch, he placed it into his bag and checked the rest of his things. His glasses, his keys, his watch. He put it on.

The wide leather band fitted snugly around his wide white wrist. The silver face shone brightly in the bathroom light, and he gave the glass face a tap with his fingernail. The watch was an old Omega, circa late 1960s. It had belonged to his father and was the only thing of his that he owned.

His poor father.

The throb behind his right eye started.

His father hadn't deserved the life he had. Or the ending he received. But he'd made up for that by getting the vengeance necessary. His father had been stoic, tall, and well-built, physically adept, psychologically adept, but emotionally *inept*. And the life he'd had had worn him down. And then *let* him down.

The man breathed deeply and let it out in a sigh. He refused to be like his father in that sense. He certainly matched the physical aspect, but he refused to match the emotional. He was in charge of his emotions and abilities, had already been practising before that night when he was fourteen, and it was that night that made him a man. And he liked the man he had become.

Carrying his bag into the bedroom, he saw his tan jacket carefully laid on the bed. He was always careful with his clothes. They were always neatly pressed, but also crease-resistant, and he always laid or hung them with extra care.

Next to his jacket was the letter. Always on white paper, A4, blank. Always folded into three. Always using cut out letters from magazines. Always the same. Everything always was.

Routine was uniform, and uniform was routine.

He picked up his black sunglasses and slid them into his shirt pocket, placed his glasses case into his bag and zipped it up. He carefully laid his jacket over his left arm, hung his bag over his left hand, and picked up the letter with his right hand. He thought a moment before placing it into his left hand, so he could smooth down the leg of his pants.

Taking a good look around, he walked down the hall and into the lounge room before stopping at the French doors leading to the backyard. It was a nice backyard with a lovely patio porch terrace type area running the full length of the house with white railings and pillars. A few steps down, and the terrace led to the blue tile inlaid pool, glistening in the light. Trees lined the fences on all three sides, and no one could see in. No one could see the spectacle. Only he.

He didn't have a pool. He'd wished for one when he was younger, but was always told to play in the creek, or at the local pool with the other boys. And as an adult, he'd never had one. Never managed to acquire a place with one, and never wanted to go to the local on his own. So…sometimes he went down to the beach at night and waded up to his knees, imagining he was an Olympic swimmer, doing backstroke or breaststroke across the waves. He quite liked the water lapping at his calves; he just didn't like it pouring onto his head.

That memory sent a shock wave down his spine and his right eye throbbed. Those memories were best kept in the past. Not the present. And gazing across the scene now, he was glad he'd gone for a swim in the pool before it had become contaminated. It had been pristine blue water before.

Quite refreshing and cool against the early summer heat and his skin. He was lily-white all over and was glad no one had seen him swimming. That would have been embarrassing.

A wistful sigh left him, and he gazed up at the sky. It was time to go. He'd been there long enough and had used up the hospitality of the owner. Showering in the bathroom and using the bedroom to change was not something he did often; quite rarely actually. But it had been a rather messy meeting and he'd needed to clean himself off. But not before giving into the temptation of the pool. Oh, how he'd loved it. But it was ruined now. Not that the rest of the house was. In fact, it was rather luxurious.

Turning to gaze over the interior, he walked around doing one last sweep of the house. A designer cushion here, an expensive vase there. Peach coloured couches and blue coloured curtains. He stopped in front of a glass bookcase against one wall and stared at the glass-framed pictures. The home owner, his wife and children, friends, family, the family dog. All rather sweet, for some. But not for him. He didn't have children, he didn't have a wife, he didn't have parents or siblings. He didn't even have a family dog or cat. He didn't need them. Sure, there had been times throughout his life when he'd questioned whether he did. He'd had many dates and girlfriends when he was young. His twenties had been very full with women. But he knew having one permanently in his life would be a mistake. The same with children. After his own childhood, he'd vowed to never inflict that kind of life upon another and so he had chosen to never reproduce.

With a twitching right eye, he turned away from the memories and walked out onto the patio, unfolding the note as he walked over to the edge of the pool. It had been a week since the last one, and still the police were no closer to catching the culprit. Catching *him*. Because they never would. There was no way they *could*. Because he always made sure he left no part of himself behind. *Always*. No matter *what* he did. No matter *how* it went down. He *never* left a part of himself behind.

Bending down, he tucked the note into the belt of the rumpled costume so it didn't blow away before the police arrived. It would be a shame if it did. If they didn't find it they'd think a copycat was at play. And he couldn't have anyone else taking credit for his work. He *hated* people who took credit where credit was definitely *not* due.

Sighing, he turned on his heel and disappeared.

*****

The next morning, Roland slammed a dozen papers onto the kitchen table. "And here we go again," he muttered. "And I can't do any-bloody-thing about it."

"You're doing your best, Ro, you know that." Merrilee rubbed his shoulder and handed him a glass of juice. "You going in?"

He accepted the glass and kissed his wife, who looked as exhausted as he was. "This time my best just isn't good enough, Merri." He stared down at the papers and muttered, "It just isn't good enough."

"Stop being so hard on yourself." Merrilee grabbed his lunch bag from the island bench. "I've packed a nutritious lunch instead of those bars you seem to be going through a lot of. And here's your coffee. I've added extra coffee sachets to your lunch bag so you can make your own instead of that horrendous rubbish from the station." She kissed his cheek and rested her chin on his shoulder. "Don't forget to take care of yourself and invite the others around for tea tonight, so I can take care of them too with a big feed."

Roland grinned softly. "How'd I get so lucky to have a wife like you?"

"Because I pursued you in college and made sure you *knew* you'd be lucky to have me." Merrilee grinned back and quickly kissed him.

"God, you two, get a room." Oliver padded into the kitchen, his friends in tow. "You both going out today?"

"Yes, we are, and didn't you boys eat here last week?" Merrilee picked up her lunch bag from the counter and flung her tote over her shoulder.

"We did. But we're back coz you have better food." Trent smiled brightly at the Nashes. "And I suck at cooking."

Roland managed a small smile and Merrilee's laughter tinkled around the open kitchen diner.

"Good to know. But in that case, we might have to start charging you boys for eating here. You go through way too much food."

Oliver shrugged a shoulder and pulled the eggs out of the fridge. "Don't you peads docs tell us we need good food for growing bones? We're growing boys after all."

"Yes, we do. But the way *you lot* eat is not normal. Regardless of the fact you're still growing." She eyed the boys up and down. All were fourteen years old and already an average height of five-eight to five-ten. "The four of you are vacuum cleaners and can start buying your own food. Now, Jean's away for the weekend and I'll be home after five." She glanced at Roland who looked exhausted. "And I'll see if I can drag your dad home at the same time. Bye, boys." She hustled her husband towards the door and managed to grab her son and plant a kiss on his cheek. "Bye, Ollie. Be good."

"Geez, Mum, you make me sound like the family dog," Oliver complained as his friends snickered.

A whine came from Goldie, their Golden Retriever mix, who sat in the kitchen wagging his tail and waiting for a feed.

"Oh, and don't forget to feed the dog," Merrilee called from down the hall. "And I mean Goldie, not you. Although you can feed yourself, too."

The boys burst out laughing, but Oliver shook his head in humiliation. "Get out you two and don't come back until you can be mature adults," he yelled down the hall and saw his parents grin before shutting the door behind them. He fed the dog and waited for his parents' cars to leave the drive. Once the sounds disappeared, he got to work on their breakfast and Trent went to work on the pile of papers Roland had left on the table.

"Spread them out on the counter so I can see while I make you drongos your breakfast." Oliver set the pan on the stove top and sliced a rectangle of butter into it. It was scrambled bacon and eggs again. Pretty much the only thing he knew how to cook.

"Okay, here, look." Trent spread one paper out to the current affairs section and followed it up with another and another. Soon, all the papers covered the length of the island bench. "This one is new. A week after the last. That's a total of how many now?" Trent read through the article. "This is the sixth clown to die in as many weeks, family man…left wife and children…nice home…family pets…dressed up as a clown for parties…note left behind…same as others…resident of Greensborough…wait." His head sharply lifted, and he glanced at each friend in turn. "That's the next suburb over," he pointed behind them, "thataway."

Oliver stopped fluffing the eggs and looked at his friends. "I wonder why Dad didn't say anything."

"Maybe he didn't have a chance to." Chase shrugged. "Your mum was all over him like a rash."

The boys giggled and Oliver doled out breakfast to hide his embarrassment.

"What else does it say?" he asked Trent who was going through the papers for more information.

"They all pretty much say the same thing. That it's an angry serial killer killing clowns in their place of residence. No eyewitnesses, no leads, no clues, nothing." He pushed the papers aside to sit and eat, but realised the others were at the table and joined them. "They say no evidence of an intruder, and they can't figure out how it happened."

"Sounds like someone's leaking information to the newspapers and station." Oliver munched on bacon and egg-laden toast. "Dad will *not* be happy, and neither will his boss. Especially so close to Christmas time."

"So…then maybe it's time we stepped in to help." Trent gave them his most mysterious smile.

Oliver stared at his friend. "What are you up to now?"

CHAPTER FOUR

"So, once more, we have *no* DNA, *no* fingerprints, *no* forensics of any kind." Roland slammed down the latest note onto his desk. "Six murders, six deaths, whatever you want to call them as we don't actually know *what* they are." He ran a disinterested hand through his hair before placing it on his hip. "We have nothing. We *literally have nothing.*"

"That's not true," Andrew told him. "Regardless of anything else, we have bodies and notes." He was sitting on the edge of his desk, arms and legs crossed, and watched Roland as he paced. "We just need to make the connection."

"The *only connection* is they're wearing clown costumes," Dt Constable Barbara Cartland said. And yes, she was named after the famous author, and her parents thought it was hilarious. Her, not so much. At thirty she'd trained for five years as an officer before moving to homicide and wasn't about to let her name get in the way. She watched Dt Denny Gibson cross his feet on her desk beside her before pushing them off. Giving him a dirty side-eye, she turned her back on his blushing face.

"And where are we on that?" Roland rubbed his eyes and then pinched the bridge of his nose. It had been a long six weeks in homicide.

"They all came from different stores. We've spoken to the owners and managers, they only rented the outfits to the victims, nothing more, and all have an alibi for the times of the victims' deaths."

"So...*no leads* on that front." Roland stood in front of the window gazing out at the cityscape before him, hands on hips, and a throbbing behind his right eye. It was always the right eye. It throbbed when he frowned, it throbbed when he thought, and was never the left. Never the left. Always the right. He rubbed it again. "What we have are six murders, with six bodies, in six different clown costumes, from six different stores, with six notes all saying the same thing. All made from magazine cut-outs. *None* of the victims knew each other, that we know of. *None of them* work in the same field, that we know of, *none of them* live in the same suburbs, and *none of them* were physically injured even though all six were *very clearly, technically dead*. There are *no* fingerprints or DNA of anyone besides the victims and their families. But upon autopsy, all of them had the same internal wounds in death. McQuarrie has no idea how that could happen even though he's the pathologist doing the autopsies, and Jessie Jo has no idea how no DNA is found, especially on those notes. So, we have sweet eff all." He turned around to face his team. Besides the three other detectives, they had ten officers from different units lending a hand. "Is that it? Is that *all* we have? *No* hard evidence of anything, and six dead men whose cause of death no one can explain. Is that *all* we bloody have?"

The officers and detectives glanced among themselves.

Andrew shrugged slightly and looked sheepish. "Sorry, Ro, but that's *all* there is. We're all stumped, mentally and forensically, and unless we want to become the laughing stock of the force and bring a psychic in, I have no idea how we're going to solve this one."

"Psychic," Roland replied dryly. "You want to take that up with the commissioner?"

"No." Andrew chuckled, despite the tense atmosphere. "But what else can we do? Where else do we turn?"

"Psychics *have* come forward, you know." Barbara shuffled through the papers on her desk. "Here, a list of at least ten people claiming to be psychic and that the murderer is also psychic which is how he's managed to kill six men without leaving a mark or DNA."

"You can't be serious?" Roland asked, but he saw the look on her face. "*They* cannot be serious? Ten psychics think a psychic is killing those men?" he scoffed. "Did they say *why*? *Why* he killed them. *How* he killed them?"

Barbara glanced through the statements; fully aware all eyes were on her. "No, just that they believe he has to be psychic to have left nothing behind and that it's a very strong ability to kill someone by using your mind." She picked up one statement. "This one says for any one person to have psychic ability to the point they're able to kill someone with just their mind, is utterly outstanding and beyond belief. It's the possibility of telekinesis, tele transportation, that the human psyche can leave the human body and still be able to achieve physical acts such as murder, and the leaving of an actual physical note. This is not a mere mortal you are dealing with; this is a person of incredible mental powers that even when caught, will not be able to stop himself from psychic travel."

"Oh, for Christ's sake!" Roland exploded. "What is this? A freakin' Batman cartoon? We'll need to put him in Arkham Asylum next. Did *any* of them say *if*, *when*, or *how* we'll stop him?"

Barbara quickly scanned through the papers. "They all say before Christmas."

"Well, that's *when*, what about *how*?" Andrew asked.

Barbara kept on reading. "One person says kids, one says a group of four teens will figure it out and stop him. The others don't say."

"Great," Roland complained. "*Now* we're getting help from teenagers to catch criminals." He swiped both hands through his hair, rumpling it, and sat on the edge of his desk. "Just great."

"Well…" Andrew offered. "They are the next generation of the force."

*****

"We *really* need somewhere bigger," Trent complained as he rustled through the newspapers on the kitchen bench. They were using the table for their laptops, googling for any news on the clown killer, and all the latest updates.

"We'll have to get out of here before five when Mum's due back." Oliver grabbed four sodas from the fridge and handed them around. "We can't use the office because Dad does, and my room's not big enough."

"The basement? The attic?" Chase asked and sculled back a couple of mouthfuls of cola.

Oliver gave him a puzzled glance. "You know we don't have an attic, but we do have a basement and it's neat and tidy—"

"And big enough," Trent finished off the sentence. "Let's pack it up and get downstairs."

They collected the papers and their laptops and headed down. The entire basement was split in two, with one half being for storage, and the other a bright and spacious living area for when the kids had friends over.

"You guys set up on the pool table and I'll see if we still have the whiteboard in the storage room." Oliver opened the storage room door and flicked on the light. "Neat and tidy like everything else." He grinned, and rolled the old whiteboard out and over to his friends. "Here she is. Just need to grab the textas." He raced back and searched for the labelled box he was after, finding markers of all colours. He left the room and turned off the light. "I don't know if these still work; they could be dried out." He pulled the lid off one and made a squiggle on the board. "That one still works."

"Okay, let's get this going." Trent clapped his hands and appraised their workspace. "We've got the papers on the pool table, laptops on your laps, and we have the whiteboard to draw up a map. And speaking of maps." He slid one out from his computer bag. "I brought this along so we can mark off where the men were found and have already done that." He clipped the map to the board and stood back. "As you can see, I used different colours for different things. Red signifies the dead men and where they were found. Blue for the costume shops they got the costumes from, and the other colours mark out different routes to either connect the men, the times, or the places."

"Is that a pentagon?" Scott asked. "Why is there a pentagon on the map?"

"Because it's one of the connections I made, or was *trying* to make, and I could only make it to five of the men and not six," Trent told him. "I took down all of the notes from the papers, everything online, and made bullet point lists of each man." He pulled a pile of papers from his bag and started handing them out. "I made lists for everybody."

"Then why do we even need the whiteboard?" Oliver asked.

"For taking notes *now*." Trent shoved a list at him. "Or for making more connections."

Oliver glanced down the list. Bullet point notes of

each victim and his life.

"I can't make a personal connection between the six victims, different schools, suburbs, different life. Some were single, some married. Some did clown work full-time, some did it as a side gig. I can't find *any* connection *any*where. *At all.*" Trent crossed his arms and sighed. "And it's really bugging me."

"Now you know how my dad feels," Oliver muttered.

"The costumes came from different costume shops." Chase flicked back and forth between the lists. "All clown costumes, obviously, the news and papers say the person's out for the clowns, so he must know when people are going to be wearing them, when they get them, where they live."

"That would mean he works at one of the shops?" Trent snapped his fingers. "But it says all employees were interviewed and no connections were made there either. And there've been no arrests of employees—"

"Or anyone else," Oliver interrupted and looked up from his papers. "It's frustrating the hell out of Dad. Not having enough evidence to arrest someone for the crimes."

"Yeah, that's gotta suck," Trent murmured. "Ah…Ollie…"

Oliver looked up sharply. Only his family got away with calling him that. "Trenty?"

Trent grinned at the name. "Do you think your dad, or one of the other team members, could give us some info we don't know?"

Oliver rolled his eyes and scoffed. "*Are you shirtin' me*? Like he or his team's gonna tell us anything about a serial killer crime scene."

"Are you shirtin' me?" A puzzled frown crossed Trent's face. "What the hell does that mean?"

Oliver shrugged and his grin was back. "It's something I heard my sister say. *A lot.* It sounded good, so I went with it."

"O-kayyyy." Trent traded a glance with Scott and Chase who were grinning. "Oliver thinks "are you shirtin' me" is a "*thing*"." He made the quote marks with his fingers and received a light smack on the back of the head in return.

"Yeah, dork, *it's a thing*," Oliver told him. "Get used to it. Let's get back to the case. *No* my dad won't tell us. *No* his team won't tell us, either."

"Are they coming tonight? Didn't your mum say something before we walked in?" Chase shifted his laptop as it was burning his legs.

"Yes." Trent turned excitedly back and forth between his friends. "That means all the cops will be in the one room and unable to *not* talk about what's going on. Even if we're in another room, I happen to have a little doodad that plugs into my phone and picks up on other people's conversations and I just happen to be able to record it."

"You're going to record my dad's private conversations with the other detectives about something that we're not legally privy to. You know it's illegal to record in someone's home without permission." Oliver stared incredulously at Trent.

"You sneaky little—"

"Don't thank me." Trent held up his hands, palm side out and grinned. "It's all my idea and since I'm going to be a detective—"

"Or lawyer," Scott cut in and grinned at Chase.

"Or lawyer." Trent threw him a dirty look. "I've been collecting items that I've thrown together into a detective kit—"

"*You* have a *detective kit*?" Oliver asked.

"Yes." Trent flashed him an annoyed frown. "Stop interrupting. I've thrown together a detective kit based on what I've seen on TV, and what I could get online. It's quite impressive."

"Will *we* get to see this kit of yours?" Chase shoved a cushion under his laptop to stop the burning.

"Of course." Trent raised a brow and a smug smile slid across his lips. "When we go and investigate all of the crime scenes of the victims."

CHAPTER FIVE

Oliver's mother arrived home at ten past five and the food delivery van arrived five minutes later. "I ordered everything on my lunch break," she told Oliver and handed him two bags. "Take these inside, love. Your dad called and said he's bringing everyone home."

Fifteen minutes later, she had the boys chopping vegetables while she marinated the steaks. "You boys are obviously staying for tea."

"Yes, Mrs Nash," they said, and kept on chopping.

Once the vegetables were in the oven and the steak in the fridge, Merrilee had time for a shower before her husband and his colleagues turned up just after six.

The boys had already decided to stay quiet for most of the night to overhear anything that might be said among the detectives. And they kept a close eye on them so as not to miss a thing, getting their drinks, and hovering nearby.

"You're being attentive, Ollie." Roland accepted the drink from his son. "That's not like you." He watched his son blush and shrug a shoulder.

"You got a lot on; it won't kill me to get you a drink." He grimaced at the use of the word *kill* and saw the detectives grimace as well. "Okay, bad choice of word, but it won't, besides," he went into joke mode to lighten the mood, "you've had it hard and it's aged you heaps. You may not be able to get to the fridge yourself. Will you be able to cook the steaks, old man?" He dashed out of the way of his father's hand.

"Who you callin' old man, little boy?" Roland quipped and heard his colleagues laugh. "I'm not that old, regardless of how I look."

Oliver's grin shone throughout the kitchen, and he went and huddled with his friends in the corner. "We'll see when you cook the steaks, old man."

"We'll see," Roland repeated to the others. "What a hide!"

"Your son definitely takes after you, Ro," Andrew said, glancing from a sniggering Oliver to his father. "But he's right. It's taken a toll."

Roland sighed and leaned heavily on the table. "Yeah, well… Hasn't fared well for any of us." He scratched his forehead and his fingers moved into his hair to scratch his head. "Not even a hair fibre, not a skin flake, not eyelashes, saliva, follicle, absolutely bloody nothing. How?"

Andrew sighed and leaned back in his seat. "No idea. Unless he's a forensic expert, CSI, cop—"

"He could be hairless," Denny suggested. When they looked at him in confusion he continued. "You know, like those ugly cats. A lot of people don't have any body hair. It all falls out early and never grows back."

The four of them glanced at each other and Roland stroked his chin.

"You just might have something there, Den. *But*, he could also be wearing a suit. Some kind of forensic suit, completely wrapping himself up."

"But someone would stand out if dressed like that," Barbara said. "They can't be going into the houses with a case full of stuff and getting dressed in the house. And they certainly wouldn't be walking into the house with a full hazmat suit on. *No one* has seen *any*body entering or leaving the premises in any such outfit. Or with a large case. They have to be getting in another way, or else committing the crime elsewhere."

"And elsewhere is where you'll be talking about it." Merrilee walked into the kitchen. "Time for the steaks, so get that burner going." She watched her husband and his colleagues slowly wander out to the back patio and crank up the massive barbecue for the steaks before checking on the vegetables. "Half done. They'll be ready in time for the steaks. Boys, start setting up the table outside. There are nine of us." She replaced the vegetables and pulled the container of meat from the fridge. "Trent, you've got spare hands." She saw the others with cutlery, plates and napkins. "Take this out to Mr Nash."

"Yes, Mrs Nash." Trent took the container, and once he'd turned away from her, gave the boys a wink before hurrying outside.

The boys followed and started setting up the outside table.

Trent stood beside Roland holding out the container while he set the steaks onto the sizzling grill, the recorder on his phone going in his pocket.

"Is that what we've come up with?" Roland set the second steak on the hot plate. "A hairless man in a forensic suit who leaves no evidence behind." He laid a third and fourth steak on the plate and the sizzle grew louder.

"Well, if no one's seeing anything or anyone, the only other option is a ghost, or some person with extreme psychic ability who can kill people with their mind," Barbara replied and rested her hands behind her on the railing as she leaned against it.

Trent's brows rose in excitement and his eyes widened, but he remained silent.

Roland picked up another steak with the tongs and saw Trent's expression. "Pretend you didn't hear that." He placed the steak onto the grill over the charcoal and watched the flames fire up. "We shouldn't be talking about it in front of the kids."

"Maybe the kids are the teens who crack the case according to the psychic." Denny chuckled, not realising what he'd done.

"What!" All four boys turned to him. "What? What four teens?"

"Ah, damn it, Denny." Roland laid the remaining steaks on the grill. Ten steaks, nine people, one dog. Goldie always got his own.

"Sorry." Denny shrugged his left shoulder and

looked remorseful. "But is it *really* considered part of the case? It's only what some psychic said when they rang into the station thinking they knew what was happening. I thought we'd dismissed all of that."

"All?" Trent set the empty container on the table and moved closer. "How many psychics rang up, or came in, or whatever they did?"

Roland sighed. "That's not for you to know, Trent."

"But if you've already dismissed them, then they're not part of the investigation," Trent persisted. "So why can't we know?"

Roland glanced at his colleagues who seemed unsure. "*I'm* not saying anything." He went back to the steaks.

Andrew glanced from Roland to the boys. "We had that tip line, and a lot of people called in. Some claimed to be psychics and not much else. One said it would be over by Christmas, and kids, or teens, would be responsible for cracking the case. Which is why Denny shot his mouth off and said what he did. But don't think anything of it, and pretend we didn't tell you," Andrew warned with a wave of his finger. "None of that really matters towards the case, but those calls were private and confidential."

"Did they say *how* the teens crack the case?" Trent desperately wanted to know more. Because the more information the better.

"Not that I recall." Andrew looked at Barbara who shook her head. "We don't have any more details on that."

"And you still have no leads on the perp?" Oliver asked and watched his father. "It looks like it's wearing you all out."

"It is." Andrew nodded in agreement. "It definitely is."

Merrilee popped her head through the patio doors. "The vegetables are done now, how about the steaks?"

Roland lifted one up halfway. "Nearly done. May as well bring them out. Ollie, help your mother."

Oliver motioned for the boys to follow him, and they each took an oven pan of veggies, or a container of gravy. As they set them on the table, Roland piled the steaks onto a plate and turned off the burners.

After everyone served themselves, they kept talk to simple things and not about the clowns or murder, and afterwards, Goldie got to enjoy his own steak.

The adults retired to the lounge room to chat, and the boys were delegated to the basement. Just the place they wanted to be.

"I hid my phone in the lounge room when they weren't looking," Trent said and started making notes on the whiteboard. "I can't wait to hear what they say."

"What was all of that about the psychics ringing up the tip line?" Scott asked. "I wonder what they actually said."

"That it'll all be over by Christmas," Chase remembered. "And that kids, or teens, help solve the case."

"I bet that's us." Trent finished writing and turned to the group. "Was that surprising, or what?"

"Yes…" Oliver thought the conversation through. "But I feel awkward knowing Dad might get into trouble for telling us."

"Technically, *he* didn't tell us. Mr Dalton did." Trent slapped him on the back. "We now have more information. He could be hairless; he could be wearing a forensic suit like a CSI—"

"Or he could be killing them psychically," Chase cut in.

"Which I think is bizarre *and* exciting." Trent stared down at the newspapers on the pool table. "Do any of them say that?"

"Not a one and you should know that since you compiled the bullet point lists." Oliver yawned and checked his watch. "God, I'm buggered. One week left of school and then it's holiday time."

"And Christmas time." Scott rubbed his hands together in glee. "I can't wait for all of my presents. I know *exactly* what I'm getting."

"How do you know that?" Chase asked.

"Because my parents asked me what I wanted, and I told them. Why would I get anything else except what I asked for?" Scott replied.

Chase started to answer, but he was cut off by Trent.

"Those men got more than they asked for." Trent's brows furrowed as he thought. "They all wanted to play the clown for some reason and hired their suits from shops. Different shops, but what if the costumes all came from the same place."

"You just said they came from different shops. The owners were interviewed; they all had those costumes for hire and the victims hired them," Oliver said.

"Yes, *but*," Trent rolled his eyes, "*Where* are the costumes from *originally*. As in where were they made, what factory were they sold from, and who might know which stores those exact costumes were going to…?"

The light dawned on Oliver. "You're saying, it's nothing to do with the costume shop owners, but the factory slash business that made the costumes in the first place." Oliver thought about it. "But that wasn't in the papers, or on TV. And I don't think Dad would tell us if it's in his files—"

"We're not telling your dad," Trent butted in. "We can't. *We* need to search for this ourselves. And if I'm right, it might crack the case wide open, and *we'll* be the ones solving *The Clown Killer Case*."

"Isn't it *The Red Nose Killer Case*?" Chase piped up. "I like that title better."

"And besides," Oliver went on. "We don't know that Dad hasn't already checked out that lead. We should tell him in case he has, so we're not wasting time. And if he hasn't, then he has the resources to go digging into it."

"Are you deaf?" Trent demanded. "I just told you, we're not telling your dad, or anyone else. We're going to those six costume shops and finding out for ourselves, and if I'm right, then we'll check out the factory, or business, or whatever, and find out what's going on."

"And what if they're made in China?" Scott asked. "You planning on going there, too?"

That made Chase and Oliver snigger, but Trent just rolled his eyes and sighed in frustration.

"Even though they're *made* in China, there must be a warehouse company here importing them, and *that's* where we'll end up. Because *that's* where they'll be bought by the stores and then shipped from. I bet it's someone from there. I'll bet you a hundred bucks it's the dude from the factory." Trent nodded authoritatively.

"I don't have a hundred bucks to bet, so I'm already out," Chase told him.

"I'm out too, and no, you're not getting my Christmas presents," Scott added.

Oliver shook his head. "I ain't bettin' you nothin'." He crossed his arms over his chest. "But I can't wait to see how wrong you are—"

"Oh, dude…" Trent stuck out his hand to shake Oliver's. "I won't be wrong."

CHAPTER SIX

The boys waited until the other detectives had left and Mr and Mrs Nash were in the kitchen having a late-night tea before sneaking into the lounge room for Trent's phone. Even though it was a Saturday, they had all rung their parents for permission to stay the night.

After retrieving the phone, they dashed downstairs to the basement and eagerly listened to the files they'd recorded that day. The first few were of early conversations before and after eating, and they made notes on their paperwork. But it was the last file where they found the most information.

"I'm not sure we should be listening to this." Oliver sat back in his chair. "It feels wrong. Like we're eavesdropping or doing something illegal."

Trent scoffed and saw Scott and Chase nod their heads. "So far the information is basic and stuff we already know. And some of it made its way to the papers and TV news, so it's not like we're finding anything out that we shouldn't." He hit play on his phone.

"*We're no closer to finding the killer than the day of his first crime.*" Roland's voice wafted out from the phone. "*Every lead has been checked, every alibi, every employee of the costume shops. Nothing. No DNA, no evidence, no anything. There is absolutely nothing.*" A weary sigh of exasperation came from him. "*I feel like giving up and handing it to someone else. Because if I can't do it after twenty years in the force, then what good am I? I may as well end it all here, all now.*"

Oliver's eyes widened and his jaw slowly dropped. He'd never heard his father talk about quitting. At least, that's what he *hoped* his father was talking about.

"*Come on, Ro. Don't give up. I know what you're talking about. Maybe fresh eyes will do wonders on the case, and if we can't bring in one of our own profilers, what about reaching out to the FBI in America?*" Andrew asked. "*They've dealt with many a serial killer and may have another take on this that we just can't see.*"

"*We could bring the psychics in,*" Barbara suggested. "*It wouldn't hurt for a couple of hours to see what else they have to offer, and if it's nothing, then it's just a couple of hours out of our day.*"

Roland scoffed. "*And they're to be believed because?*"

"*No idea,*" she replied. "*It's a shot, regardless of how long it is.*"

A short moody laugh came from Roland. "*I have no idea if it will hurt or hinder, but at this point, I have six men dead and no bloody clue.*" Another weary sigh. "*May as well talk to them. Bring them in if you can or go to them. Take Denny…do it on Monday…"*

Trent raised a brow in interest and gave a slight nod of his head.

"Oh, and Denny," Roland went on. *"Try not to talk about the case in front of the kids, or anyone else, for that matter. We don't need them having nightmares or getting any ideas in their heads."*

"Slip of the tongue, boss," Denny said. *"But I didn't think that stuff was important."*

"Maybe not, but it doesn't matter. It's all confidential, like any crime, or file," Roland went on. *"Were the crime scenes released, Drew?"*

"Yep. All six homes were released back to their owners. Although, I don't think some of them will be doing much with them. And I'm not sure the wives or families of the deceased will want to live there anymore."

"No…they probably won't," Roland murmured. *"As if seeing the body of a loved one lifelessly thrown wherever in the house or flat wasn't bad enough, why would you want to live there? And they saw it. Some of them. Some of them are the ones who discovered the bodies and called triple zero. They saw their husbands and fathers tossed limply aside like a rag doll in their clown costume with no blood, no cuts or wounds. Nothing. Nothing but a note tucked into the costume, or left lying on the body."*

"That note's a weird one," Barbara muttered. *"No fingerprints, no DNA. We couldn't even figure out what magazines the letters were cut out from."*

Trent excitedly glanced at his friends. Were they finally going to find out what all of the notes had said?

"And just to say one sentence," Barbara went on. *"It makes no sense. There's no question, no demand, no long-winded diatribe about why he's doing it. In fact, with all of the research I've done on serial killers, trying to learn about them, a lot of them have left similar letters. Simply a couple of sentences almost like an afterthought. While others are long winding letters, almost like love letters to the police. Others are a catch me if you can concept, simple and to the point. But this one..."*

She paused, and Oliver could almost envision her shaking her head.

"This one is just weird," she finished.

"It certainly is," Andrew agreed.

"Yeah, but what is it?" Trent almost yelled, shaking his phone for answers. He was so nervous *and* excited he'd been clutching it with both hands the whole time and didn't want to miss a single word.

"Shhh," Oliver warned and quickly glanced over his shoulder at the door. "We don't want the olds coming down here and finding out you recorded them. Keep it down."

"Shhh, yourself," Trent shushed back. "Listen, we might hear it."

"What does it tell us about the killer?" Denny asked. *"Because I have no idea."*

"It tells us he has a story to tell, but he wants to tell

it his way," Roland replied. "He clearly has a hatred of clowns, and it probably stems from childhood."

"So...what? He was scared by a clown as a kid?" Denny asked. "Did he watch Stephen King's IT as a kid? What?"

"Maybe he was assaulted by a clown as a child?" Barbara offered. "And waited until now to do something about it."

"But he's doing the wrong thing," Roland snapped. "I mean, for heaven's sake, who goes to the bother of cutting out letters from a magazine six times over, enough letters to spell out all clowns must die on six pieces of paper. Whoever and whatever he is he's sick and we're gonna find him and put him away. But in the meantime, I need a good sleep and some time with my wife. So, get lost, you lot. We've fed and watered you, and now it's time to leave."

The boys finished listening to the recording to see if anything else was said, but apart from *thanks for the meal, goodnight,* and *see you on Monday,* there was nothing.

Trent finally turned off the recording. "Well, that's interesting. We know for a fact there were notes left at every crime scene, but we never knew what they said."

"Yeah, they never released that to the press, but they found out about the notes anyway. Just not what they said." Oliver leaned back in his seat and checked his watch. Ten p.m. "Time for bed soon."

"Who has time for bed when we know that detail about the notes?" Trent frantically scribbled on his printed-out notes.

"But where are they gonna get us?" Chase asked. "It doesn't tell us who made them, who's been killing the clowns, it tells us nothing. So…" He shrugged. "What are we to do with any of it?" Looking from friend to friend he saw Oliver and Scott nod in agreement. "I say we just let Mr Nash and the other detectives deal with it." He noticed Trent hadn't stopped writing. "We have one week of school left, if that, and then we're out for the summer."

"Mum said I could leave now," Oliver told his friends. "I said I'd stick around to hang out with you drongos."

Scott snickered. "It's free babysitting for another week."

"Boys, time for bed," Roland yelled down the basement stairs. "We're heading up. You need to as well."

The boys froze at the sound of his voice, even Trent whose hand had stopped halfway through a word.

"Uh…sure Dad. We'll be up in a minute," Oliver called.

"Okay, not too much longer. I've locked up the house, turn the lights and anything else off when you come up."

"Okay." Oliver twisted around to stare at the stairs and waited. But Roland said no more. "He's gone."

Everyone else unfroze and went back to what they'd been doing.

"Okay, here's what we're gonna do," Trent ordered.

"Thanks to the news stations tracking down the costume shops, we know which ones to go to. And thanks to the news stations for sharing the addresses of the crime scenes, we know which ones to go to. So, tomorrow we'll come up with a plan of attack, and start executing it after school each day. We should be able to check out three or four shops per day, and three or four crime scenes each day in the days following. By then it'll be the end of the week and school holidays and we can investigate the murders full-time until Christmas or whenever this is solved—"

"Didn't one of the detectives say teenagers solve it before Christmas?" Chase asked. "That's two weeks away and he's only been striking on Fridays, which means there's another to go next Friday."

"Are clowns out at Christmas?" Scott asked the group, looking from Chase to Trent to Oliver. "Are they a thing at Christmas? Because there seems to be a lot of men dressing up as clowns these last few weeks. They're out in abundance leading up to Christmas."

Trent snapped his finger as an imaginary lightbulb turned on over his head. "That's it! We'll also go and talk to other clowns to see if they know anything, or where they get their costumes from, or if they knew the dead men. They might know who did it, or who has a grudge against them. Awesome idea!" He nodded in excitement and looked at his friends, noting their wary expressions. "What?" Shrugging a shoulder, he made notes on his paperwork.

"It's not my fault I have all the ideas."

"Ha!" the rest of the boys scoffed.

"*You*! Have *all* the ideas!" Chase exclaimed. "This is the *only* time you've *ever* had *any* ideas. Usually, you're riding on *our* coat tails."

"Rubbish!" Trent shuffled his papers into a neat stack and slid them into his bag in case someone found them. "I have lots of ideas, lots of the time. You monkeys just don't know about them."

"That's because you don't have them." Scott snickered. "We know you don't have a lot up top." He tapped his temple with his forefinger. "We know, Trent. We know."

"Hardy ha-ha," Trent mocked. "Isn't it time for bed?"

The boys left everything as was, but they kept sniggering as they walked up to Oliver's room where they were bunking on the floor in spare sleeping bags.

*****

After breakfast the next morning, they laid out their plan of attack for the coming week. With a map and a list of addresses, they set up a route for each day and decided on how to get there, then made a list of equipment they'd need. They were going to hit those stores if it was the last thing they did.

CHAPTER SEVEN

Monday, after school, the boys headed to the first costume shop. They were riding their bikes and needed to get there fast, so they wouldn't be home too late.

It was a good twenty minutes ride down back streets to avoid the traffic, and they leaned their bikes against the shop window when they arrived.

"God, I'm glad we've got extra drinks," Scott gasped and took a swig from his water bottle. "It's warm out today."

"Yeah." Oliver had a quick drink from his own bottle and asked Trent, "Are you doing the talking?"

"Of course, since this is my plan," Trent boasted and pulled out his list of questions. "Let's go and get this done." He led the way into the store armed with his phone for recording and the questions he was going to ask. He'd spent all day Sunday coming up with them to get specific answers. As he approached the counter, he looked around the store, making a note of where the CCTV cameras were, and of any other exits, as well as how many people. "Hello," he said to the person behind the counter. "I'd like to speak to the manager if possible."

"Sorry." The girl blew her gum into a bubble and waited for it to pop. "He's not in today." Chewing loudly, she eyed all four boys. "Can I help you with something? Are you here to rent costumes?"

"Actually, we're here to do interviews for *The Bayview Times*. It's a small local paper that's run by one of the bigger conglomerates in town and we'd like to interview you about the clown case that's all over the news. We understand that one of the victims rented his costume from this shop." Trent had spotted it coming from a mile away. The young blonde had teased, coloured hair, and dressed like an '80s Madonna, and she seemed to be obsessed with social media. And she just might want to talk about it if she believed she was going to be in the paper.

"The newspaper? You want to do an interview for the newspaper?" She wrinkled her nose. "I've already been on TV. Haven't you seen me on the news?"

"Yes, we have," Trent smoothly lied. "Which is why we're here. Because you were so knowledgeable about everything, we knew we had to interview you. Isn't that right, boys?" He looked at his friends who all nodded and stayed silent.

"But you just asked for the manager when you walked in," the girl said, suspiciously eyeing them. "You didn't ask to see me."

"That's because I was being polite and trying to find out if the manager was in, because if they were, we may not've been able to speak to you. And we might've got into trouble if we didn't ask them, but, we're lucky they're not, so we can spend time interviewing you. Is that okay?" Trent gave her his best and brightest smile. It was one he gave when he wanted something, and this time he was after information.

"Oh…" The girl stopped leaning on the counter and stared back. "Thanks. Are you going to take my picture?'

"Of course." Trent turned to Oliver. "Can you take some pictures of the lovely," he turned back to her, "I'm sorry, I've forgotten your name."

"Marlene," the girl replied.

"Marlene," Trent said to Oliver. "And Scott, can you take photos of the store and these lovely costumes. Chase, take notes."

The four of them went into reporter mode with Trent firing off question after question. When did you rent the costume to the victim? How long did he rent it for? Where was it originally bought from? Who made it? Where do you get these incredible costumes from? "And how old are you, Marlene?" Trent finally asked. "Are you single? Our readers might want to know."

"Oh." She blushed. "I'm nineteen and single, which is a pity." She posed one last time for Oliver. "Did you get everything you needed?" She had gone all out, even supplying them with copies of various rental receipts and manufacturers' paperwork. Desperate for more fame, she'd willingly handed it over.

"I think we have everything we need, Marlene.

Thank you so much," Trent told her. "You've been an absolute pleasure to work with and we'll let you know when the story goes to print. Thank you again." He shook her hand and they left.

The boys biked around the corner and stopped for a drink.

"Get all that?" Trent checked his phone recording.

"Got the photos," Scott replied. "Cameras, exits, office, costumes."

"Pictures of Marlene. I got…" Oliver checked his phone. "One hundred."

"Do you realise how incredibly easy that was?" Trent capped his bottle and shoved it back into his cooler lunch bag in his backpack.

"Won't be so easy next time," Chase said. "Especially if we *do* get the managers. They may not be so forthcoming with info."

"True." Trent nodded, and wiped the sweat from his brow before fixing his cap. "Let's keep our fingers crossed that we get something. Six shops and one down. Let's try and get to the other two."

They biked on to the next shop and spoke to the assistant and the manager who were both wary of mentioning anything, even though Trent led with the same questions. While they weren't given any proof, they were told the name of the company the costume was bought from and the name of the victim who rented it. Reluctant to give the boys any more details, the manager asked them to leave.

"Well, that went well," Trent spat sarcastically as they sat on their bikes in the shade of the building.

"Did you get photos?"

"When they weren't watching." Oliver had wandered the store looking at costumes and inconspicuously taking photos. When he'd nearly been caught he'd motioned to a display and exclaimed how awesome it was, which set the manager at ease somewhat, and made the assistant preen, for the display had been his idea.

"We did what we could when he wasn't keeping an eye on us," Scott added, having also taken photos and looked at a lot of costumes.

"Let's hope the next store gives us more because this heat is doing me in, and I can't wait to get home and into the pool." Trent strapped on his helmet, and they rode on to the next store.

When they arrived at the store, Trent told the boys of his change in plan. Since they weren't getting much, he'd get straight to the point and see what happened. Nodding, the boys entered and went straight for the counter.

Luckily, the manager, while wary of answering questions, consented to doing an interview and gave short, sharp answers which was exactly what they were after, especially the answers to the two most important questions.

After thanking the man, they made their long trip home and arrived well after six at Oliver's house.

"I know you boys said you were going to be late, but it's nearly seven. What have you been doing this long?" Mrs Nash asked. "And do your parents know?"

The boys grabbed sodas from the fridge and

slumped down at the kitchen table, sculling the drinks back in record time.

"We told them last night," Trent replied and burped. "Excuse me. I needed that. Are we eating here?"

"And what is it that you're doing, or need I ask?" Merrilee went on. "And we ate at six, but I could offer you boys some pizza. There's a few in the freezer."

"Dad's home?" Oliver asked and went for another soda.

"No, just your sister and me. Your dad will probably be late."

Oliver grabbed four more drinks and handed them around. "Frozen pizza it is, then."

"Well, you know how to put it in the oven, so just make sure you don't set the house on fire," she told her son. "I'm going to relax in the air-conditioned comfort of the lounge room and veg out in front of the TV. Your sister's heading out with friends at seven-thirty."

Oliver pulled the pizzas from the freezer. "After being out all weekend? That's rich." He turned the oven on and ripped the boxes from the pizzas before placing them onto trays and sliding them into the oven. "Seems she's hardly ever home."

"True," Merrilee said. "But she's twenty and has a part-time job and uni. She's bound to be gone a lot these days. Just don't make a mess, and I want you boys to be home by eight-thirty." She pointed at the others. "It's still a school night regardless of it being the last week of school."

"Yes, Mrs Nash," the boys said.

"Good. I'll leave you to your pizzas." She picked up her large drinking cup and grabbed a small carton of decadent ice cream from the freezer before leaving them to fend for themselves.

Sighing, Oliver slumped down at the table. "I'm buggered, and it's nearly seven. Are we going to do this every night?"

"Every night until we solve the case," Trent replied. "We've marked off three shops and have three more tomorrow, and then two days of visiting the crime scenes. That will lead us to finding when another murder is due."

"Do we know that for a fact? No," Chase said. "We have no idea where the murderer is, no idea of when or where he'll strike or *how* he'll strike."

"But we do know the name of the import business who sells the costumes to the stores." Trent's lips curled into a secretive smile. "All these shops bought them from the same factory. And if the next three managers tell us the same thing, we'll have a winner, and can hit up the factory on Friday afternoon."

"What? When the killer's out killing clowns?" Scott frowned at the thought. "And when are we supposed to be interviewing clowns? Weren't we doing that as well? If we're this buggered after one day, how are we going to get through the rest of the week? And school's not out until Friday, and Christmas is next week."

"Stop your whining, we're taking the bus tomorrow, so make sure you've got your school bus passes. We won't be so tired," Trent told him.

The oven bell went off and Oliver went to serve pizza.

*****

On Tuesday after school, they took the bus to the next costume shop, did their spiel, and rode another bus to the second, and then onto the third. By the time the boys got home to Oliver's house, Trent was ready to scribble down a game plan. All six stores had bought their costumes from the same factory import business. All six victims had been wearing their costumes when killed. The import factory was the key in the plan, and they intended to visit it on Friday.

*****

After school on Wednesday and Thursday, the boys travelled to the homes of the murder victims and stood studying them from the street. Unfortunately, five homes were still occupied by the families, or locked up by the owners, but the small flat behind Dingles' factory was empty. And since there were no curtains at the windows, they could peer in and see the crime scene for themselves.

"Keep an eye out to see if anyone's watching." Trent cupped his eyes with his hands to cut out the glare on the glass. "I'd love to get in there for a closer look."

"Doesn't that fancy detective kit of yours come with a lock-picking kit?" Oliver joked as he gazed at the houses up and down the street. "And you call yourself a Hardy Boy."

Trent heaved an annoyed sigh. "Wasn't me calling myself that, you dork. Anyone checked the door, yet?" He walked around to the front door and turned the knob. To his surprise, it opened. "What the…?" Peering inside, he checked the wall to the side of the door for an alarm system, but found none. "Oooh, let's do this."

"Are you kidding!" Oliver exclaimed. "We're trespassing and'll get caught. And if my dad finds out—"

"He won't." Trent wandered inside, dropped his bag in the middle of the lounge room, whipped out his phone, and started taking photos. "This is *so* cool."

"This is *so* wrong," Oliver muttered and shook his head, but followed him in anyway, as did Chase and Scott. Being in a house he knew someone had been murdered in was creeping him out.

"This is so right." Trent moved into the bedroom for more photos, followed by the bathroom. "It's such a small place, how would no one have not seen anything?" He walked back into the kitchenette dining room. "How is there no blood, not hair, no fibres, no anything to solve this case?" He took a video of the room and saw through the front window an elderly woman across the road standing on her front porch in her dressing gown watching them. "Looks like we've been spotted." He nodded at the woman. "Better go." He gathered his bag from where he'd dropped it and headed for the door that Oliver swung open, only to find two guns pointed at their faces.

"Oliver?"

"De-de-tec-tive Cart-land," Oliver stuttered, staring down the barrels of their police-issued guns. "De-tec-tive Gib-son. Ah…"

"Oh, sorry." Cartland holstered her gun and stared at the four ashen-faced boys. "What are you doing here? We got a report that teens had broken into the flat."

"Being nosy," Trent said from beside Oliver. "And we didn't break in, the door was unlocked."

"What he said." Oliver's right forefinger shakily pointed at Trent. "What he said."

"Right." Cartland placed her hands on her hips and glanced at Denny who was looking rather amused. "Well, you boys shouldn't be here, and since we can't take all of you in our car, we'll follow you to the bus stop and make sure you don't go breaking into any other houses."

"It's not like we do that on a daily basis," Trent retorted. "Oliver's dad is the lead detective and we got nosy—"

"*You* got nosy!" Oliver snapped at him and turned to Cartland. "You don't have to tell my dad, do you?"

"Yes, Oliver. We do. It came through to us because we're the detectives on the case. Your dad sent us here to check it out." She smiled lightly. "What we *didn't* expect to find, was our boss's son and his friends breaking and entering."

"Again with the breaking," Trent quipped. "It *was* unlocked, we didn't *break* anything."

Oliver's face fell. He knew he was in *big* trouble. "Ah… Bugger!"

"Does that mean we're *all* in trouble?" Chase asked.

"Yes, young man," Cartland said. "It does."

*****

"And what did you boys think you were doing breaking into the flat behind Dingles' factory this afternoon?" Roland Nash had the boys lined up side by side in the living room. It was six-thirty and he'd just got home and was standing with his hands on his hips, and being incredibly intimidating.

Silence.

"Well?" he demanded.

"Being nosy," Trent murmured. "It's a big case, you're the lead detective, and the door was unlocked. We didn't break into anything."

"That's not the point." Roland stared pointedly at Trent. "This is a dangerous serial killer and I want none of you near it. Do you understand me?"

"Yes, sir," came quietly from all four boys.

"And Oliver." He stopped pacing in front of his son.

"Sir." Oliver's eyes were downcast and his cheeks were flaming.

"It's bad enough that I've brought this case home. I don't want you involved in it. Do you understand me?"

"Yes, sir."

"Good. Make sure you do."

CHAPTER EIGHT

On Friday morning, Trent came to school with a massive grin on his face. "Guess what's happening today? A massive clown rally in town. It's happening because they're sick and tired of being hunted and want the police to do something about it." He shoved the newspaper in front of the others. "Who's up for a ride into town?"

"Are you kidding?" Oliver frowned at him. "After the bawling out we got last night because *you* couldn't help yourself and had to go and break into that flat behind Dingles. We got *ripped* because of you."

Trent shrugged a shoulder. "Sorry. But we didn't break into anywhere. The door was unlocked, and the place was empty."

"That didn't mean we had any right to enter," Oliver snapped back. "*I'm* lucky I'm not grounded."

"And *we're* lucky Mr Nash didn't tell our parents," Chase added, pointing between him and Scott. "We could've been skinned alive."

Trent rolled his eyes. "But you weren't. Look, this

is the last day of school, it ends early, and we can catch the bus into town to attend the rally. We can interview as many clowns as possible and see what they say. Who knows...?" He looked between the boys. "We might get even more evidence than we have."

"Except we have none," Scott complained. "All we have is the name of a factory that imported the costumes all six men wore. That means nothing."

"*And it could also mean something,*" Trent argued. "Look, you all had no problem coming every day the last four days, and because we got caught in one *empty* flat while investigating, you want to chicken out. What a pack of sooks you are."

"*We got ripped by my dad last night,*" Oliver repeated, angry that last night had even happened. He rarely got into trouble simply because he didn't want to be confronted by his father and punished. "It's *all your fault.* Why should *we* continue doing *any of this* for *you*?"

"It's not for me, it's for your dad," Trent said matter-of-factly. "If we can find evidence that'll lead to the perp, then that'll help your dad wrap this case up."

"They have no evidence of anyone, let alone a perp," Oliver said. "Even if we found someone, or something, they would still need evidence of them *actually committing* the crime. *That's what evidence is.*"

"*I know that!*" Trent's eyes rolled harder in their sockets. "Jesus, Oliver! Why can't you just help me finish this off so your dad can find the guy killing clowns?"

"But what if he *is* doing it psychically?" Scott eyed his two friends standing toe to toe in the schoolyard quad going at it. He also saw other kids standing around watching. "If he's not *physically* killing them, then what kind of evidence would they need to arrest and put him away?"

Oliver shook his head and sighed. "I don't know. I just…" He stepped away and rubbed his puffy and throbbing tired eyes. He'd spent the night crying in his room, something he hadn't done since he was eight when he'd broken his favourite superhero action figure and that was nearly six years ago. A small pounding at the back of his right eye told him he'd been frowning the whole time they'd argued. His eye always throbbed when he frowned. It throbbed when he thought. But certain things triggered the pounding behind his right eye. Always the right eye. Never the left. Always the right. "A confession, I suppose. But even then, without any actual cold hard physical evidence it might be hard to prove anyone did it."

"And what if the dude kills another clown in the meantime?" Trent asked, knowing his friend had it harder than the rest of them. He also knew when Oliver had been crying or was upset. "Today's Friday; he's due to kill today."

Oliver's body heaved another sigh and he glanced at Trent over his left shoulder. "Then we go to the rally and speak to the clowns."

*****

They made sure to wrap things up that morning, and left school at lunchtime without anyone noticing. They took the bus into town as they'd left their bikes at home, and arrived in the mall at 1:30 p.m., when the crowd was at its peak.

"Holy Jesus, this is a coulrophobic's worst nightmare," Chase murmured.

"That's it!" Trent snapped his fingers and glanced at the men in the crowd. "The killer must have a fear of clowns, which was mentioned on the tape. Something must've happened to him when he was little."

"Which would give him a reason to hate them," Oliver replied and was pushed aside by an alley of clowns. "Hey!"

"Sorry, kid. Didn't see you there," one clown called over his shoulder. "Hey, you're not in costume. Are you here to support us?" The man and his friends came back to where the boys were standing. "I didn't know this was gonna attract kids."

"Actually, we're here to do interviews for our local newspaper, *The Bayview Times*. We wanted to see how everyone was faring under the dire circumstance of *The Clown Killer Case*." Trent thrust his phone forward to record every word. "Do you mind if we interview you?"

The man laughed at his friends. "Get a load of this. Kids want to interview us about *The Red Nose Killer Case*. Do you think we should give them an interview?" The others nodded and they all started talking at once.

While Trent asked questions, the boys snapped photos of all the clowns in their costumes, as a record of outfits. Once the interview was done, they moved on and managed to get quite a few statements before the leader of the rally spoke on a stage in the middle of the mall. While he did so, the boys kept an eye out for any suspicious-looking people, which, considering they were in an alley of clowns, was hard to do.

"Come on, let's skirt the crowd," Trent suggested. "We might see more." The others nodded and he led the way to the outskirts of the gathering where they could catch their breath. "Crikey! That's a mob. Let's go clockwise and take photos."

They walked around the crowd, keeping an eye out for people that looked as though they didn't belong there, took photos, and Trent kept recording the speeches given by the clowns on stage.

When they'd walked all the way around they stopped at the side of the stage and waited for the big reveal that was about to happen.

A contraption rose upward, tilting to a ninety-degree angle until it was facing the crowd, and with some big ado, the leader of the rally pulled off the sheet covering it to reveal what was supposed to be a huge sign. Instead, it was a clown, strapped spread-eagled on the board, wrists and ankles tied to different corners, and pinned to his torso was a piece of paper with cut out magazine letters declaring that *all clowns must die.*

An audible gasp rippled through the crowd, shocking them into silence except for the odd scream popping up among the shoppers who were watching.

"Uh-oh, that's not good," Scott murmured as he stared in horror at the spectacle.

"Nope," Trent replied, staring at the dead clown on display for all to see. "That means Oliver's dad will be on his way and we need to get out of here. But first, I gotta take photos." He hurried through the crowd, filming the whole thing, trying to get as close as possible to the stage. He started climbing the stairs for a better look, but security held him back while others threw the sheet over the dead clown.

Oliver, meanwhile, filmed the crowd around him, scanning his phone to the left until he saw a blur against a shop window. Puzzled, he glanced at the window, but saw nothing. Again, he looked at the phone and the blur was still there. It looked like a blob of white on top of a blob of tan on the bottom. "What's…?" The blob turned his way and rushed at him, but looking up, Oliver saw nothing. A cold chill went through him, and he gasped and stepped back, clutching his phone to his chest.

"Oliver, what is it?" Chase asked, seeing his friend in shock. "You okay?"

Oliver shook his head violently, but stopped when his ears picked up the distant wail of police sirens. "Gotta go, Dad's coming."

"Okay, let's get Trent and get out of here." Chase grabbed Oliver's arm and dragged him through the crowd towards the stage. "Trent? We gotta go. The cops are coming."

Trent manoeuvred his way to them. "What's that?"

"The cops," Scott replied. "Let's get out of here."

They took off running down the mall from the stage and away from the closest laneways that the police would be blocking off, making it to the end of the mall. They hailed a bus and slumped down into the seats at the back, peering over the window edge to see if any police vehicles were on the lookout.

"Do any of us know where this bus is headed?" Scott asked.

"Nope," Trent said. "But we'll get off soon enough, meanwhile, Google the bus routes. We need to get to the factory where those costumes are from."

"Hey, Oliver, what happened back in the mall? You looked like you'd seen a ghost," Chase asked, noting his friend's quiet demeanour and ashen face.

Breathing in, a glassy-eyed Oliver looked at his friends. "I think I did. I think I saw the clown killer."

"What!?" All three boys sat stunned.

"But how?" Trent asked.

"Here." Oliver shoved his phone at Trent. "Near the end of the video. The white and tan blobs that come at me. I felt it rush through me. It was cold and made me gasp and feel sick." He faded off and sat in silence while Trent played the video and sped through to the end.

They peered closely at the screen and did indeed see blobs of something, but they couldn't make out what.

"So…" Trent replayed it. "Are you saying this is the clown killer? But…it's not an actual person." He watched it a third time. "It's nothing except a mist-like thing."

"The psychics did say he was doing it psychically. Maybe he can teleport his soul to a crime scene." Chase saw their befuddled frowns and shrugged. "How the hell should I know?"

"It came at me," Oliver murmured. "It *saw me* and knew I could *see it* and tried to scare me by coming at me and going through me." He stared at his friends. "It was *so* cold, and it went *through* me. *Through*…me."

The boys watched him, concerned by what had happened and how he looked.

"We need to get out of here." Scott pulled on the lever. The bus pulled to a stop at the next bus stop, and they disembarked, standing in the shade of the bus shelter while consulting the schedules and bus routes pinned on the back of it.

"Looks like we can take the 303 to here, and then the 308 all the way to the road down from the factory. We can walk to it easily enough." Trent checked his watch. It was already 3:30, a half hour after school break up. "Were the olds expecting us home straight away?" He cast a glance at his friends and received shakes of their heads in return. "Good. Coz it could take a while to get there and closing time is five. And it's another fifteen minutes to wait for the 303."

They sat on the seat discussing the plan of attack for when they reached the factory. They didn't have their bikes, so they couldn't ride away, but they did have extra chargers for their phones, and Trent had his camera. They also had food and extra drinks, which they had before the bus came as they hadn't eaten lunch.

On the 303 they charged their phones, switched them to dark mode, and turned off all ringers and notification sounds, then saved all videos and photos to their respective dropboxes. They didn't want to be interrupted with what they were about to do. Not that it was anything important. They were just talking to the manager of the factory about clown costumes; the costumes that had been sent to the stores, who rented them to the men who ended up dead. For all they knew, there was no connection other than that.

"What if he does have power?" Scott asked as they sat on the back seat of the 308. "What will we do if he tries something on us?"

"That's why we have our plan," Trent replied. "*If* it's the dude running the factory, then we'll know. But for *all* we know, he has nothing to do with it and is just the dude importing clown costumes for stores to buy. We have no idea who the clown killer is, let alone what he looks like." He shrugged and physically deflated. "I'm buggered and can't wait for this week to be over."

"School's over, and we missed it," Oliver mumbled, staring out the window at the passing scenery. "School's over."

"Finally!" Trent crowed and went for a high five,

but none of the boys was interested. He shrugged. "Meh, okay, but Christmas is in another week. Yeah."

"If we make it that far," Oliver mumbled.

CHAPTER NINE

The man paced back and forth, sweating in the afternoon heat, even though the air-conditioner was going full blast. Stains were growing larger under his armpits, making his white shirt cling to him, and he held out his arms to dry them off.

"What am I going to do?" he murmured. "That boy saw me. I can swear he saw me. He was looking straight at me and filming me with his phone, looking from it to me. Oh, why did I hang around to see my masterpiece? How stupid, stupid, stupid could I be?"

His pacing slowed to a stop. *But what did he see? He certainly wouldn't have seen me. I technically wasn't there. So, what did he actually see?* The thought surprised him. He'd never wondered if anyone could see him. See what he became when his powers were in control, while his physical body was in one place, and his metaphysical was in another. And he never once stopped to think about what it was he became after the transformation, or what people could see. But a boy had seen something. All because he'd been stupid enough to hang around after a kill to see everyone's reactions. And it had been beautiful.

A smile slid across his lips, and he savoured the sound of the crowd. The audible gasps that came as one with the odd scream thrown in for effect. "Beautiful, just beautiful," he murmured, remembering his seventh kill. Pinning the man to the board, spread-eagled for all to see. He'd estimated that there were a good five hundred plus clowns there, and knew it was going to have an impact. And as much as he'd hated seeing them all, he'd stayed to get their reaction, and by God, had it been beautiful. But by God, he'd hated all those clowns.

"Now, how did that boy manage to see me?"

*****

At five-fifteen, Merrilee arrived home and called out for her children. "Jean… Oliver… Anyone home?" Hearing silence, she hurried to the kitchen for an ice-cold wine and a tub of decadent ice cream to eat while soaking in the bathtub. But on her way upstairs, she noticed a piece of paper caught under the door leading to the basement.

"Mmm, what's that?" Placing the glass and tub on the hall table, she opened the door and pulled the paper free. "Must be something from the boys. They've been down here a lot." It looked like the corner of a ripped printed sheet of paper, and she hurried downstairs to see if they were there and found the whiteboard against one wall.

"What's that doing out? And why didn't Ollie put it away." She pulled it away from the wall and saw the map clipped to the back, along with all of the boys' written notes. "Now what the hell are they up to?" she murmured and pulled her phone from her pocket. After taking a snapshot, she texted it to her husband before calling him.

"Merri?"

"Ro, did you get the photo I sent you? What on earth are the boys up to?"

"Hang on." Roland clicked on his texts and looked at the photo. "What the bloody…? That damn boy and those friends of his have been looking into this case, that's what."

"But is it important?" She was reading what Trent had written. "They seem clued in. Did you know this stuff?"

"No, but I do now and wish he'd come to me with it. Is there anything else?"

Merri glanced around the room. "Nope."

"Okay, we'll enlarge the photo and have a look. You go and have your bath."

She chuckled. "How you know me. Just make sure our boy is okay."

A loud sigh came from Roland. "Will do." He hung up and handed his phone to Denny. "Get this photo off and blow it up. The kids have been playing junior detective."

*****

It was a quarter to five by the time the boys got off the 308 and they still had to walk down the road to the factory.

"Let's eat and walk, and walk fast," Trent suggested. "We haven't much time."

They hurried down the street until the factory came into view and then slowed their pace.

"When's it open till?" Scott asked, capping his water bottle.

"Five or five-thirty," Trent replied. "But still, I want to get this over and done with so we can go home. Let's stop in the shade under those trees and get our stuff ready."

They packed their drinks and food away and pulled out their phones. Trent hung his camera around his neck, and all of them pulled up the record app on their phones.

"Ready?" Trent got three uncertain nods in return. "For all we know it's just the guy who runs the factory, and nothing more. But be on the lookout and stay on your toes. Chase, you and Scott stay in the background and look around. Oliver and I will deal with the manager." He checked his watch. "Five to five. Quick, let's go."

They hurried through the empty carpark towards the door and saw the sign for the closing time on the front.

"Five minutes," Trent said. "May be all we need." He pulled open the door and they rushed into the small, barely furnished reception room. "Hello?"

No one answered, and no one was behind the desk.

A sound came from behind the only closed door in the room and Trent silently pointed to it. "Through there, I guess," he whispered, moving over and twisting the knob. The door opened into a large factory floor full of clown supplies. It was somewhat dark, with clown faces on every wall, and every bit of floor space, and hanging from the roof, giving it a very eerie feeling indeed.

"Of all the bloody stupid things to do..."

A clown mask went sailing by and the boys realised someone was there.

"Is this place a mess or always like this?" Scott whispered.

"How could you be so stupid as to let that kid see you when you've been so careful with every crime scene?"

The boys' eyes widened in shock and Trent quickly pushed the others behind large barrels lined up against the wall to their right. Racks of frilly accessories hung above them, so they had some visibility protection.

"Get your phones out and record this," Trent whispered, and all four held their phones up while the man went nuts. "Oh, my God, he's throwing stuff everywhere."

Oliver's gaze finally latched onto the man and saw he was dressed in a white shirt and tan pants with black shoes and belt. His black-framed glasses made his eyes bigger, and his brown hair was neatly parted on the side and slicked back. "A white blob on top of a tan blob," he whispered. "Oh, my God." He looked at the others in a panic. "That's him! That's what I saw."

Trent's brows rose and he went back to watching the man throw one of the biggest tantrums he'd ever seen an adult have.

"How could you be so stupid as to hang around a crime scene just for the adulation of the crowd? To see how they reacted, and how could that boy have seen me? How could *anyone* have seen me?" His pacing on the factory floor was frenetic, and with each of his hand movements, objects ended up flying through the air. How he did it stumped the boys, but the man knew. His powers had developed as a child and into teenhood. He had the power to move objects with his mind and emotions and to project himself into other places to do things he really shouldn't be doing. Like killing people.

"Well, it's not like it's the first time," he muttered. "Seven down, seven to go, another seven must go, she did the deed, and paid for her greed, seven down and seven to go, another seven to go."

The boys exchanged puzzled frowns. None of what the man had said made any sense, but looking around, Trent came up with an idea.

"Give me your phone," he whispered in Oliver's ear and took it before Oliver could say no. He quickly tapped out a text but didn't hit send. Instead, he carefully passed it to Chase and whispered instructions in his ear. He slid his own phone into his t-shirt pocket, so it could still pick up sounds, and turned his camera on. When the coast was clear, he indicated for Oliver to move back to the door where they stood up and he quickly opened and closed the door to the reception room. "Hello? Is anyone here? We'd like to ask some questions."

*****

"Well, what is it?" Roland asked as Denny pinned the blown-up photo to the whiteboard in police headquarters.

"It's a convoluted list of the dead men, crime scenes, and costume stores," Denny replied and stood back with his hands on his hips. "I have no idea, otherwise."

Roland stood staring at the lists. "What's that address?" He pointed to the one on the right of the six others for the costume shops. A bracket surrounded them with six arrows pointing to the address on its own.

"Ah…" Barbara quickly flicked through her papers. "Don't know."

"Is it another costume shop?" Roland asked. "Although, from the way it's written, I'm getting a feeling that these six stores are connected to that address…" He spun around. "How far back did we go with the costumes?"

"Just to the stores that rented them," Andrew replied, sitting on the edge of his desk with his arms crossed. "Why?"

"Did we not follow up with them? Go back further?" Roland looked at each member of the team. "Come on, find that address and tell me what it is."

They googled for it and found it was a clown costume and party supply wholesale importer.

"And it took my son and his friends to figure that out?" Roland's hands went to his hips and his stern expression bore down on them. "Find out everything you can about that factory. Who owns it, and who runs it. Now!"

*****

"Hello?"

"Ah, hello." Trent craned his neck and pushed Oliver forward. "Can we speak to the person in charge, please? There was no one at the reception desk, and we heard noises back here, so we came back. Hello?"

The man walked up to them. "Yes, hello. What can I do for you?" His gaze landed on Oliver and widened. "You!"

"Him?" Trent asked innocently. "Do you know my friend? As far as I know, we've never met before. We came to ask some questions."

"Questions?" The man's eyes flickered back and forth between the two. "What type of questions? About what?"

"About whether or not the costume stores where the dead clowns hired their costumes bought them from here or not." Trent clicked a photo. "Do they buy from you?"

"Ah, why?" The man's gaze flickered to the door behind them. "Why do you want to know?"

"Because I think they did," Trent went on. "And I think you knew exactly where they'd gone and targeted the men who rented them. I think you're the one killing clowns. You're the clown killer, aren't you, Mr Dudley?" He'd seen the name on the front door and decided to use it.

Dudley's eyes turned the size of saucers and flicked back to Oliver. Items around them quivered. "What makes you say that?"

"Because I saw you," Oliver murmured. "A white blob on top of a tan blob. You ran right through me." He hadn't taken his eyes off the man the whole time. "You're the killer."

Dudley suddenly calmed. "And what are you two boys going to do about it? You're what, twelve, thirteen?" The smug smile slid across his lips. "You can't do anything."

"We're fourteen, Mr Dudley," Trent stated. "How does that sound?"

More objects quivered and a red tone washed over Dudley's face. "Fourteen?"

"Yes," Oliver said. "Were you killing clowns at fourteen?"

Dudley hardened as the memories came back and his right eye started to throb. "As a matter-of-fact, yes, I was. Fourteen of them. All at my mother's house after she killed my father. I was fourteen years old. Do you know what it's like?"

Chase looked at Oliver's phone and hit send.

*****

Andrew ran into the room and handed the papers to Roland. "You have no idea who runs that factory, and yes, the costumes came from there."

Roland quickly read through the papers. "Jesus. Is that the address?"

"Yes." Andrew waited for more, but Roland's phone beeped.

Roland pulled it from his pocket and read the message, his brows crossing in anger. He glanced at the address on the paper and back to the phone.

33221 forestville rd glenview clown killer HELP!

"Get squad cars to that address NOW. Oliver's got the clown killer. It's the manager of the factory!"

CHAPTER TEN

"No, because I'm not a killer," Oliver replied, hoping his racing heart didn't give him away. He stayed as still as he could, so no one could see him shaking.

"Neither was I until I was fourteen," the man said. "But I was abused, and I have no idea where my powers come from, or how I got them, but they happened. *Especially* on my fourteenth birthday. And then I killed fourteen people, and no one guessed it was me." He smiled. "Got away scot-free because I had used my powers. No evidence, no proof that I did it."

"Why?" Trent asked. "Why fourteen?"

"Because that was the number of people at my party. None of them were *my* friends. They were *mother's* friends, her *sisters'* friends, and *their* mother's friends. She'd already killed my father, so then I killed her," he stated matter-of-factly.

"Is that why you're killing clowns? What did they have to do with it?" Oliver asked, never taking his eyes from the man.

"Because she and the others dressed as clowns."

The man's right eye twitched at the memory. "They dressed as clowns and did bad things to children."

"Are you included in that?" Trent kept his voice calm and even.

"Yes," the man spat. "She and her cronies had done it for years, and when I finally had the courage to tell my father, she killed him because he'd confronted her instead of going to the police. Problem was…" his face became dark, "the police were in on it which is why she got away with killing my father. She knew I'd told on her and punished me by tying me up in an old shed under a tap and made the water from the old well pour on my head. I *hate* water pouring on my head!"

Items in the factory swirled around them as his anger grew. Trent and Oliver stepped back, watching the display of emotion.

"What do the men you killed have to do with that?" Trent yelled above the sound of the swirling items. "What did they do to you?"

The man laughed and the articles swirled faster. "They're the descendants of the abusers and they're abusers themselves."

"Why not tell the police? And why now? And why fourteen?" Oliver asked.

"Because…" The man's anger made the articles fall to the ground. "One, the police would hardly believe me when I'm connected. Two, because they're the descendants and it's now forty years since it happened, and three, because I was fourteen and there were fourteen abusers. See…" He smiled maniacally. "All works out to the number fourteen. So…" He clapped his hands. "Since seven are down and I have seven to go, that means I'm going to have to do something with the two of you."

"No." Oliver took a stand and could feel the anger rising inside of him. "No more. No one should have died then, and no one should have died now. It ends."

"Ah." Dudley stood in half awe, half shock at Oliver. "You…have it…in you."

"I don't know what you're talking about, but we will not let you kill again." Oliver took a step towards him. "This ends now."

While Oliver had been talking, Trent had sneaked off to the side and donned a clown costume and wig. He'd whispered to Chase earlier to do the same, and now waved the other boys out. "Let's get him," he yelled, giving a rebel yell and running around Dudley.

"What are you doing?" he demanded, feeling the stress levels rise. "Stop it, stop it. What are you doing?" His hands covered his face and he screamed.

Trent, Chase and Scott flung everything they could pick up at Dudley while Oliver just stood opposite him.

Watching the horror of his fourteenth birthday party replay in is head, Dudley collapsed to his knees. "Stop it, stop it. Daddy, make it stop. I hate her, I hate her." Everything in the factory whirled around them and the boys kept grabbing what they could and hitting him. "Daddy, make it stop, make it *stop*," he screamed, his head falling back and his eyes glowing red as he stared up at the ceiling.

Everything stopped and Dudley fell to the floor.

"Oliver." Roland Nash, his detectives, and a dozen police officers came flooding in to the factory. "Ollie." He grabbed his son in a bear hug. "Are you okay?" He looked over his son's shoulders to see three clowns, and a man in a heap on the floor. "Boys."

"Mr Nash." Trent pulled off his wig and costume. "We've got a confession on camera. He killed the seven men, plus his own family when he was fourteen."

"We know." Roland held his son at arm's length. "Your mother found the whiteboard and the name of the business, texted me the photo, and we traced it down and then tracked the manager and his past down. And then got your text."

Oliver looked up in surprise. "I didn't—"

"Yeah, that was me," Trent said waving his hand. "Well, *technically* Chase hit the send button, but I wrote the text and told him to send it."

"Daddy…is that you?" Dudley asked, curled up in the foetal position on the ground and sucking his thumb. "Please take me home, Daddy."

"He's had a psychotic break," Oliver told his father. "He'll never get better."

Roland's brows rose. "And how do you know that?"

Oliver shrugged his right shoulder. "You could see it in his eyes."

"Huh," Roland muttered. "So, you're an expert on psychology now."

"Daddy, please take me home," Dudley whispered. "I'm scared and I hate what they do to me. I don't want them to do it anymore, Daddy. I want to live with you. Please take me to live with you."

"His parents had separated before his fourteenth birthday. His father wanted to take his son with him, but his mother refused. His father died a week before his mother did," Roland explained.

 "We know, he mentioned it," Oliver said, gazing upon the man with compassion.

Roland nodded. "And with all of the information we managed to gather there were photographs of his parents. The irony is, I look like his father."

Oliver glanced sharply at his father as he walked over to Dudley, getting an incredibly bizarre feeling that his father was descended from Dudley's father. But that would make them…

"It's okay, Winston; I'm here to take you home." Roland gently stroked the man's head. "I'm here to take you home. Come now, up you get." He helped Winston Dudley to his feet. "My good friend Andrew will take care of you. You can trust him. I promise."

"Please take me home to live with you, Daddy. I want you to take me home," Winston whimpered and folded in on himself, arms curled against his chest, head bowed, only looking up under hooded eyes.

"I know, and I will." Roland passed him off to Andrew. "I'll be right behind you. It's okay now, Winston. No one's going to hurt you anymore. I'm taking you home."

THE DEMON RESIDES

CHAPTER ONE

"Ugh, dude, did you watch that movie last night?" Jude Lennon bounced the basketball twice and threw it to his best friend, Keegan Watts, who hit it with his cricket bat.

"Which one?" Keegan watched the ball sail into the air and land neatly in the basketball net. "Score!"

Jude grinned and ran after the ball. "That Elm Street movie with the claw dude." He picked up the ball and quickly threw it at Keegan.

It surprised him, but Keegan reacted and managed to hit the ball in the direction of the hoop. It bounced off the metal ring. "No fair, I wasn't ready," he complained and stuck a hand on his hip while his friend retrieved the ball. "You mean *Nightmare on Elm Street*?"

"Yeah, that one." Jude walked over to him, bouncing the ball. "Was that weird shit or what? Enough to give you nightmares."

"Dunno. Didn't watch it." Keegan eyed his friend. "What? You sayin' it gave you nightmares?" Laughter burst out of him. "You're kiddin' ain't you? *You,* having *nightmares*? Since when?" He'd known Jude since he was little. Being neighbours, they'd grown up together, attended the same school, and played on the same sports teams. He'd also never known Jude to have nightmares.

"No...I'm not." Jude frowned at his friend. "I may be a horror buff, but no movie has ever given me weirdo dreams before. I've heard about Elm Street for years, read about it, know what the plot is, but had never actually seen it. So, since there's a movie-fest on TV of all eight movies, I thought this is the perfect chance to see them. But that...ugh, I don't like Johnny Depp, but did you see what happened to his character? Yikes!" He shuddered. "Exactly what nightmares are made of."

"You scaredy-cat." Keegan chuckled. "You know full well horror movies aren't real. That it's all make-up and green screen special effects." He tapped the ground with his bat. "Come on, throw it, scaredy-cat."

Jude's eyes narrowed. "Oh, is that how it's going to be?" He bounced the ball hard in Keegan's direction, and watched it fly into the air.

Keegan managed to hit it, but it landed on the garage roof and lazily bounced down into the hoop. "Score!" Keegan threw his hands into the air and ran around the backyard.

"Ah, bum!" Jude stomped his foot and crossed his arms. "No fair!"

"Neither was you bouncing the ball so hard," Keegan chastised. "Just coz I called you a scaredy-cat."

"Which I'm not," Jude spat crossly. "It just gave

me weird nightmares, is all. Have you seen it? Coz you can't tell me not to have nightmares if you haven't seen it. I'd like to see how you go."

"I think I saw it years ago." Keegan tried to remember back. At fifteen, it wasn't a movie for his age group anyway, and he wasn't into horror like Jude.

"I mean, seriously…" Jude held the ball to his chest and contemplated his next move while talking. "How would you like that claw to come out of the bed? How many times did we think there were monsters under our beds as kids…and that movie has to go and be made about it. The ultimate monster and it looks like that. I sure as hell wouldn't want to be sucked into my bed." He dashed left and darted right, threw the ball back over his shoulder and turned around to watch it fly right past the hoop. "Ah, bum!"

"Well, if you dedicated the time you spend on horror movies to learning how to play basketball, you'd be able to take the shot," Keegan teased.

"Bugger off," Jude sniped and ran after the ball. Walking back to his friend, he added, "You wanna come over and watch movie number two?"

"Now *I'm* telling *you* to bugger off," Keegan replied. "There's *no way* I'm watching that stuff if it's as scary as that. Why would *I* want nightmares? Besides, that, I just realised that we *actually live* on Elm Street."

Jude's eyes grew wide. "Bloody hell! No wonder I'm having nightmares."

"Dude, that's not why." Keegan motioned for him to throw the ball. "It's coz you're a scaredy-cat." He barely managed to duck before being hit on the head with the ball. "Oi! What'd you do that for?"

"Why do *you* think?" Jude snickered. "Dare you to watch the first movie this afternoon, then the second one with me tonight, and then go to sleep and tell me it didn't give you nightmares."

Keegan rolled his eyes. "Are you that much of a—"

"Don't say it," Jude warned, and stuck out his hand. "Deal?"

Reluctantly, Keegan extended his hand. "Deal."

*****

The boys managed to find the first movie online and watched it that evening before the second movie that night.

"Well?" Jude asked after it had finished. "Enough to give you nightmares?"

"Meh, I doubt it." Keegan stretched his muscles out and rested back against Jude's bed where they'd been sitting on the floor watching TV in his bedroom. "Personally, I don't think it's scary enough to bring on nightmares."

"Well…something made me think of that damn claw last night," Jude muttered. "I'm gonna go the bathroom and grab some snacks from the fridge. Want anything?"

"A soda," Keegan replied and changed the channel to see what else was on. He'd thought the movie was rather boring and wasn't really into watching the second. But a deal was a deal.

They watched *Nightmare on Elm Street II* and lasted until the credits rolled and the network played an ad for their latest reality show.

"Well?" Jude turned to his best friend. "Not as good as number one. Something tells me they'll just get worse."

"*That* would be all of the reviews we read online." Keegan sniggered. "Yeah, still don't think much of it."

"It probably *is* the ultimate monster under the bed movie. I mean, really, who'd wanna sleep knowing that was gonna happen?" Jude changed the channel to see what else was on. "I certainly don't want claws to come up and get me in the middle of the night."

Keegan shook his head. "You daft sod, still acting like such a child. This thing ain't real. It's just some dude in make-up and a glove." He wearily climbed to his feet. "I'm gonna go. Sweet dreams, dude." A chuckle left him as he climbed out the window and through the tree between their houses.

"At least he didn't call me scaredy-cat," Jude muttered and turned the TV off to get ready for bed.

"Sweet dreams, scaredy-cat," Keegan called from his room.

Jude heard his chuckle and stuck himself halfway out his window. "I'm not a freakin' scaredy-cat, you simpleton."

Keegan flipped him the bird and closed his window.

Jude did the same and hoped his locked window

kept the monsters at bay.

It was after twelve by the time Jude finally got into bed. He'd faffed around doing other things to get his mind off the movie, made sure there was nothing under his bed, and that the doors and windows in the house were locked. Finally, lying back, he watched the tiny coloured stars dance across his ceiling. He was into all things celestial and had a lamp that spread the galaxy over his room. It also helped him relax enough to fall asleep.

Most nights.

Tonight, though, was a different story.

His brain worked overtime telling him the movie was nothing but that. A movie. An actor in a suit playing a part. A piece of Hollywood movie magic that was not real. He tried counting sheep, stars, and planets, but finally turned the TV back on and watched a late-night show, hoping the droning of the host talking about himself would make him fall asleep…

*****

Tap tap tap tap.

Tap tap tap tap.

Tap tap tap tap.

Tap tap tap tap.

Jude's eyes slowly opened and registered where he was. In his bed, in his room, with the TV off. The stars had stopped spinning, and he was breathing slowly.

Tap tap tap tap.

Tap tap tap tap.

In stereo now. The taps reverberated off every wall and surface around his head and into his ears.

"What the hell?" He sat up and listened closely, just making out the shape of everything in the dull starlight. His head swivelled to the window and his ears tuned in. *That's where the taps are coming from. Bloody Keegan!*

Jude threw back his covers, stormed over to the window, and flung the curtain aside to find nothing. No Keegan, anyway, but a tree branch tapping against the window. Breathing a sigh of relief, he opened the window to break off the branch, and after throwing it into the tree, he closed the window on the chilly night. Back in bed, he flicked off his bedside lamp and tried to straighten out his bedding, but his feet became entangled in the sheets. With a huff, he turned his light back on. "How the hell did this get so messy?" he muttered, pulling his top sheet over the bed. As he reached for his quilt, something caught his eye and he stopped and stared and dropped the quilt, exchanging it for the top sheet. Slowly holding it up, he saw four slashes down the middle.

*****

"Are you kidding?" Keegan asked the next morning when he saw his friend's sheet. "Sure you didn't do that yourself?"

They were standing in Jude's bedroom changing the bed as Jude didn't want his mother to see his sheet.

"*Of course* I didn't do it myself, you twat," Jude snapped. "I *told* you, I thought you were tapping on the window to scare me, but it was the tree branch. When I was sorting out my bedding, I found it this way." Holding the sheet up, he shook his head. "You can see this, right? What the hell happened to cause this? Coz they're not normal wear and tear holes, but full-on straight cuts like someone took a knife to it." He turned his gaze from the sheet to his best friend. "Like someone took *four* knives to it."

Keegan burst out laughing. "You still got Freddy Krueger in your head? Dude, we may live on Elm Street, but this ain't a nightmare. That sheet is definitely cut, and it can only be by human hand."

"It wasn't me," Jude declared defiantly. "I'm telling you. *I did not do this.*"

"Well, it sure as hell wasn't Freddy unless he came out of the TV. Or you're doin' stuff in your sleep you don't know about." Keegan noticed his friend's frown. "You still gonna watch the next movie tonight?"

"Yep!" Jude gave a sharp nod. "This crap is not going to get the best of me."

CHAPTER TWO

That night, Jude sat on his bedroom floor and watched the third instalment of *Nightmare on Elm Street*.

"Ugh." He pulled the quilt off his bed and covered his eyes at the gory scenes and grabbed the remote to change the channel. But something stopped him. It wasn't the fact that *another* teenager had died in the movie, it was the fact he'd vowed to watch it and Keegan knew it. He didn't want to be called a scaredy-cat, and didn't want to be weak, or be *seen* to be weak. He was fifteen and could deal with horror films. Usually. Deciding he'd better finish off the movie, he pulled the quilt over himself and left just his eyes peeking out. He was going to finish watching it if it was the last thing he did.

Once it was over, he took a few deep breaths, watched a late-night chat show, and got ready for bed.

"This is not going to get me," he muttered, and checked his sheet to make sure it was okay. Finding it was, he turned off the light and crawled into bed.

Lying back, he counted the stars on the ceiling and finally drifted off.

The neatly placed quilt slowly shifted and continued moving until it slid right off the bed. A hole appeared in the sheet just under Jude's knees. A second hole appeared beside it, followed by a third and fourth.

The holes grew longer until they were slits. The slits grew longer until they were cuts, and silently moved through the sheet towards Jude's face where they stopped once the hem had been cut. The sheet was now neatly shredded into four pieces. Four pieces of sheet started moving on their own.

The middle two pieces wound their way under Jude's neck, crossed, and came up the other side, crossing again until his neck was fully wrapped.

Jude's hands went to his neck, his eyes still closed in sleep, his brain working through the movies trying to convince him the sensation wasn't real.

The sheet had other plans.

The middle pieces slammed down across Jude's face, covering his mouth and nose.

Jude woke, his hands grasped at his face, his eyes widened in fear. But the two outer pieces of sheet darted around his forearms and wrists and pinned them down to the bed.

The sheet was a malevolent force out to do what it wanted, and it wanted to keep Jude pinned to the bed while it took its prey.

Jude struggled, kicked his feet out of the tangle around his legs, tried to scream, tried to breathe. He tugged on the sheet around his wrists, pressed against the bed with his feet to push himself up, and tried to get his head to his hand by bending at the waist.

But all to no avail.

He remembered back to the first Elm Street movie where the same thing had happened. One of the characters had been hanged in the same way and not wanting to befall the same fate, Jude had to decide to give up or keep fighting. Not knowing if it was a dream or reality, and quickly losing steam, he decided to give in because it was *just* a dream. Nothing like this could happen in reality, so it *had* to be a dream. It was just his overactive brain working feverishly to scare him and he needed to make himself calm down.

Falling back onto the bed, he stopped moving. Stopped moving his legs, stopped moving his arms, stopped moving his head. Every single muscle in his body stopped struggling and he went limp. So limp, he fell asleep.

*****

"Jude, time to get up. You've got football this morning." Mrs Lennon flung back the curtains and turned to see her son tangled up in the sheet and the quilt on the floor. "For goodness sake, how did you manage to make this mess?" She pulled at the sheet and found it wrapped around his arms and wrists. "Jude?" A frown crossed her face. "Jude?" Holding the sheet up, she saw four strands limp in her hands.

"What the hell…? Jude." She shook him awake and his eyelids lazily rose to half-mast. Holding the four pieces in front of his face, she noticed the dark circles and bags under his eyes. "Are you having nightmares?"

Jude breathed in and eyed the sheet, noticing it was ripped into four strands. His eyes widened, and the realisation hit him like a tonne of bricks. "Crikey!" He shot up and rubbed his arms, checking them for marks before feeling his face to find everything was in order.

"Jude. How the hell did you do this?" Mrs Lennon's frown deepened.

"Um." He gulped and quickly thought of something. "It must have been cheap cotton and ripped when I was asleep." He inwardly shrugged. It was the best he could do in such circumstances.

"Sheets aren't cheap, Jude, and this isn't even the one I put on your bed. Why is this one on your bed?" She watched him guiltily grab his footy shirt and pull it on.

"Um, something kinda happened," he mumbled and grabbed his shorts.

"Sheets aren't cheap, Jude," she repeated. "If you're going to continue with this attitude, you can stitch them up and reuse them."

Jude found his football boots under a pile of clothes in his closet and dug out a pair of socks to go with them. He sniffed them and shrugged…at the smell *and* his mother's comment. "Okay."

"What do you mean, *okay*?" She watched her son

as he dressed. "Aren't you going to have a shower? What's got into you? You've never ripped up sheets before."

"They're pretty cheap cotton." He shrugged and picked up his bag. "I didn't mean to rip it." He looked at his mother's puzzled expression. It wasn't as if he could tell her some movie character ripped his sheets in the middle of the night. "Look, I'm sorry the sheet ripped." He tried to sound as sincere as possible. "I didn't mean it. The cotton's probably thin and I must have ripped it somehow. I'll stitch it up and reuse it. Try and get some wear out of it." He batted his big baby blues at her. "Can you change the bed and set up your sewing machine for me? I'll do it when I get home. I gotta get to footy practice with Keegan."

His mother raised a brow at her son and wondered what was going on with him. "Will that be before *or after* you shower? And while I'll set up the machine, I won't make your bed. You can put this sheet back on once you've fixed it." She let it fall from her hand onto the bed. "Your father's making omelettes. Get downstairs and eat before you leave."

Jude opened his mouth. "I don't have—"

"Eat! Now!" She extended her arm to point at the door. Watching him sulk out the doorway, she could do nothing but keep wondering what was happening with her son.

*****

At football practice, Jude told Keegan what had happened.

"Sure you didn't do that yourself?" Keegan grinned and kicked the ball in Jude's direction. They were warming up before they got into the real practice.

"Of course not, you twat." Jude frowned. "Why would I cut up a sheet? Now I have to sew it back together and keep using it because it's not like I can afford to go and buy more."

"Are you sure the sheet wrapped itself around you?" Keegan picked up the footy and handballed it to his friend. "Are you sure you just didn't have nightmares and end up ripping the sheet and then getting twisted up in it?" He saw Jude's expression and managed to put his hands up in front of his face before the ball hit it. "Hey! Don't take your nightmares out on me. You're the idiot that keeps watching the movies."

"Yeah, I know," Jude grumbled, and dodged the ball as it came flying back. "But it was just the first movie when the sheet wraps around that dude's neck and hangs him in jail. Not only did it wrap around my neck, it pinned my arms to the bed. I just couldn't move them. I was kicking my legs, craning my neck, and nothing." Jude shook his head and heard the whistle blow for practice. "I just couldn't do anything. I couldn't even breathe."

"So, how come you've watched three movies, but only stuff from movie number one is happening to you?" Keegan threw the ball back and forth between his hands. "You stuck on number one, or something? Is it in replay in your head? Has anything happened from the second and third movies? What about number four tonight? You still gonna watch that? I mean, what's the point?" he asked as they walked towards the coach. "Maybe you should just watch them in the morning and then you'll have forgotten about them by the time you go to bed. Or, how about just not watching them at all?" He stopped at the outer edge of the crowd and waited for either Jude to reply, or the coach to speak.

Jude sighed and shoved his hands in his shorts. He'd grabbed the wrong ones that morning and instead of being his footy shorts, they were his normal ones he wore when playing outside. "Yeah… I know." He listened to his coach give orders and before they started practice heard, "And Jude, wear the right shorts next time." Seeing the whole team turn to him and snigger, he blushed. "Yeah, sorry coach. I was in a rush and didn't realise."

"Then realise for next time," Coach Stretton warned and blew his whistle. "All right everyone, into your lines."

The team sorted themselves into four lines and started their manoeuvres, but Jude's mind was elsewhere.

Why the hell am I scared of a movie? Why does some stupid fake-clawed, fake-skinned actor freak me out? And what the hell is he doing in my nightmares? I don't have nightmares. I'm Jude Lennon. I love horror movies and have never had a nightmare in my entire fifteen years on this planet. Not even as a little kid.

He kicked the ball across to his teammate and caught the next one coming. *What is it about these stupid movies that's making me think Freddy Krueger's in my head? I mean, that can't be me ripping my sheets up, and I know I didn't wrap the sheet around my neck and arms that way. Nope, defo wasn't me.*

They stopped for a drink and quarters of orange while the coach pointed out all the things they were doing wrong.

"Well?" Keegan asked, lightly jogging on the spot to keep his leg muscles pumping.

"Well, what?" Jude replied.

"What are you gonna do about those nightmares? You gonna stop watching those movies, or what?"

Jude sighed. "I don't know." He pulled the juicy orange pulp off its peel and chewed on it. "Dunno. I'm *not* a scaredy-cat. I've never had nightmares, regardless of what movie I've watched. *And* I'm fifteen years old. How stupid would I look if I let some stupid movie get the better of me?"

"Maybe it's like *The Ring*?" Keegan cut in. "You've seen *that*, haven't you?"

Jude's brows furrowed. "Yeah, what of it?"

"Well, maybe the Elm Street movies are like that. You watch the movie, and then the character comes out of the movie to kill you."

"Oh, for Pete's sake." Jude threw his orange peel at his friend. "Now *you're* being stupid. That movie wa'n real either."

"Just sayin'." Keegan shrugged and threw his orange peel into the bucket one of the assistants carried around. "Neither's *Nightmare on Elm Street,* but something's got you turning into a scaredy-cat."

"Stop freakin' calling me that!" Jude punched Keegan's arm.

"Boys!" Coach Stretton called. "Back to practice."

"Yes, coach," they said and walked back to the field.

"Why don't you come over and watch number four and then when something happens, you can see whether it's real or not?" Jude hooked a football with his foot and kicked it.

"Dude, I can't see your nightmares anyway. And since nothing else will be happening, what's the point in me being there? Besides, I don't care to watch another one of those stupid movies. I had enough of the first two." Keegan shuttled the ball between his two teammates. They were standing in triangles, three a piece, and Jude was beside him throwing and kicking his ball to two other teammates.

"Even for me? Your best friend of how many years?" Jude batted his eyes at Keegan. "Go on, you know you want to."

"Jude and Keegan. When you two have finished flirting with each other, get your heads back into practice," the coach yelled, making the rest of the team laugh.

Embarrassed, the boys put their heads down and got back to what they were doing.

CHAPTER THREE

When practice was over, Jude and Keegan went their separate ways. Keegan went off with his family for his younger brother's soccer practice, and Jude went home to stitch up his sheet. After showering, he dug out the first sheet and walked into his mother's sewing room where she'd set everything up for him. Being an only child, he'd been raised to do basic sewing, cooking, and washing. The rest of the housework was easy enough.

He laid the sheet on the desk, pinned the edges together, and in record time had sewn double layers of stitches. "Now, for last night's," he mumbled and laid out the slashed material. He had four edges and a hem to do. Once completed, he checked his handiwork and ran upstairs to make his bed. "Sheet…quilt…pillows…" he muttered and fluffed all four of them before plopping down on the bed. "What am I gonna do tonight? Do I want to watch the movie? Do I leave it for the morning? Do I need to bother? What the hell is happening to my sheet?" He tried to remember it happening, but drew a blank. "Well, something happened, and I wish I knew what it was. It's not like Freddy popped out of the TV like that girl in *The Ring*." He chuckled. "Trust Keegan to bring that up. We watched it together." Looking around his room, he had his desk by the window where his laptop was set up. The bookcase full of electricals was beside the desk, and the TV unit was beside that. His eyes darted back and forth between all three and slowly it dawned on him.

"Hey!" Keegan's head burst through the window and his body followed.

"Dude! Jesus, don't scare me like that." Jude clasped his chest and felt the pounding of his heart through his ribcage.

"What?" Keegan grinned. "Scared I'll give you nightmares?" He flopped down into the bean bag in front of the TV unit. "You still freaking out? Come up with a plan, yet?"

"A plan for what?" Jude threw one of his pillows at him and got him in the head.

Keegan gave his friend an arched brow and then promptly managed to get up into a half-crouch, shove the pillow under his butt, and sit back down. Wriggling into it, his grin returned, wider than before. "Was that your sleeping pillow? You'll be dreaming of me tonight, breathing in my sweet scent."

Jude's face screwed up in disgust. "That is seriously disgusting, dude. I'll have to burn it now."

Keegan lifted his right butt cheek and farted. "Here, that will help ignite it."

"Ah, dude!" Jude ran to the window to make sure it was wide open and breathed in great gulps of air. "What the hell is wrong with you? That's even more disgusting than you just sitting on it. And what the hell did you eat?"

"Curry." Keegan settled into the pillow and bean bag, not minding his own smell. "For tea last night and lunch today."

"Aw, far out, dude, that's gross, but enough about you." Jude waved air into the room hoping to push the stench out the door. "Before you turned my room into a toilet bowl, I was trying to come up with an idea to try and find out what's happening."

"And did you?"

"No. Your big head and backside interrupted me." Jude sat on the window ledge. "You got any ideas?"

"Are you still going to watch the movie tonight? And the one tomorrow night, and the night after?" Keegan watched his friend pout and frown while he thought.

"I dunno. I probably shouldn't. But I just feel…" Jude shrugged. "Compelled."

Keegan's brows rose. "Compelled? How? *I'm* not making you watch it. *Freddy's* not making you watch it. Your *parents* aren't making you watch it. Wait…they're not making you watch it, are they?"

"No." Jude scowled. "I'm compelled to watch it because a horror movie has never got the best of me. Not a one has ever given me nightmares. Not even *The Ring*." He snickered at his best friend. "But it's like; I started this, now I have to finish it."

"You know you actually *don't*," Keegan told him. "*No one*, not *even you*, is making you do this. You can say, nope, I'm done. No more for me."

"But, I've never let a horror movie get the best of me," Jude replied. "I'm not about to now. So, why don't you come over and watch it with me, and then if anything happens tonight, you'll be here to say it did."

"And what if *nothing* happens?" Keegan argued. "Then you're just a wussy boy scaredy cat who's been having nightmares from a movie, and I get to tease you about it for the rest of your life and tell all the kids at school about it."

Jude's scowl was back. "You'll do no such thing, Keegan Watts! Or I'll tell all the girls at school that you practise kissing on the bathroom mirror." He watched the blood drain from Keegan's face and his eyes grow to the size of saucers.

"You wouldn't," squeaked out of Keegan's mouth. "How do you…?"

"Oh…yes I would." Jude smirked. "And I know because I saw you and took a video of it." The lightbulb went off over Jude's head. "Video!" He snapped his fingers and went to his cabinet to check the DVR. "Yes, it records." He searched the shelves for his video camera. It was old, but still worked. He found his normal camera, his phone, his iPod and opened up his laptop.

"What *are* you doing?" Keegan was now intrigued. "What did you come up with?"

"We're going to set up all of these to record

overnight." Jude fiddled with buttons on devices and searched for power cords to recharge. "I can leave my laptop recording all night. Set up my camcorder to record, set up my camera to take shots with movement. I can set up my phone as well, and most can stay plugged in all night, so they won't run out of power at the critical moment."

"Are you leaving a light on?" Keegan went to his friend's side. "You won't pick up anything, otherwise."

"Ah…" Jude glanced around the room. "I guess the bedside light. It's by the bed, so will be better than the overhead light."

They went to work setting up the equipment, making sure they had the right angles and a clear view of the bed. All the cords led back to the power board, and all were in and charging.

"There." Jude brushed his hands off and placed them on his hips. "All set to record once I go to bed."

"What do you think will happen?" Keegan reclaimed his seat on the bean bag.

Jude flung himself across the bed. "Nothing, I hope."

"Then it's all in your head." Keegan nodded. "Which we already know. Has anything matched the movies? You're watching number four tonight."

"Just the clawed sheet from number one. And I'm not in a mental hospital."

"Yet," Keegan joked. "Seriously dude, we may live on Elm Street, but this ain't no movie and we don't live in Springwood. This ain't real, it ain't happening."

Jude rolled over to glance at his friend, a million

thoughts flooding through his mind. "I hope so, dude. I really do."

*****

Nightmare on Elm Street IV aired at eight-thirty that night. It was a continuation of number III, with some of the same characters until they were killed off and new ones were sucked into the nightmare.

Jude was alone. Keegan had wanted nothing to do with it and gone back to his room, sniggering all the way, leaving Jude to huddle on the floor in front of his TV with his arms wrapped around his legs which were pulled up to his chest. "This is just a movie," he muttered over and over, unable to tear his eyes away from the screen until the credits rolled and the ads came on. He sighed in relief. "Okay, that's done." Unwinding from his position, he rubbed his stiff muscles and climbed to his feet. "Time to set everything up and head to bed."

After going to the bathroom, he set his electricals to record, turned off the TV and the overhead light, and lay back in bed. He breathed in through his nose and out through his mouth, counted stars on the ceiling that weren't as bright due to his bedside light being on, and tried to think of anything other than Freddy Bloody Krueger.

At some point, he drifted off.

The quilt slowly slid off the bed and the stitches on the sheet started popping one by one. Each layer of stitches popped and broke and flung apart until the sheet was again in four strips. And once they did their dance around Jude's neck and wrists, the bed opened wide and sucked him right in.

Jude woke and found himself still in bed. Sighing in relief, he glanced towards his bedside table for his clock, but didn't find his bedside table. He found another bed with a person sleeping in it.

"What the hell?" he muttered and sat up. He saw another person beside them and another bedside them. His head swivelled to his right and he saw more beds with more people. And in front of him across the room to the left and right were even more. "What the bloody…? Where am I?" He pushed the covers back and swung his feet to the floor. It was ice-cold and they recoiled in shock. Looking down, he saw he was dressed in a white hospital patient gown. "Why am I…?" His brows furrowed and he stood up, ignoring the coldness of the floor, turning to see if he could make out where he was.

It was the mental hospital from movie number three.

I've jumped to number three, so I should be able to get out of here. It's just a dream, Jude, it's just a dream. Maybe you should go back to sleep, and you'll wake up at home. It's just a dream. This is not real. His feverish brain darted in different directions trying to come up with a plausible plan, but no matter how hard he thought, nothing came to him.

He silently stepped over to the bed beside his and looked at the person sleeping. It was one of the characters from the movie. Frowning, Jude checked on the others. All characters from the movies, all in a deep sleep on their cots, all wearing the same hospital gown and covered in the same hospital blanket. His eyes took in their surroundings. A long dark room, cold with an icy air when he breathed. High windows with metal bars at one end, and a wide door at the other. The floor was frozen concrete, and his feet were starting to stiffen with the cold. "This can't be good," murmured from between his near-frozen lips. And his brain, despite the cold slowing it down, decided he'd make a run for the door to see if freedom was on the other side.

The echo of his near-frozen feet on the concrete resonated loudly in his ears. His hands reached out for the doors and pushed on them, and as they opened, the stifling fiery heat from a furnace smacked him in the face. His eyes closed against the heat, and his hands flew up to cover his face. "What the hell? What now?" He could feel his extremities thawing, his hands and feet warming him to the point of boiling. "God, I go from freezing cold to boiling hot." He turned around to go back into the institute, but found it had disappeared and all he saw was a boiler room.

"Just like the one Freddy likes to play in," he muttered, spinning back around to find a doorway out. The heat was unbearable and he was parched and scorched. "There's got to be a way out of here." Deciding to run, he ran away from the heat down corridors that led back to the boiler room. "What?" he whined. "This is ridiculous."

"Oh…Ju-ude…" a very raspy and rough sing-song voice echoed all around. "Ju-ude…I'm coming to get you-oo…"

"Bloody hell!" Jude gasped and took off running. He heard a scraping sound behind him, following him down corridors and hallways that kept leading back to the boiler room. No matter which way he turned, which hall or corridor he ran down, they all led him back.

"Ju-ude…" The scraping turned into multiples and Jude knew it was the four knives of Freddy's glove.

"Gotta get out of here. Ow!" He yanked his arm away from a hot pipe and as he inspected the burn, he saw the door he'd originally come through. He took off running and smashed his way through, back into the asylum, back into his cot bed where once more the bed opened up and swallowed him whole.

CHAPTER FOUR

Jude woke with a start, his whole body twitching and jerking awake. His eyes darted around the room, taking in details and information until his brain finally comprehended that he was actually in *his* bed, in *his* room, and *not* in the asylum.

"Bloody hell!" gasped out of him and he kicked and threw off the sheet covering him. "What the hell was that?"

The bedside light was still on. His quilt was on the floor, and the sheet was in four pieces. He gingerly picked up one strand. "Naw, bum. I thought I'd stitched this properly." Dragging the sheet over to his lamp, he studied the stitches and saw they had been cut. "Bloody hell!" The realisation hit him. That maybe he had clear proof that something was going on. "The videos!" Lurching towards his desk, he realised how soaked he was and looked at his shirt and shorts. Even his bed was soaked through, and he realised he should shower and change first. He dashed into his bathroom, stripped off, and was in and out within a minute and looking in the mirror while he dried off. "What the hell?"

His face was red as if he had a bad sunburn, and checking the rest of his body, he noted the insides of his hands and arms were too. Was this more proof that something had happened? He remembered his feet being frozen and looked down at them. His toes were blue, but not cold. After giving himself a determined look in the mirror, he marched into his closet, dressed in shorts and a tank top, grabbed clean sheets and a mattress protector, and changed his bed. Once everything was back in its place, he turned off all the electricals and set to work looking at the footage.

They all caught the same thing.

Absolutely bloody nothing!

"Aw, what!" Jude threw himself back in his chair. "What! How can there be nothing? *At all!*" He sped through each video again and saw nothing but him sleeping in bed and occasionally twitching. Shaking his head, he slumped against the desk. "How could nothing have happened? My face is red, my arms are red, I was freezing and then sweating and soaked my bed. Ugh!" Lifting his head, he glanced at the time on his computer. "7 a.m. Not much point going back to bed. I guess that means it's just my nightmares after all. Nothing's happening. Just me and my overactive imagination."

*****

"So...what happened?" Keegan shoved his head

through Jude's open window and his body followed. "Did you catch anything?"

"Nothing!" Jude complained. "On *any* of them. All I did was twitch in my sleep. But I woke up in a complete sweat with red arms and hands." He held out his hands, palm side up, and Keegan peered closely.

"Not really red. A little pinkish maybe." Keegan glanced at the bed. "No ripped sheet last night?"

"Oh, it ripped all right." Jude hurried over to the pile and held it up. "I stitched this back together yesterday and now look. Ripped *again* in the same place."

Keegan wandered over to him. "What's your mum going to say about that?" He held out one side of the sheet. "Gonna stitch it again?"

"I'll have to," Jude grumbled and dropped the sheet back on the pile. "And I'll have to wash them as well. She'll be ticked as, but at least I put the other ripped and repaired sheet on. I'm trying to get as much use as possible out of them. But it's looking pretty hopeless."

"*You're* pretty hopeless." Keegan grinned at his best friend. "All those recording devices and you didn't catch *anything*?"

Jude shook his head and threw himself across his bed. "Nope." With his arms hanging over the side, and his head hanging half over, he mumbled into his quilt. "And I don't know what to do about it. *Something is* happening and I don't know what that is, or what to do about it."

"What happened last night?" Keegan flung himself backwards onto the bed and stared up at the ceiling. "What movie was it from?"

"Number three." Jude felt himself drifting off. "I was in the asylum in a bed, and the other characters were in beds beside me, and it was freezing, so I ran for the door and the boiler room was on the other side. Suddenly it was burning which is why my face and arms are red, and Freddy was calling out to me, and I finally got back to the asylum room where all the beds were, and I fell through mine and that's when I woke…"

Keegan glanced at his friend and grinned. Jude had fallen asleep and was now drooling into his quilt. He shoved Jude awake. "And then what happened?"

"Huh, wha?" Jude's head flew up and he blinked rapidly. "What happened?"

"You tell me. What happened when you fell through the bed in the asylum?"

"Ah…" Jude gathered his thoughts and leant on his elbows. "Ah…I woke up back here, dripping in sweat. Although, it felt more like swimming in it, and then I remembered the videos, had a quick shower and changed the bed."

"So, falling through your bed brought you back to here…" Keegan mused and chewed on his bottom lip. "Well, the whole falling through the bed thing was movie number one, and the mental home was movie number three, you've completely bypassed movie number two, and number four was on last night. Anything about that in your dream?"

"Nope." Jude yawned and shook his head. "Didn't get much sleep, but, man, I'm glad it's Sunday. I might sleep all day."

"What…and stay awake all night like they're supposed to do in movie number one. Yeah, that really worked for them. Johnny fell asleep even though he had headphones on, and the TV blaring, and he was still sucked into the bed."

"Yeah, yeah, I know." Another yawn escaped Jude and he rubbed his tired eyes. "But what else can I do? Filming it proved nothing. Living it is a bloody nightmare. So, staying up all night couldn't do any harm."

"Thank God it's school holidays; otherwise you'd have to go to bed. Which you'll have to do at some point because how many more movies are on?" Keegan rolled over and sat on the side of the bed. "Plan on staying awake for all of them?"

"No, of course not," Jude said almost defensively before scowling. "It's movie number five tonight and then there are three more."

Keegan counted on his fingers. "That takes you to Wednesday night. Have you come up with anything else? If you're not doing anything in real life, according to all of your recording equipment, then that means it's in your dreams just like in the movies. It's telling you not to fall asleep, but…" He shrugged.

"Yeah, yeah," Jude mumbled and sat upright as his father walked into his room. His father was wearing a red and green stripe t-shirt. "Why are you wearing a red and green striped t-shirt?"

"Wearing what?" Mr Lennon glanced down at his top. "It's a blue and orange t-shirt. You know…it's the one you gave me for Father's Day." He chuckled and looked at the pile of bedwear beside the door. "Your mother's been telling me about your sheets. Better get those washed and dried before she gets home. She's out at one of her women's meetings. And also…" he stared at his son. "You might need glasses if you think this is red and green." With another chuckle, he walked out the door.

"Seriously, dude." Keegan stared at his best friend with a bemused expression. "You thought that was red and green? It's *so* obviously blue and orange."

"Yeah, well, in the light it looked red and green," Jude mumbled. "And those colours are next to each other on the colour wheel, not so hard to get confused in dim lighting."

"Dim!" Keegan looked around the room. "It's broad daylight and the sun's coming right in your window. *Do you* need glasses? I'll get to call you four-eyes."

"Ah, hell to the no!" Jude snapped back. "I do *not* need glasses and can see just fine. And *no*, you *can't* call me four-eyes."

"Nerd?"

"No!"

"Geek?"

"No!"

"Glass head?"

"No! What?" Jude's brows rose. "Glass head? What? Oh, for God's sake, get out, you dipshit. I've got sheets to wash."

"And since I won't be helping with that, I'll take my leave." Keegan headed for the side window, but he stopped before climbing out. "Bye, four-eyed scaredy-cat."

"Get out!" Jude shouted and threw his balled-up sheet at him. It missed because Keegan had fled through the window, so he went to collect it.

"Four-eyed scaredy-cat," Keegan called from his room.

"Freakin' simpleton dipshit," Jude called back and picked up the sheet. As he walked back across the room he happened to glance out of his front-facing window and saw an old car slowly drive past his house. He did a double take, turned toward the window and watched the car move with the speed of a snail past his house. It was old, with a leather roof that looked to be retractable which meant it was a convertible. It registered in his brain, looked familiar, *was* familiar, and he knew it was the car from the first Elm Street movie. From the end of it, when the four teens drive away from Heather's house and it locks them inside. His eyes narrowed and he peered closer, swearing the person in the driver's side was wearing a red and green striped jumper.

"No…" He leant back and inhaled sharply. "It can't be…" Quickly rubbing his eyes, he managed to catch the end of the car as it drove beyond his house. "It can't be…no." He shook his head a couple of times. "Can't be. There is no way that was red, no way, I'm awake." He slapped his face on both sides and punched both of his arms. "Okay, I'm awake. That definitely wasn't red. I didn't see that. That was *not* the car from the movie. That was *not* Freddy Krueger driving it, it was just an old car with a driver wearing a striped top. End of story, that's all there is to it. I need to get these sheets washed and dried before Mum gets home."

Leaving the window, Jude collected the rest of the bedwear and hurried downstairs to the laundry where he quickly put the small load on. "Okay that's going to take ten minutes, what else can I do?" Gazing out the window, he spotted something caught on one of the backyard trees. "What's that?" Hurrying outside, he ran over to the tree and looked up. "What the bloody…?"

It was a red and green striped piece of fabric caught on a branch. "You have *got* to be kidding me?" Shaking his head, Jude blinked rapidly to adjust to the light and looked again. The red and green fabric was still there. Sighing, he went in search of a rake from the garden shed and proceeded to snag and pull the fabric free. But once he held it in his hand, he could see it wasn't red and green at all. It was blue and pink, and looked to be an old tablecloth that must have flown in from someone's clothesline.

"Okay, well, that's bloody weird." Fingering the fabric, he put the rake away and went inside to finish off his laundry load. But when he pulled his bedwear from the washer, he noticed small patches on the top sheet. And a closer inspection revealed the small patches to be along the four slashes on his top sheet.

"And that's strange…" He lifted the sheet closer to his face, and once his eyes focussed found those patches to be very faded patches of red and green.

"Oh, for God's sake," he groaned. "How the hell did that happen?" Holding the sheet from the bottom, he lifted it as high as he could and studied the slashes. Small patches in red and green dotted the sheet either side of all four rips. They were faded, but noticeable upon inspection, and upon that inspection, he found no spots anywhere else on the sheet. Nor his bottom sheet, nor the mattress protector. He ran his hands inside the washer and found no dye leakage, or any other item that might have been trapped inside when he'd shoved his stuff in.

"What now? Mum's going to kill me. *And* I'll have to pay for another sheet and they're not cheap," he mimicked his mother. Holding up the sheet for another inspection, he found the patches had disappeared. "What the hell!" Jude examined the sheet closely. All the patches of red and green had disappeared. "What the hell are you doing to me, Freddy?"

CHAPTER FIVE

On Sunday night, Jude sat down in front of his TV to watch *Nightmare on Elm Street V, The Dream Child.* He was determined to beat this idiotic nightmare he was actually living, and even more determined to prove something was actually happening to him physically and not just metaphysically.

At fifteen, he'd decided to be an adult about it and take it on as an adult. He was grown up enough to know that movies weren't real, but what was happening to him was *more* than real, and not just a nightmare. Regardless of what the footage revealed, he was determined to not only get the better of things, but to convince himself it was all just a figment of his overactive imagination.

He tried not to pull the quilt over himself, or over his eyes, and breathed a huge sigh of relief every ad break, and *especially* when it was over.

"That's done and dusted," he muttered and switched over to a comedy. "Five down, three to go. Breathe, just breathe." He swiped his hand over his face and through his sandy hair. The wavy lock fell over his forehead, and he pushed it back. "Just have to make it through tonight."

The comedy finished and he changed the channel to find a news bulletin. "The world is bat shit crazy enough without Freddy Krueger making it worse." Jude changed the channel and came across *The X-Files*. "Don't need more of that stuff." On another channel, he came across *Paranormal Caught on Camera*. "Ah, bugger! That stuff's on every channel." Finding a talk show, he got ready for bed, made sure all locks, doors, and windows were closed tight, and turned on the record button on his electrical devices. "May as well see if I can get it again, but it will probably be blank tomorrow morning." Stretching back in bed, he watched the rest of the talk show as his eyes slowly lowered themselves to a close.

*****

The clawed hand made its way up through the bed until the arm was fully extended. It flexed its fingers and waved hello at a sleeping Jude before waving for the other hand to come up. It followed the same path as the first. Making its way up on the other side of Jude until it was fully extended, it flexed its fingers and waved hello to Jude as well as the other hand. The first hand counted down to one and that's when both hands crossed over Jude's body and pulled him into the bed.

He didn't scream. He didn't flail. He didn't even wake as he disappeared into the mattress. When he *did* wake, he was in a bedroom that wasn't his.

"Ugh, what is this?" Groggy, he sat up and looked around. "Wait…" His brows furrowed. "This isn't my bedroom. This is…oh…" With wide eyes, he scurried off the bed and stood staring at it while trying to get his wits about him. "This is the bedroom of Johnny Depp's character from the first Elm Street. When he tried to not fall asleep, but still did, and he was sucked into the bed." He saw all of the paraphernalia on the walls and the bed, and he wondered why he was there.

"Okay, I'm clearly dreaming, I've gone back to number one for some reason. Maybe I'm walking through each movie, maybe I'm meant to experience all of it. Who bloody knows? But what the hell do I do now?" Knowing he'd be sucked into the bed if he lay down, he went to the window and flung it open. All he saw were the trees and stars in the black sky.

"Hello," he called. "Hello-oh…" Only the rustling of the leaves replied. "Okay, that's not a plan," he muttered sarcastically and went to the door. Flinging it open, he saw the car at the end of the path with four teens ready to drive off to school and waving goodbye to him. But it wasn't him that was there.

"Hello, Jude!"

Jude was grabbed by two clawed hands and flung backwards towards the bed, while the door slammed shut. He landed face down on the mattress with claws springing up either side of him and pulling him down into the abyss. He landed with a thud in another bedroom and saw it was from the second movie, after Nancy's family had moved out and new tenants had moved in. He saw an open book on the bed, and, reading a few lines, he realised it was Nancy's diary, telling her story to all future owners. "This is the movie that's five years after the first and the dude wanders the street, kills his friend, attacks his girlfriend, and ends up supposedly killing Freddy." Jude's fingers slid over the pages before turning them. He flipped until the writing stopped and he found something that made him gasp.

Jude Lennon, you're next! was written in red scrawling letters.

Jude touched a finger to the writing and found it wet. When he examined his finger, he realised the substance was sticky and wet. "Well, dang! If it doesn't look like blood," he muttered.

"That's because it is, Jude Lennon," the voice came from behind him before two hands shoved Jude into the bed that opened and swallowed him whole.

"Ah…ow!" He bounced onto a narrow cot bed and his head bounced a second time, giving him a chance to see where he was.

Back in the mental asylum from movie number three.

"Ah, damn it!" He managed to sit up and saw all the characters asleep on their cots. Just as they had been the first time he'd experienced that part of the dream. "Now what? I'm going to freeze to death? Do I stay here, or head for the door and get burnt instead?" Shivering, he made a quick search of the room before realising there were only two ways out.

The door, or the bed, hoping it would open up and swallow him whole again. But if it didn't, he could possibly be there forever in a comatose state like the rest of the characters.

Resigning himself to his fate, he pulled a sheet from the cot, wrapped it around himself to protect him from the burning heat, and headed for the door.

But instead of the boiler room as he'd expected, he was outside and standing a short distance from two men digging a hole in the ground.

"What the hell are they doing?" he muttered and tried to recall the scene from the movies. As he watched, he saw the two men stop digging, but before they could do anything, bones from the grave came to life and killed one of the men. "Oh, my God, it's from movie number three when they find his bones. "No, stop!" he yelled and started to run towards the men. But he was too late. The second man was subdued, and the bones collapsed into a pile. "Damn it!" Jude landed on the grass beside both men and felt for a pulse. One was dead, and one unconscious.

"Damn it!" Jude sat back on his heels, panting, trying to remember what happened next. "Okay, he's gone for now and won't be back, but we have to put the bones back into the grave and…and…" He glanced at the items beside the men and picked up the bottle. "Holy water. Yes! Douse them in holy water." He shoved the bones into the hole and poured the water over them. When the container was empty, he looked around for the cross that was supposed to go in next and threw it in on top. "There, that's supposed to do it. But what if it doesn't?" Racking his brain to get the right order and sequence, he remembered that the female lead was supposed to be dying at that moment.

"I can't do anything about that." Tightening the sheet around him, he started walking away from the grave, but was stopped by a clawed hand on his chest that sent him flying backward to land in Freddy's grave.

"Ow. What the hell." He shifted aside and shoved Freddy's skull away. "Be dead already, damn it." He struggled to his feet and saw the actress from the movie levitating above the ground, screaming in pain and clutching her stomach. "Oh, my God."

"Hello, Jude," Freddy growled, gazing at him with balls of fire emanating from his eyes. "Say hello to my friend, Nancy." He thrust his clawed hand forward and the actress flew backwards towards Jude, landing on him. Both of them collapsed into the grave.

"Ow, God, are you okay?" Jude grunted at her.

She said nothing, just limply relaxed on top of him before the dirt started pouring in.

"Hey! What's going on?" Jude yelled. "Help, help, somebody help…" was all that came from him before the dirt covered him whole.

"Hey, dude, you okay?"

The covers were flung back, and bright sunlight poured into Jude's room.

Keegan had noted that Jude was still sleeping, so

proceeded to bounce up and down on him. "Wake up sleepy head; it's time to see what happened."

Jude's left eye popped open, and he gasped in air. "What! What the hell?" Scrambling out of bed, Jude stood staring at Keegan who stared back in shock.

"What the hell are you doing? Oh, I can't breathe." Jude bolted for the window and flung it open, breathing in great gulps of air. "What the hell!?"

"Dude, you okay? What happened? You have another nightmare?" Keegan chuckled and slapped Jude on the back. "That's what happens when you watch horror movies. Nightmares follow. And what number was it last night?"

"Five," Jude gasped and pulled his head in from the window. "Number five. But that's not it. This nightmare was different."

"How so?" Keegan flopped down on the end of the bed. "Was it worse than all the others? Better than all the others? The same as all the others?"

Jude hurried over to his desk and clicked on the video of last night. While waiting to find something, he grabbed his video camera and phone, and turned the TV DVR on to see if they caught anything.

"Jude?"

Jude fast-forwarded through the laptop video, finding nothing of interest, then did the same to the footage from his phone, video camera, and the DVR.

Keegan sat watching him, peering at the footage when he could, brows furrowed, lips pursed in thought. "Jude?"

Jude got to the end of the laptop video and banged his fist on his desk. He ended the phone and video camera footage and cleared his DVR.

"Jude?"

"What!" Jude's head spun around in anger at being interrupted. "What?"

"Dude…*what* is going on?" Keegan's head shook in worry. "Look at you. You look like you haven't slept in a week, with dark circles and bags under your eyes. Your sheet and quilt cover are shredded to pieces." He held up both. The strips of fabric hung from his fingers. "And even your t-shirt's ripped. Which I only just noticed."

"My what?" Jude's gaze moved from his slashed bedwear to Keegan's face. "My what?"

"Your t-shirt." Keegan pointed at Jude's t-shirt that he wore to bed. "On the back."

Frowning, Jude pulled the shirt over his head and straightened it, so he could look at the back of it. Four slashes ran from the top hem to the bottom hem. "Jesus!" He dashed into the bathroom and craned his neck to look at his back in the mirror. "Jesus!" he exclaimed louder. "I've got four slashes on my back. What the hell?"

Keegan stood staring from the doorway. "Dude, what the hell?"

"Do you believe me now?" Jude demanded, throwing his t-shirt towards the laundry bin. "Just look at my back. I couldn't've done that to myself." He stormed back into the bedroom and over to the window that overlooked the street. There idled a red convertible, the roof down, a person sitting in the driver's side wearing a red and green striped jumper, and a brown fedora style hat. And while Jude couldn't see the person's face, he certainly saw the four clawed glove hand wave to him as the car drove off.

CHAPTER SIX

"There, did you see that?" Jude pointed at the car. "Did you see that car with that person? Just like in movie number one at the end when Nancy gets into the car with her boyfriend and friends, but Freddy locks the car and grabs her mother. Did you see it?" He looked over his shoulder at Keegan who stood silently by the bed. "Did you see it? It's the second time I've seen it and God knows how many times it's driven past, and I *haven't* seen it. Did you see it?"

Keegan stared in concern at his best friend. "No, dude. I didn't see it and haven't seen it at all." He paused before continuing. "Are you sure *you're* seeing it?"

Incredulousness fell over Jude, and he stared in silence at his best friend. His heart hammered in his chest, his back now hurt from the four slash marks, and his sanity was under question. "Get out."

Keegan frowned. "What?"

"Get out," Jude demanded and started gathering his sheets. "Get out and don't come back if you don't believe me."

"Jude—"

"No!" Jude stared pointedly at his friend. "*You're* questioning my sanity even though *you've* seen my shredded sheets, even though *you've* seen my shredded t-shirt, and even though *you've* seen my shredded back. Yet you *still* don't seem to believe me. So, you can get out and don't come back."

"Dude, don't be stupid." Keegan placed his hands on his hips. "I didn't say I didn't believe you, I just said I didn't see the car. I *can* see your sheets and back, and while I don't think it's Freddy Krueger doing this from beyond a movie on TV, I *do* think something serious is happening. And no, I know you didn't do that to your back. Calm down and take a breath."

Jude dropped the two balled up sheets onto the bed and took a deep breath. It shuddered on the way out and he breathed in again, hoping to settle his nerves. On a third deep breath, he spoke. "I meant what I said. If you don't believe me, then get out and don't come back. What I *don't* need, is a so-called best friend who doesn't believe me, making jokes and mocking me." He grabbed at the quilt and jerked the cover off. Its shredded pieces fell into his hands. "What I *need* is a best friend who *is* going to believe me. Who *is* going to help me find out what's going on. Who *is* going to be here for *me*." Glancing from the shredded linen to Keegan, he added, almost sullenly, "So, you're either here, or you're not. Make up your mind." Gathering the bedwear, which he knew was no longer viable to use, he walked down to the laundry to dump it in the bin.

His mother saw him, saw the linen, and saw the marks on his back. "Jude?"

He stopped in the laundry door opposite the kitchen, and they stared each other down across the hallway. "Couldn't be helped. I'll save up and pay for another set." He walked off down the hall.

"Jude, just a minute."

He stopped mid-stride, but he didn't turn around. "What?"

"Your back. What happened?"

He thought quickly. "I don't know. I was itchy and used a metal ruler to scratch my back. It must have left marks, but I didn't notice until this morning. They'll heal. I need to shower and change the bed. Anything else?"

Frowning, Mrs Lennon slowly stepped along the hall towards her son. "No."

"Okay, I'll be down for food later." Jude hurried back upstairs and dug out another set of sheets and a quilt cover from a shelf in his closet before turning to his bed.

"Here, let me help?" Keegan reached a hand for a sheet, but Jude just stared at it. "I don't bite." Keegan motioned for the sheet with his hand. "Let me help."

Heaving a deep sigh, Jude dumped the top sheet and quilt cover on the floor and unfurled the fitted sheet towards Keegan. Within minutes they made the bed and Jude quickly showered.

He felt the sting of the marks on his back and winced. Hot water wasn't doing them any favours, so he changed the water temperature and let the coolness soothe the angry red slashes. *What the hell am I gonna do*, he thought, running his hands over his face. *If I sleep tonight after the movie, it will happen again. It if I sleep today…mmm.* His brow furrowed. *What if I sleep today and stay awake all night? Is it only a nightmare? Or does it haunt daydreams as well?* "Maybe I should, coz I'm bloody exhausted," he muttered and turned off the taps. After dressing, he ignored Keegan and went down to the kitchen to find his mother cooking him up a plate of fried eggs and ham.

"The toast is in, the juice is cold, and I expect you to eat all of this because it looks as if you're not getting enough protein. So, fill up." Mrs Lennon plated up the food and placed it in front of her son. "I take it you ate at your house, Keegan."

"Yes, Mrs Lennon. But by gosh that does look good." He knew if he buttered her up he just might get a serve, too.

"Just as well I made two lots, then." Mrs Lennon was used to Keegan eating a second meal at her house, even though she knew he ate like a horse at his. But somehow, he managed to stay skinny. "Here you go." She put the plate in front of him and noticed the tension between them. "You boys got any plans today?"

Jude looked at her under hooded eyes. "No."

Keegan glanced from Jude to his mother. "Not at the moment, Mrs Lennon."

Jude's mother looked between them, noting the sullen air her son was giving off. "I suggest you try and get some sun for at least ten to fifteen minutes. Maybe your vitamin D is low, Jude. I expect to see you out in the backyard after breakfast." A quick glance at the clock told her it was later than that. "Make that after brunch since it's almost eleven. I had planned to cook steak for lunch at one, but considering the food you've just eaten, I might make it for an early tea, instead. Keegan, will you be staying for that as well?"

"Don't know, Mrs Lennon," Keegan managed around a mouthful of ham. "No idea what we're doing today, or if I'll even be here."

"I guess we'll have to wait and see, then." She saw her son down his juice and stand up.

"I'm finished." He left his dishes in the sink and headed into the hall. "I'm going back upstairs."

"No. You're going outside before it gets too hot and the sun gets too high," Mrs Lennon called. "Jude! Go and get some sun."

Jude had stopped in the hall, his hand on the stair rail.

"Jude."

Sighing, his head dropped back, and he looked up at the ceiling.

"Jude, I know you heard me." Mrs Lennon stood in the kitchen doorway. "Sun, now."

Another sigh, and Jude turned on his heel and stormed down the hall, out the back door, down the porch, and over to the back fence. He huffed and sat down, leaning against a tree, and crossed his arms over his chest. "Ow." He shifted against the tree, so his back didn't hurt, and heaved another sigh.

"Seriously, Jude, dude, *what* is going *on*?" Keegan flopped down beside him, the sun warming his face. "Spit it out and maybe I can help."

"Huh," Jude scoffed. "You didn't want to help this morning. All you wanted to do was question my sanity."

"No…I didn't." Keegan crossed his legs and rested his hands in his lap. "I just said I hadn't seen the car and asked you if you were sure if you had. It's in the movie; you would be remembering it from that. I seriously doubt anyone in this town has *that* exact car, make and model, and is sitting there like Freddy Krueger waving at you."

Jude's brows plummeted. "How do you know he waved at me? I didn't mention that. I didn't say anything about it. I just said he was in the car. I didn't say he waved at me." He turned to Keegan. "Who are you? You said you didn't see it and questioned my sanity, and yet here you are saying he was waving at me when I never mentioned it. Who are you? How did you know unless you're Freddy Krueger and this is a dream? Is this a dream?" He scurried to his feet. "*Are you* Freddy Krueger and this is a dream? Tell me." His fists balled up by his sides and he stomped his foot.

"Will you calm down? You're being a dick." Keegan stood up and faced him. "It was just a guess that he was waving at you because *no* I didn't see it, and while I don't know if you did, or didn't, see it, or it's just a figment of this weirdo dream-mare you're having, there's not a lot I can do to help you if you don't tell me what happened last night. But I can very well see that something *did* because of your back and your sheets. So, calm down and tell me what happened." Staring at his defiant friend, he noticed Jude's frown soften.

But then Jude huffed, and a scowl spread over his face. With crossed arms, he recounted the dream from the night before. "I didn't even know if I was awake when I woke up. *Sure*, you were bouncing on me, but that didn't mean I was awake. I don't even know if I'm awake now."

Keegan punched his friend's arm.

"Ow." Jude slapped his hand away and rubbed the red splotch on his arm. "What'd you do that for?"

"Are you awake or not?" Keegan asked.

"Well, since I felt it, I suppose I could say I am. But *who's* to say I am? Who's to say I am, and this isn't a dream as well and I'm feeling it in my dream." Jude's scowl was still in place as he stared back.

Keegan shook his head and chuckled. "Geez, dude, Freddy's got you twisted in knots. Just stop watching the movies. You've got what…three more to go?"

Sighing, Jude rubbed his eyes. The throbbing behind his eyeballs was growing and he didn't know if it was from being in the sun, or from a lack of sleep. "I don't know, maybe at this point I should."

"Maybe after number one you should've," Keegan replied. "No one made you watch them except you. I have no idea why you did, because the whole, *I need to confront my fear thing* just didn't cut it. You *never* needed to watch them, and you certainly don't need to *keep* watching them."

"But I gotta see it through to the end. I need to know how to kill him." Jude rubbed his hands over his face and pushed his thick blond hair back. His hands rested interlocked on top of his head. "I need to know how to kill him, so I can finish him off in my dreams."

"Then instead of watching it, google it," Keegan said. "Maybe Wikipedia has the plot lines online. Or some website dedicated to the movies does. Jesus. Look at you. White as a ghost, dark circles and bags, throbbing headache, by the look of it, and you look like crap. You need to finish this, Jude. Finish watching the movies. *No more.* Finish having the nightmares. *No more.* Finish worrying, or thinking, about Freddy Bloody Krueger. *No more.* Be done with it. End it now."

"Or I could just finish watching the rest of the movies today in broad daylight." Jude's arms fell to his sides. "Maybe I should just get the rest of them out of the way today and then I'll know how to fight Freddy in my nightmares tonight. *If* I have a nightmare tonight, that is." Jude snapped his fingers, becoming excited while Keegan shook his head in dismay. "That's it. I'll just finish watching the rest of the movies, so I'll be prepared for tonight, and after tonight, it should all be over."

"You wish," Keegan muttered. "You wish."

CHAPTER SEVEN

They raced inside and upstairs, but before they could hit up Google on Jude's computer, Jude veered off and flopped onto his bed. "God, I'm so tired." He yawned. "Wake me in an hour and you can google…"

Keegan shook his head and gave a soft grin at his snoring friend. "Let's hope he doesn't dream in broad daylight. In the meantime, though…" He pulled out the desk chair and made himself comfortable in front of the laptop and started googling *Nightmare on Elm Street.*

Jude drifted off into la-la land and believed he was having quite a nice time of it until Robert Englund popped into his brain.

"Hello…who's this? Whoever this is, I need to tell you that Freddy is real. It wasn't just a movie. It was an actual evil. An evil entity that took possession of a body, a person, and that happened to be a functional body and person. Whoever is out there and whoever can hear me, I am here to tell you that Freddy is real. Be careful. Try not to dream about him, try not to let him into your head because he will take control. Not just of your dreams, but your body, your mind, your persona, your life. Freddy Krueger is real. Take it from the guy who played him. How do you think I did it so well? I'd be left drained at the end of every day, and by the end of the movie, I'd feel as though I was another person and not myself. If you can hear me, contact me via social media. Reach out and let me know. Tell me if you're dreaming of him, if he's invading your life, and I'll try and help you. His presence is strong. I can feel it. I sense it. He's here and he's after new victims. New blood. New kids to destroy. He did that in eight movies and countless TV shows, and he's here to do it again. Contact me on social media and I'll try and help you the best way I know how."

A four-fingered claw slashed through Jude's black vision, cutting off the transmission from Robert Englund.

Jude jumped back and gasped, waiting for something else to happen. But the blackness surrounded him. There was no more Robert Englund. No more clawed hand. No anything. Just blackness all around him. He tried to calm his breathing, tried to regulate his pulse, but he *knew* something was out there. Waiting, not breathing, not moving, just waiting. His gaze darted to every millimetre of blackness. It was suffocating, except for his own breath and heartbeat. Oppressive. Blacker than black. And something other than he was there.

Jude slowly straightened from the partially

crouched stance he'd jumped into when the claw had slashed through. His arms slowly lowered to his sides. His breathing became quiet, and he tried to figure out what this was. *Where* he was? Was it a dream state, or a static state? A psycho paranormal state? *Something* was making the air around him black and thick. So thick he could barely breathe it.

Deciding to make a move, he slowly walked to the right, but kept an eye on the space in front of him. He didn't want any more surprises. But regardless of how far he thought he'd walked it was still black. There was no light, and he couldn't see anything. He was blind.

Taking a chance, he walked forward and slowly waved his arms back and forth in front of his body, hoping to find something to end this, and also hoping he didn't find *someone* who might end him.

"Jude…Jude…"

Jude froze to the spot, an ice-cold sensation rushing through his veins. The blackness made it impossible to see, so he had to rely on his other senses. He dared not breathe, he dared not move…

"Jude…Judie dude. Wake up. You've slept an hour and you told me to wake you up in an hour."

One eye popped open to see Keegan leaning over him.

"It's been an hour. If you want to get these movies out of the way, it's time to do it now. You awake?" Keegan peered into Jude's open right eye. "You awake? Do you want me to poke you?" His finger moved towards Jude's eyeball and almost made it before Jude rolled onto his back.

"God, has it been an hour already?" Jude yawned, and putting his arms above his head, he stretched his back. "Seriously?" His body went limp and he stared glassy-eyed at the ceiling.

"Yep." Keegan glanced at his watch. "Bit longer, actually. I got lost in cyberspace as usual. But I found the final three movies online and we can hook the computer up to the TV and watch them."

"Yeah…" Jude was so mellow he felt boneless.

"Did you have a dream? I didn't hear a peep out of you." Keegan grabbed the laptop and carried it over to the TV unit. "Didn't see you do anything, either."

"Yeah, actor Robert Englund popped into my head. Oh, my God!" Jude sat up with a start. "I need to find him on social media. Do you know if he's got Facebook or Insta?" He bounced off the bed and grabbed the laptop from a startled Keegan before landing bum first on the end of the bed. "I need to find him on social. He said Freddy was real and to contact him." His fingers flew over the keys as he searched the internet for Robert Englund.

"He what now?" Keegan frowned and sat beside Jude. "He said what?"

Jude replayed his nightmare scene for scene to Keegan. "Ah, here he is." He pulled up Robert's Instagram account and started scrolling through for signs of anyone else seeing Freddy in their dreams. "Nothing. Let's hit up his website." He clicked the link in the bio and a page for his website popped up.

Scrolling down, Jude didn't see any links for other socials. "Looks like Insta is all there is. But there is a contact page, so let's hit that." Up popped the page and Jude found a comment section. "Cool. It's time to write." He started typing and quickly described his dreams from the first to the last. Signing off with, *if Freddy is actually real, any idea how to kill him once and for all*? Jude hit the submit button and watched his email go through. "There. *Now* it's time for those movies."

They hooked up the laptop to the TV and proceeded to watch Elm Street VI, while waiting on an email ding from the computer. Movie number six showed them exactly how to kill Freddy. Movie number seven showed them how fake life became real life with Wes Craven, the creator of Elm Street and Freddy Krueger, making the movie a spoof of the evil in Freddy becoming real.

"Jesus!" Jude exclaimed. "That's almost like my dreams." They watched as Freddy died *again*, and then moved onto the final movie where Freddy was versing with another horror movie villain, Jason, from the Friday the 13th movies.

"Ah, well this is just getting stupid," Jude complained, watching Freddy and Jason duke it out with their respective weapons of choice. "How the hell is anyone meant to be scared by this?"

"How is anyone meant to be scared by any of them?" Keegan rolled his eyes. "But this *is* just stupid and clearly just for the money. You know what studios are like. Anything for the moolah." He rubbed his fingers together to indicate money, and then snorted as Freddy's head was decapitated. "Yeah…coz *that's* gonna stop him."

"Well," Jude said after the credits rolled. "I got nothing out of that one. And I completely agree. It *was* stupid and had nothing to do with the previous seven."

"And even I think they got a little bit wayward," Keegan added. "Sure, some of the characters were continued into the next film, but then they were killed off. So, then what was the point?"

"Continuity." Jude flicked off the TV and checked his emails.

"And yet, not even TV shows can get *that* right," Keegan muttered. "Anything?"

"Jesus! Look at this." Jude clicked on the email and up came the reply from Robert Englund.

Dear Jude,

My God, you've been dreaming of him. You've watched all of the movies, haven't you? That's always the one thing I recommend no one ever does. Watch all of the movies. He gets stronger with every one and seeps into your brain and your nightmares. Which he seems to have done. All I can say, dear boy, is do what they did in the movies when it comes to killing him. Try everything they did. Try to watch other things before going to bed to take your mind off it, and him, come up with a plan to execute in your dreams for when the time comes, because you will need to know what it is you're doing and what your next step will be. You need to be prepared, even if it kills you — ha ha, a little horror humour there, but this is no joke. Freddy's no joke, and you do *need to be prepared no matter what you do. You are in my thoughts and prayers, Jude Lennon.*

Robert Englund.

"Whoa," Keegan muttered. "Cool, he replied."

"Yeah, but couldn't really help me with anything, could he. And you'd think he could, *and* would." Jude shut down the open windows on the screen and closed the lid. "Regardless of the fact, he psycho-whatever-it-is contacted me."

"Mentally," Keegan offered.

"Yeah, whatever," Jude went on. "He couldn't help anyway, so what was the point in making contact?" He dropped the laptop on his bed and paced around his room. "All night, I have nightmares. During the day, I have daymares. Freddy's in my head, Freddy's in my bed, Freddy's in my freakin' dreams."

"Maybe that can be the new rhyme." Keegan chuckled. "Instead of that one the little girls in white sing while they're playing jump rope at the end of movie number one."

"The end?" Jude frowned and stopped pacing. "I thought it was the beginning."

"Whatever." Keegan shrugged. "It would make a great song. If only you knew how to write music and play instruments."

"Don't need to these days with Garage Band and a whole assortment of music apps." Jude went back to pacing. "Okay, so we know how to kill him. I've dreamt pretty much about the first five movies. No…"

he paused, "It's been mainly movies one to three. I don't think I've dreamt about four and five yet."

"That should have been last night's dream, right?" Keegan watched Jude think through his nightmares.

"Yeah…maybe…" Jude's fingers played with his lips absentmindedly. "Maybe. But now that I've rushed ahead and watched the final three, it might all come to a head tonight. So, I need to come up with a plan."

"Use the one they did, in the movies." Keegan climbed off the floor and dusted himself off before sitting on the bed. "Or, at least, take what they did and craft it into your own plan."

"Mmm…" Jude thought the plans in the movie through. "It's not like I have a pipe bomb, but I can use my own hand to stop him. I'll just have to pull him into the real world somehow for it to work."

"You want me here?" Keegan asked, swinging his legs back and forth to get the circulation going.

"Don't know." Jude sighed and flopped onto the bed. "I—"

The doorbell interrupted him.

"Jude, can you get that," his mother called from her room across the upstairs landing.

"Ugh," Jude groaned. "Sure." He rolled his eyes at Keegan and wandered into the hall and downstairs. The doorbell rang again. "Coming," he called irritably. "Coming." He flung open the door to find Freddy Krueger on his doorstep, tipping his hat with his clawed hand.

"Hello, Judie, Dudie. Miss me?"

CHAPTER EIGHT

Jude said nothing, just slammed the door on the entity standing on his doorstep. He turned to walk upstairs when the doorbell rang again.

"Jude…didn't I tell you to get that?" Mrs Lennon leant over the upstairs railing.

"I did. There was no one there." Jude stared up at her.

"Then why did the doorbell ring a third time?"

It rang again.

"And now a fourth." Mrs Lennon raised her left brow at her son.

Jude sighed, spun on his heel and answered the door. It wasn't Freddy, but their neighbour, Mr Feinstein. "Oh." Jude breathed a sigh of relief. "Hello, Mr Feinstein, you're…" he paused and his brows rose, "wearing a red and green stripe jumper."

"Yes." Leonard Feinstein's eyes narrowed and his lips pursed. "Do you have a problem with that, young man?"

"Um…" Jude's gaze moved up to his neighbour's face and shook his head. "No. Not at all, Mr Feinstein.

It just looks like Freddy Krueger's."

"Whose? And how would another person have this jumper when it was made for me specifically." Leonard Feinstein sniffed. "My mother made me this jumper. No one else would have one, so you have no idea what you're talking about." His snotty attitude was always directed at Jude when he stopped by, but the appearance of Mrs Lennon changed that. "Hello, Marcia, lovely to see you. I seemed to have received your mail by mistake again." His smile shone brightly at her, but dimmed a little when he cast his cool gaze at Jude. "You don't happen to have any for me, do you?" His brows rose at Jude, who backed off.

"I'll be upstairs," Jude told his mother and left her to converse with Feinstein about the lack of manners the mailman had for dropping off the mail at the wrong house. He made it to his bedroom and told Keegan what had happened. "I bet he stole our mail, so he could bring it over to see Mum."

"Got a crush on her, hasn't he?" Keegan chuckled and plopped down in the bean bag. "He does the same to my mum and probably every other woman his age in the neighbourhood. Has it hard, the poor soul. He's single, in his forties, and still lives with his mother who knits him Freddy Krueger jumpers."

Jude burst out laughing and quickly shut his bedroom door. "That's hilarious, but true, sadly. I hope I don't end up like that." He sat on the end of the bed and sighed. Gazing out the window, he thought about what had been happening in his life for the last six days. "I hope it doesn't happen," he muttered. "I don't want to end up like Feinstein."

Keegan noted his friend's serious expression. "You won't. Unless you end up like Freddy Krueger instead."

Jude's head swivelled towards his best friend. "Don't *even joke* about that. It's not funny. These nightmares have been freaking me out."

"Yeah, I can see that…" Keegan paused a few moments before continuing. "So…what are we going to do about this? Do you want help? Do you want me to stay tonight?"

"I don't know." Jude deflated and fell backwards on his bed. "I have no idea what *I'm* going to do, what I *should* do, *what's* going to happen. Where do I even start?"

"Start with what time are you going to bed? Do you want to fight in your dream, or just let it happen? You know this is a load of bunkum, so you can fight it."

"Can I? Do I? *I* don't know that this is bunkum. I thought Mr Feinstein was Freddy when I opened the door thanks to that God awful jumper."

Keegan sniggered. "Yeah, well, you can't go around thinking the neighbours are a fictional movie character. You might accidentally kill them in your sleep thinking they're Freddy."

"What if Mr Feinstein *is* Freddy?" Jude joked. "He hates me, probably wishes Dad and I were out of the way."

"*Don't even joke* about it," Keegan cut him off. "That's *so* not funny, dude, because he probably wishes the same thing about my dad and me. And besides which, you don't want to be a murderer. You're *not* Freddy Krueger."

"Didn't say I was." Jude sat up and rested his hands on either side of his legs on the bed. "But I *need* to do something and I need to get a plan in motion."

"So, let's get to it," Keegan said.

Once they were done it was time for tea and the steaks had been cooked.

"Are you staying for tea, Keegan?" Mrs Lennon asked when the boys entered the kitchen.

"Mmm…I'd love to, Mrs Lennon." Keegan breathed in the heady scent of barbecue steak. "But I better get home. Mum will be wondering where I am."

Mrs Lennon smiled at him. "I doubt it. She always knows you're here getting up to mischief."

Keegan's eyes widened and his hand went to his chest in mock shock. "Me! Get up to mischief? I think you have me confused with your son, Mrs Lennon."

"Ha!" Jude exclaimed. "Hardly. Get lost so I can have your share. I'm starving."

"And you have more colour in you." Mrs Lennon quickly glanced at her son. "Good to see you still have your appetite."

"Never lost it and not about to when such delicacies as barbecued steak are on the menu." Jude leaned over the stovetop grill and breathed deeply. "Yum."

"Glad you like it, but then what don't you like," his mother said. "Keegan you'd better get home for tea, and our tea will be served in ten minutes."

Keegan said goodbye to the Lennons and Jude waved him off from the front porch, standing there, gazing at the neighbours' houses, waiting for Keegan to shut his door behind him. Watching the lights pop on in the houses across the street, and seeing a red convertible with the top down slowly roll past with a man in a red and green striped jumper and brown fedora hat wave at him.

"You might be smug now, Frederick Charles Krueger, but I *will* kill you." Jude closed and locked the door and went to eat.

*****

That night, he watched a comedy movie on TV and set up his electricals to record all night. "Even if I don't get anything, I'll be prepared." He nodded at his handiwork and followed the movie with a talk show, laughing at some of the host's jokes, booing at others.

Once the clock struck midnight, he got ready for bed and turned off the TV and the main overhead light. Just his bedside light was on and casting a few menacing shadows on the wall opposite. He settled into bed, took a deep breath, and closed his eyes.

This had to end once and for all.

"Oh, Ju-uuude."

Jude's eyes flew open and his heart raced. He was

in Nancy's bed, in Nancy's room. "Damn it!" He threw back the covers, and raced through the door and down the stairs, flinging open the front door, only to find himself in Glenn's room with Glenn being sucked into the bed. "Okay, looks like I'll have to play instead of run. Let's go then." He dived into the bed after Glenn and landed back in Nancy's room, but it was different.

"Okay, now I'm in Dan's room five years after Nancy's family moved out. So, here we go again." Once more he raced from the room, down the stairs, and opened the front door and found himself in jail watching Rod Lane be strangled by the cot sheets. "And we're back to number one. Okay, what next? Let's run."

Jude ran from the jail and found himself watching the two men digging up Freddy's bones. "Movie number three. He kills Nancy and her dad. Let's go, Frederick." He ran over to the two men and grabbed the bottle of holy water, dousing the bones just as they came to life. "Suck on that, Frederick Charles Krueger." He picked up the cross and threw it onto the bones. "And take that for good measure." He nodded at the two surprised men and jumped into the grave.

He woke up in the asylum, back in the same cot, next to the same characters as he had in previous dreams. "And this time I came prepared." He bounced out of bed and ran for the door, the ice-cold floor not bothering him because he'd fully dressed before going to bed. His sneakers took the brunt of the cold, and his jeans kept his legs warm. He smashed through the doorway into the boiler room. "And here we go again."

Taking off to his right, he ran down passage after passage only to find his way back to the ward. "Ah, bugger," he panted, and rested his hands on his knees as he bent over. "I really am running in circles. But if this is where I'm meant to be, let's do this." He untied his track jacket from around his waist and pulled it on to ward off the cold, and ran from bed to bed trying to wake the rest of the characters.

"Okay, no luck with that." He wiped the sweat off his forehead. "May as well head back to bed myself." He took a running dive at his cot and fell right through, landing on old concrete. He immediately shoved himself up and saw Freddy facing off against Alice who was holding up a piece of broken glass. He watched as the souls Freddy had absorbed ripped him apart. "Well, that's a new one. By why am I doing the watching?"

Not sure which way to go next, he stood still and watched the remainder of the movie. Because that's what he was technically in. A movie. Or to get even more technical, all *eight* movies. When the characters had walked away, he turned around and saw Amanda Krueger absorb her baby son. "Ah, movie number five from last night. And there's Alice again." Feeling the chill of the air, he zipped up his jacket and wondered what to do next.

"Oh…Ju-uuude. Judie, Judie, Judie, Jud-eah!"

Jude turned around, but no one was there. "Come

out, you gutless coward." In the distance, he saw a person in a hat walking towards him, his arms outstretched. "Was that from movie number one?" Jude frowned, made a choice. He turned and bolted.

"Oh, Ju-uuude…come back and play-aaay…"

Jude ran through the labyrinth of passageways. He couldn't remember which movie they were from, but he kept on running. "It would be *really* useful right now to know where I'm going." Bursting into a large room, he skidded to a halt in time to see Freddy's daughter pin Freddy to a post with his own glove and then throw a pipe bomb into his chest. Freddy exploded and the dream demons escaped his body.

"That went well." Jude nodded and shoved his hands into his jeans pockets. "What next, because there's not much point to this dream I'm in."

"Oh…isn't there, Judie, Judie, Judie, Jud-eah," came from behind him.

"And I'm off." Jude took off running and found himself on a movie set. "Ah, number seven, the recreation." He watched Wes Craven, Robert Englund, and Heather Langenkamp being directed in a scene and then all freak out when a metal claw hand came scurrying across the ground. "Damn, that's creepy, but damn that's good work." Watching everyone scatter, he took off into the crew and headed for the house which turned out to be a replica of Nancy's.

"And here we go again." He threw his hands up in despair before rubbing them through his hair and messing it up. "I either head up to the bedroom, or head down to the basement." Deciding to not get locked in the basement, he ran up the stairs to Nancy's bedroom and threw himself onto the bed. He fell through and landed with a bone-cracking thud on the floor of the boiler room.

"Ah," he screamed in pain and managed to roll over and grasp his right hand. "What the hell!" He knew it was broken. The pain told him that. And he struggled to his feet, clutching his hand to his chest.

The heat permeated right through his sweat jacket and he tugged it off and wrapped it around his hand. "God that sucks," he yelled at the top of his lungs. "*You* suck, *this* sucks, *the pain* sucks, *this freakin' dream* sucks."

"But why do you think it sucks, Judie?" the voice came gravelly and low. "It's only *you* who does, Judie. But then, you haven't realised yet."

"Realised what?" Jude pouted, the pain in his hand becoming unbearable.

"That it's not *me* you're running from, Judie Jude. It's yourself."

Screwing up his face at the stupidity of the answer, Jude started moving, trying to remember where the door to the asylum was. "Go away and let me get back to sleep."

"It's not sleep you want, Judie. It's the truth."

"Ha! And what truth would that be, *Frederick*?" Jude kept on, but couldn't find the door, so he turned down another passageway into the boiler room.

"The truth that is *literally* in your hands, Jude

Leonard Lennon."

"Ha! My middle name's not Leonard. That's the next-door neighbour's."

"Exactly!" Freddy's voice came from behind him. "Neighbours can sometimes become such *good* friends. But then again, the future is in *your* hands, Judie. Your *right* hand."

"You mean the one that just broke?" Jude scowled and glanced at his hand. Except it wasn't *his* hand. Because *his* hand didn't have four knives attached to it. "What the hell!"

"The future is in *your* hand, Judie, and it wasn't *me* you were running from."

Jude stared at his hand. Glove, four knives. "What the hell?"

"It wasn't *me* you were running from…"

Breathing deeply, Jude turned around to confront Freddy face on, but there was no one there. "Where are you, you coward. Show yourself."

"It isn't *me* you're running from, Judie."

A light glinted off to Jude's right and he turned towards it. The heat from the boiler room seared his flesh, making sweat drip from every pore. He walked slowly towards the glinting and found it to be a shiny metal meter box. He stared into it and saw himself. Except he wasn't himself. His left hand touched his face. His skin was burnt and red and a brown fedora style hat sat on his head. He glanced down and saw he was wearing a red and green striped sweater, and with his gloved hand, the picture wasn't looking good.

He gazed into the shiny metal, comprehending

what he now was. Maybe what he had always been. What he thought he'd been running *from*. Not *something* else. But…*himself.*

It's not that he was running away *from* the demon, he *was* the demon. The demon resided within *him.*

He disagreed with that and took off running.

INFESTATION

CHAPTER ONE

"Marlaine, the fun drain, when she walks by everyone runs away. Marlaine Dufrane, the party pooper sends fun down the drain."

Marlaine Dufrane could barely look at the classmates singing the song she hated so much. Day after day at school, she would have some group or another chant that ditty to her face, or sometimes behind her back. But they always made sure she heard. Lunch and home time were the worst for the torment, as they were under the eye of the teachers the rest of the day. And most days she hid in the library doing homework at lunchtime, so she didn't have to worry about it during her after school job.

Barely thirteen, Marlaine was following her parents into the cotton and sawmill. All three of them worked there to make ends meet in the little country town of five thousand people. There were also coal mines and quarries to keep the folk occupied, but still, times were hard and no thirteen-year-old should be working for five hours after school each night to help her family survive.

"Hey, Marlaine! We're talkin' to you."

She glanced up from her morose self-retrospection to see the school bully. Knowing it was best to say nothing, she merely blinked at him and turned away, walking in the direction of the library to get her maths homework done for the day.

"Hey! I'm talkin' to you."

Marlaine felt the hands on her back and was thrust forward. Her shoelace caught under her shoe, and she fell face first into the ground of the school's lunch yard in front of several grades of kids. Her books flew around her and her hands and knees were roughed up. The heat rose to her face, burning her flesh to her hairline and ears. It was just one more day at that horrid school.

Laughter and jeers about her clumsiness, her old worn-out hand-me-down uniform, and her holey shoes rang around the yard. The kids that hated her tormented her about everything, even though she'd never done anything to them.

"Darius Cormack! I saw that," an authoritative voice rang out. "You just scored yourself one week of detention starting from today." Mrs Butterworth, the school's principal, stormed over and leaned down to Marlaine. "Are you all right, dear? Let me help you up."

"I'm fine, Mrs Butterworth," Marlaine mumbled, not wanting to cause more of a scene than necessary. She climbed to her feet with the principal's help and looked at her grazed hands and knees. "I'm fine." Keeping her eyes down, she quickly gathered her books.

"You are not fine, Marlaine. Go to the nurse and get yourself cleaned up and Darius…" She watched Marlaine head for the office and then turned to the sulky thirteen-year-old brat. "I saw *exactly* what happened and you still have detention."

"I did nuthin'!" Darius complained with a scowl. "She tripped over her own stupid shoelace, so it's *her* fault." He shoved his hands into his pants pockets. "It was *her* fault."

"*No, it wasn't.* And I'll be ringing your mother to let her know you have detention all week. Now…" She coolly gazed over the other teens standing around him. "Since all of you were singing that degrading little ditty, how about I give the rest of you detention as well?"

"What!"

"No!"

"I didn't do anything!"

"Oh, pish!" Mrs Butterworth exclaimed. "I saw and heard everything, so you all have detention because I know it's not the first time you've sung it. Now finish your lunch and make sure you're in detention this afternoon or I will hunt you down myself." When none of them moved, she clapped her hands sharply. "Move!"

They hurried off across the yard and she walked back inside the office, seeing Marlaine sitting in the nurse's office getting her hands and knees cleaned. A sigh left her. She knew it wasn't the first time the girl had been bullied for being poor. Most of the mill kids were, and that's why many left school when they were old enough, barely having a decent knowledge of basic English and maths. With another sigh she walked into her office to start calling parents.

"Thank you." Marlaine's voice was soft as she looked down at the Band-Aids on her palms. "I need to get to the library now." Sliding off the bed, she gathered her books. "I barely have time to do my homework before lunch is over."

"Did you eat lunch?" Nurse Rutherford asked kindly, taking in Marlaine's gaunt, unhealthy complexion and physique. "Do you need to apply for the lunch service? Many mill kids do. You'll get a decent lunch and breakfast too if the need be."

"I did." Marlaine nervously glanced at the clock on the wall, seeing the second hand tick by, counting down the minutes she had left. Her stomach growled, betraying her. "I do eat lunch," she said a little more forcefully. "Thank you, Nurse Rutherford." Hurrying from the room, she left the office and ran for the library. God, how she hated the way everyone looked at her. With such pity. As though she was someone to be taken care of. She took care of herself. Fed herself, dressed herself, got herself to school. She had to, as both of her parents worked long hours at the mill five days a week, and sometimes on Saturday.

Her father was always gone before she woke, and her mother left home when she did, with both finishing between five and seven most nights, although her father waited to walk her home from her own shift of cleaning the mill until eight. This was her job. Cleaning the mill. Sweeping floors, taking out the rubbish, picking up the remnants on the floors and putting them in the scrap pile or to be used pile. Twice a week, she cleaned the toilets, making sure to put the *being cleaned* sign on the door so no man walked in on her. The other men knew they had to be respectful of her since her father was not only their supervisor but was well known and respected as a hard worker, while her mother was the receptionist slash secretary.

But none of that meant they lived well. They didn't. Hand-me-down clothes and uniforms, anything that would fit from the five charity op shops in town also meant more ruthless teasing when other kids recognised something they had previously owned, and their parents had donated. It also meant the bills were barely paid and they had to cut corners where they could and eat as lean as they could. Breakfast was always an egg sandwich, and lunch was a sandwich with a piece of fruit from one of their trees, and water from the tap for a drink. Milk was bought once a week, along with meat and vegetables that were made to last the entire week. And sweets, soft drink, cakes and other treats were normally a twice a year treat for birthday and Christmas for which her mother saved up. They were the only two times each year that she received anything new from the local discount variety stores, and those items had to last her, so she always took care of them.

Her stomach growled as she quickly took a seat in the library and opened her book. There were ten questions to answer, and all were rather difficult, which made her fret that she wouldn't have the time.

"If you need any help, Marlaine, just let me know," Mrs Carmichael, the school's librarian and town's historian told her as she passed by to pop a book on a shelf.

"Thank you," Marlaine murmured, but didn't raise her head. A shy and quiet girl, she rarely looked anyone in the eye, refusing to make contact unless she absolutely had to. And she rarely absolutely had to.

"You're welcome, Marlaine." Mrs Carmichael walked over to a cart of books to be shelved. She knew this was Marlaine's ritual, as it was for many of the mill kids who were bullied at the school. Poorer than most other folks in town, they sheltered in the library most days to either do homework, or just stay out of their bully's path. It was a sad affair, and one she tried helping by teaching them and helping with their homework and other things. She'd often bring them food; make sure they were still on the breakfast and lunch list, that they got books out to read, and often recommended titles for them. She also sheltered them when the bullies came into the library to continue their torment. Popping two more books on shelves, she peered at the clock and then at the kids sitting at the tables or on couches. "Ten minutes left, everyone. If anyone needs help, yell out now."

A couple of kids raised their hands and called out, so she went over to help them.

Marlaine glanced at the clock and finished off

question nine, then started on number ten. It was about the same level of difficulty, but she scribbled down the answer just as Mrs Carmichael called out.

"Five minutes left. Start gathering your things or go to the bathroom now if you need to. Or have something to eat or drink."

There were water fountains to drink from, and a small bathroom, all off the entrance hall. There was also a bowl of fruit on the front desk for anyone to pick a piece from, and it was always empty by the end of lunch.

The kids scattered to do what they needed, and Marlaine closed her maths book and gathered her things. She'd left her bag in her locker which was why everything had flown from her arms when she'd fallen. Some of the pages of her books were ripped, but there was no serious damage.

Better bring my bag next time, she thought as the bell shattered the relative silence.

"Off to class, kids, and be careful. Take some fruit with you," Mrs Carmichael called and watched as each one hurried through the door. "Be careful."

Marlaine got through the rest of the day non-scarred and hurried home after school to avoid the bullies, but mainly to change for work. She quickly donned old, ragged jeans, an old, stained t-shirt, and grungy old Dunlop sneakers. All from an op shop, and all well-worn by her work at the mill. Taking her uniform into the laundry, she carefully washed under the arms and around the collar to keep it clean, and then left it to dry on a rack hanging over the sink. She whipped together a plain sandwich for later, grabbed her bag, and ate the banana she'd taken from the library as she rushed two blocks down the road to the mill. She made it on time and logged in at 3:30 p.m.

Walking through the factory, she saw the workers gathered around the far end where the office was. Her parents were amongst them. The manager was talking, and she stopped on the outskirts of the group.

"Now, as you know, Mortimer isn't here today, and we just thought he was sick. But we found out from his wife and the police that he never went home. Hasn't been home since Friday, which is why the police have been around here today."

"Do they think he disappeared from here…like the others?" one man called out. That set off a rumbling through the crowd.

"Now, now…" Reginald Sherriff, the mill's manager, put his hands up to placate the crowd. "There is no evidence that something happened to him here, or that he disappeared from home. The police just wanted to ask questions."

"But that's what they did last time," another man said. "Either somethin's happenin' to our workers, or they're all uppin' and leavin' without tellin' anyone."

"And that's entirely possible." Reginald glanced across the gathering. "But, so far, it's only been four men, counting Mortimer. It's entirely possible they're just leaving for greener pastures and not telling anyone. *Including* their wives."

Small laughter mumbled through the crowds and

Marlaine silently made her way to her mother's side.

Betty Dufrane looked down at her daughter and slid an arm around her, pulling her close. Marlaine was her only child, and a much fought for one at that. After years of trying, with depressing disappointment, she'd finally become pregnant on her forty-fifth birthday and named the baby after her much-loved grandmother.

Marlaine snuggled into her mother's side and wrapped her arms around her waist. Listening while the men bickered.

"If they're leaving of their own free will, that's one thing. But what if something *is* happening to them?" someone asked. "They've all been working at night, doing the night shift, and haven't been heard of or seen again. Maybe the night shift's haunted. Maybe the mill's haunted. Maybe there's a ghost getting them when they're here on their own. Don't ever put me down for the night shift."

Rancour rolled through the crowd and Reginald once again put his hands up. "Stop this nonsense. The mill's not haunted. The night shift's not haunted. There's no bogeyman picking workers off one by one. Otherwise, the police would have said something."

"What *did* they say?" someone asked.

"All they said was the same as the others. He didn't go home, has been missing, but there's no evidence of foul play anywhere. They think all four men simply walked away from their lives and wives. Until they find evidence stating otherwise, it's life as normal. And that means for us, too. So…everyone back to work." He clapped his hands. "It's getting late; let's get this finished."

The crowd dispersed and Betty quickly hugged and kissed her daughter before rushing into the office to finish her work.

Douglas Dufrane smiled wearily at his daughter and gave her a quick pat on the head before heading back to his workstation.

Marlaine hated how worn out her parents looked and felt it to the bone herself. They worked long hours just to make money to survive and put the bare minimum of food in their stomachs and petrol in a car they only used on weekends for outings, although her parents had been discussing selling that, too. The money all three of them made covered bills and basic food, and that was it. Most of the mill workers lived on the poverty line and had cheap rental cottages which were situated in the first two roads of houses around of the mill that were kept for the workers, so they could to get to work if they had no transport.

Marlaine hurried into the supply closet for her broom and set to work sweeping the huge factory floor which would take her an hour. It took another hour to sweep the sawmill's floor, and by the time she got back to the closet for other supplies, her mother was preparing to go home.

"I'm off, my darling. I'll have a nice hot meal ready when you and Daddy get home after eight-thirty." She slid a hand knitted cardigan around her shoulders.

"Oooh…hot roast chicken and veggies?" Marlaine was always hopeful for her favourite meal.

Betty smiled at her underweight daughter. "You know we had that yesterday, but I turned the leftovers into soup. So, it will be hot chicken and vegetable soup with bread."

"Oh…" Marlaine's face fell. "Still yummy…I guess."

"At least it's food and will fill your empty tummy." Betty tweaked her daughter's chin. "Have you signed up for the lunch service? You could get breakfast, too. There's nothing to be ashamed of in asking for help. We all need to, sometimes."

Marlaine glanced up at her mother under hooded eyes. "No, ma'am. Not yet."

"And why not?" Betty kissed her daughter's cheek. "I know the other kids have, and it will give you a better start to the day and a healthier lunch. Some days you barely eat breakfast. You need to sign up and start being fed. It will help more than I can. You'll get a good breakfast and a lunch a day, and it will fill you out a little." Her daughter's thin frame was something she always worried about.

"I'm fine, Mama, really. Safe trip home." She hurried off to the supplies closet to gather the mop and bucket. Now she had to mop the factory floors.

Sighing, Betty hurried from the mill and down the road to her home.

CHAPTER TWO

Two hours later, Marlaine had finished mopping the floors and was emptying the bucket of dirty water for the tenth time in the small bathroom sink. It was a dirty job, but it paid two pounds an hour and she worked for five hours every afternoon during the week. At ten pounds a day, that was fifty pounds a week, and forty of that went to towards the household, eight went into her bank account, and two pounds went into her purse to buy anything she wanted. But she was saving *that* too. What for? She wasn't sure yet, but getting paid was a big deal for a kid in her circumstances. *Dire* circumstances at that!

She put the bucket and mop aside to dry overnight and gathered dusting cloths from the closet. She just had the offices to go, and she'd be done.

"Ready to go, bluebird?" Douglas asked from one of the chairs outside the office. He'd been reading a magazine while waiting for his daughter's shift to end.

"Another hour or so, Daddy." She smiled slightly. "All for another two pounds."

"I know it's not much, bluebird, but it all helps.

Every last bit. And you get to save some." He tossed the magazine onto the pile on the small coffee table beside him. "We wouldn't be able to do that for you. Times are tough all round."

"Yeah…" murmured from between her lips and the smile disappeared. "I guess. Although it doesn't seem like much for all the work I'm doing."

"We only make double what you make, sweetie, and work ten hours a day. Your mother makes less because she's only nine to five, and on the odd occasion, six. Every little bit helps."

Marlaine sighed from the pit of her empty, weary stomach. "I know. Do you want a coffee before I clean the offices?"

"Yes, thanks, bluebird. And maybe we can munch on some of those biscuits Reginald keeps hidden in his desk drawer." He looked at her hopefully.

A small giggle bubbled out of Marlaine. "You mean the ones he thinks no one knows about, but what he doesn't know is that rats eat them in the middle of the night?"

"Ew!" Douglas's face screwed up. "I think I'll pass on those and just take the coffee."

"Okay, Daddy. One coffee coming up." She went to the small side cupboard kitchenette in her mother's office, filled the kettle with water, and set it to boil. She poured a couple of teaspoons of coffee into a clean cup and added two sugar cubes. It was where her mother made her boss coffee and tea every hour on the hour during the day, and where she took a couple for herself.

While waiting for the kettle, she dusted her mother's desk, filing cabinets, and the top of the picture frames on the wall, and when the kettle boiled, took her father his coffee and dusted the manager's office. It was a pigsty as usual, but she didn't dare touch anything on the desk for fear of receiving his wrath for doing something wrong. Within half an hour she was done with dusting and tidying and went back to the closet for the vacuum cleaner that she lugged into the office.

"Half an hour to go," she mumbled, and pulled the cord from the back of the cleaner. Once it was fully out, she plugged it in and away she went. Ten minutes later she was moving into the manager's office and kneeling on the floor to get between to filing cabinet and cupboard to plug the cord in, when a sharp pain fled through her finger.

"Ow!" Her hand snapped back, and she saw blood pooling on her right forefinger. "What the…?" She saw a rat race out from between the cupboards, squeaking all the way as he bolted under the desk and disappeared near a desk leg. "That was weird. He only had three legs and a stumpy tail."

"You okay, bluebird?" Douglas poked his head into the office. "Bluebird?"

"Here, Daddy." She looked over the desk top. "I'm fine. Just got bitten by a rat with three legs and a stumpy tail."

"Are you okay?" He moved behind the desk to examine her finger. "I've seen rats around here, but wouldn't want to be bitten by one. Have you had your shots?"

"Yes, Daddy. It's okay. I've been bitten before."

"Does your mother know about that? The doctor?"

"Yes, Daddy…" She sighed. "He gave me my shots."

Douglas pulled his handkerchief from his pocket and wrapped it around her finger. "There. If you're able to, finish off and we can go home."

"Okay, Daddy. Nearly done." Marlaine quickly plugged in the cleaner and got to work on the floor. She was faster than usual, as time was passing, and she yanked the cleaner out the door and back to the utilities closet. "There. All done."

"I cleaned out my cup and left it on the sink for you, bluebird, to save time, because it's nearly eight-thirty and I need to get you home. Are you finished?"

"Yes, Daddy. Just need to turn the lights off as we go." Taking her father's hand, she noted the bags and dark circles under his eyes, the unshaven face, and rumpled red check lumberjack shirt from the op shop that matched his reddish-brown rumpled hair.

They checked out of the mill and bade goodnight to the security guard who locked up behind them and made their way two blocks down the road to their cottage where the smell of chicken and vegetable soup hung thick in the air.

"We're home," Douglas called, closing the door behind them.

They hurried down the hall to the small kitchen and saw Betty scooping out ladles of steaming broth into bowls.

"Yum!" Marlaine sat wearily into her chair and

thanked her mother for the bowl she placed before her. They ate in relative silence except for the odd comment or two, and a retelling of rat hijinks in the manager's office.

"At least you've had your shots," Betty said. "So, you should be okay. But if anything happens to your finger, or you start feeling sick, tell me and I can take you to the doctor. Now, if you've finished, run along and have a nice hot shower and get ready for bed. I'll wrap your finger in something before bedtime."

"Yes, ma'am." Marlaine scooped up the last of her soup with her bread and pushed her chair back.

"I'll do your dishes. You go and clean that finger." Betty smiled at her daughter and waited for her to run off. "I hope her finger will be fine. The doctor's not cheap these days." She gathered the dishes and placed them on the sink.

Douglas leaned back in his chair, slid his hand up his wife's arm and pulled her onto his lap. "We may be struggling, but we can afford the doctor if need be. It's covered by the mill anyway, as that's where it happened."

"Yes…" she murmured. "That *is* a good thing. But Reginald might have a problem since it's not work related."

"Except it is. She was doing her work when it happened. And if he didn't hide food in his desk, there wouldn't be any rats to bite people." Douglas almost cracked a smile.

Betty giggled softly and kissed her husband. "Yes, I suppose so. But he won't agree to that."

*****

Marlaine stood under the hot water and scrubbed herself clean, then rubbed herself down from top to bottom with the pink fluffy towel she got to call her own. It was one of the few things her mother didn't mind spending a little extra on, especially when on sale, as good towelling and bedding would last longer. She braided her hair, so it dried overnight, and hurried into her room to change into her nightie. After hanging up her towel and checking on her uniform, she ran back into her room and jumped into bed as her mother walked in.

"I see you're ready for bed." Smiling at her, Betty sat beside her and dabbed her finger with a piece of antiseptic-soaked cotton wool. "How are your palms and knees?" She'd noticed them at the factory and knew something had happened.

"Sore, but I'll live. As usual," Marlaine replied, unable to look her mother in the eye.

Betty dabbed a small dry towel onto the scrapes. "I'll pop Band-Aids on your hands. Do you want them on your knees as well?"

"Yes, please."

Pulling the covers back, Betty lovingly covered her daughter in Band-Aids and then settled the covers around her chin. "Night, bluebird, sweet dreams." She kissed her cheek and left the room, turning off the light and closing the door behind her.

"Night, Mama." Marlaine snuggled down under the covers and tried to get comfortable, but her finger throbbed from the antiseptic, and her scraped hands and knees were burning a little. "Mmm…" Shifting, she stuffed a pillow under her knees and lay back. It helped her burning knees, but not her palms or finger. A sigh left her. "Maybe I should have taken a painkiller," she murmured, and flung her covers back. Dashing into the kitchen, she heard the shower going and knew it was her father, so she quickly grabbed the packet of pills from the first-aid cabinet, and a glass from the sink, and knocked back the pills with tap water. Leaving the glass, she hurried back to bed and tried to settle in. Eventually she fell into a troubled, feverish sleep.

CHAPTER THREE

Squeaking rats with three legs and stumpy tails chased her throughout the mill. She ran, screaming as they nipped at her ankles, leaving little sets of teeth marks that turned red; the same colour as their eyes which glowed brightly in the dim factory.

"Get away from me, get away," she cried, running back towards the office area and managing to shut the door behind her as the rats piled against it. "Ugh! What is going on? Why are they after me? And why are their eyes glowing?"

Hurrying into the manager's office, she closed the door and pushed a small side cupboard against it and then turned to the phone. She dialled out, but only heard a dead tone. "Hello?" She pressed the plungers a few times and tried again. "Hello?"

Nothing…

The line wasn't working.

A sound came from her mother's office, and she spun around to see the office door moving. "Oh, my God. They're trying to get in. How did they get in? And how do I get out?" Frantically searching for a way out, she saw the only viable exit was the windows overlooking the mill floor so the boss could see what was happening at all times. Hoping the coast was clear, she flung back the curtains hanging over them. Instead, she found rats piled up, covering the windows, trying to get into the office, scrambling over each other to get to her.

A scream escaped her, and she turned and leaped onto the desk. "What am I going to do? What am I going to do?" But on reflection, she realised there was nothing she *could* do, and before she had the chance to think of something else, the rats poured into the room through the door and window, covering her, suffocating her, drowning her. And as she screamed, she flung her arms up to protect her face, but she still went down in thousands of rats.

*****

Marlaine bolted upright, flinging her arms in front of her face. "Get off me! Get off me! Oh, how awful. Get off me."

"Marlaine?" Betty opened the door and hurried in. "What is it? What's wrong? Did you have a bad dream, sweetie?"

"Argh…" Marlaine lowered her arms and looked at her mother through feverish eyes. "I had a dream about rats." Raising her finger, the throb pounded in time with her heart. "It hurts. So do my hands and knees."

"Then I'll get you some painkillers to take with your breakfast." Betty smoothed Marlaine's hair. "It must have been a rough dream. You'll need to do your hair. Yell out if you need help, but hurry up and get dressed. I popped your uniform on your door and I'll get started on your egg sandwich. Hurry now." She left her daughter to get ready for school.

Marlaine freshened up and changed into her uniform before unbraiding her hair and brushing it into a ponytail. She tied it with a rubber band and slipped a hair ribbon in school colours over it. With her bag dragging behind her, she hurried into the kitchen for her egg sandwich, two painkillers, and a glass of water, while her mother finished getting ready for the day. Her father had left over an hour earlier for work.

Staring at her hands and knees, she sensed the throb subside, and upon inspecting her finger, wondered why being bitten by a rat this time had made her sick when it hadn't any other time. "Or maybe I'm just coming down with something," she murmured and swallowed the pills with her food. "I hope I'll be able to write today." After drinking the last of her water, she rinsed the dishes under the tap and left them to dry on the dish rack.

"Are you ready, Marlaine? It's time to go." Betty came down the hallway to see where her daughter was and collided with her in the kitchen doorway. "Don't forget to see the nurse for painkillers if your wounds hurt. And make sure to sign up for the free lunch service. I should have just signed you up myself at the beginning of the year. So, if you don't do it, I will."

"Yes, ma'am," Marlaine mumbled as they hurried outside into the warm sunshine.

After making sure the door was securely locked, they set off down the road towards the mill. But while that was only two blocks away, Marlaine still had to trek another five blocks to get to school.

When they arrived at the road across from the mill, Betty kissed her daughter goodbye. "See you at three-thirty, bluebird."

"Bye, Mama." Marlaine moved quickly down the street towards her school. She knew that at a fast pace, she could walk a block in a couple of minutes so she should be there within ten to fifteen minutes. And she timed it right, walking through the gate one minute from the bell.

"There's Marlaine, the fun drain, that got me detention." Darius turned up behind her with his posse in tow. "You're a pain, Dufrane. You got me into trouble, and I don't like that." He poked her in the shoulder. "I think I should teach you a little lesson."

A prickle of anger rose up Marlaine's spine, creeping up until it hit the back of her head and zapped into her brain. Her heart raced, her hands clenched into fists and heat rose with her anger, reddening her skin and blurring her eyes.

Spinning around, she flashed her furious eyes at him. "Enough! I'm sick of your bullying and I've had enough. So, stop it."

Darius shrank back, watching the red glow hover in her eyes. He'd never seen anything like it, nor seen

Marlaine fight back, as she was always quiet as a mouse and took what he dished out. He noticed his friends had also backed away. "Ah…" He licked his lips and took a step back. "You okay? Your eyes are glowing red."

A frown furrowed Marlaine's brows. "Don't be ridiculous! How would my eyes be glowing red? That's just another way for you to belittle and degrade me." Spinning on her heel, she stomped off to her homeroom with a racing heart. *What just got into me?* she thought. *I've never stood up to Darius before. Or any other bully. How did I do that? Oh, my gosh.*

Darius and his cohorts slowly trailed after her as they were in the same class. "*What* was that? *How* did she do that? She's *never* got angry or fought back before." He glanced at each friend and received shakes of their heads or shrugs in reply. "*What* just happened?"

The bell rang and cut off any more thoughts.

✶✶✶✶✶

At lunch, Marlaine spent her time in the library trying to do her homework, but all she could think about was her run-in with Darius and the rat bite on her finger. Recalling the dream from the night before, she wondered if she'd picked up a rat germ that made her dream about rats, or if it had given her the power to fight back. But fighting back wasn't in her blood. Literally. She'd never fought back against her bullies and didn't know why she had now. And that surprised her more than anything. The fact that she'd just spun around and snapped at him.

But why did they say my eyes were glowing red? Why would they glow red when they're blue? Why would they glow at all? The thoughts puzzled her just as much as how she managed to fight back did.

"Marlaine, do you need some help?" Mrs Carmichael asked as she put books away on the shelf next to her. "You seem to be off in space."

Marlaine glanced her way. "Just wondering if rat bites give you something other than diseases."

"Mmm…" Mrs Carmichael frowned in thought and stopped what she was doing to think about it. "I've never been asked that before. Why do you ask?"

Marlaine held her finger up. "I was bitten last night by a rat with three legs and a stumpy tail. Just wondering if they give you something other than germs."

"Oh…I don't think so. Did you clean the wound?" Mrs Carmichael scanned Marlaine's Band-Aid covered hands.

"Yes. Mama did last night before bed. But I had weird dreams all night," Marlaine told her.

"Could be a bit of a fever caused by the germs," Mrs Carmichael mused. "Have you had your shots?"

"The last time I was bitten. The doctor says it lasts for ages." Marlaine looked from the librarian to her finger. "Will I grow a third leg and a stumpy tail?"

Laughter burst from Mrs Carmichael. "Oh, heavens no, child. You won't. Let me look up some books on rats and diseases. You can take them home for the rest of the week." She hurried to check the files and found several books. "Ten minutes everyone," she called and set the books on the table beside Marlaine. "These are all I've found, but you take them home and have a look, and see that rat bites don't give you superpowers, or three legs and a stumpy tail, for that matter."

"Thank you, Mrs Carmichael." Marlaine packed the books into her bag with her homework. She'd only half done it but could finish it off tomorrow.

The bell rang and they filed out of the library for their afternoon classes.

*****

Marlaine left school at the final bell of the day and made it home in time to change and get to the mill by three-thirty for her shift. All went well, and she made it home with her father before nine to a hot meal and a shower. While she hadn't thought about her finger all night, she had been wary of rats while doing her work. But although she didn't see any, she still didn't want to run into another one. And she didn't for the rest of the week. Nor did she run into bullies at school; nor were there any more missing men.

CHAPTER FOUR

Marlaine turned up for work on Monday afternoon to find another group meeting.

"I hear what you're saying, Bob, I really do," Reginald said. "But Laurie didn't go home and he's not here. The police have been and can't find any evidence of foul play. Like many of you, he leaves his car home and walks to work, so the police are thinking if it's not leaving by choice, then maybe there's a kidnapper or murderer in town knocking off mill workers."

"What about you?" a man yelled out. "I'd be surprised if it *wasn't* you knocking us off, so you didn't have to pay so much. You sure you're not getting rid of us one by one, picking us off, boss?"

Reginald quickly responded, putting his hands up to defend himself. "Now, now, don't go starting silly rumours, Tony. I'm trying to keep the peace here—"

"Bull crackers!" a grizzled old man yelled and waved his fist in the air. "All the missin' men have been us oldies, the ones you're tryin' to get rid of. An' maybe you are. Maybe this is your way of gettin' rid of us. You kill us durin' the night shift an' dump our bodies somewhere or chop us up in the saw." He looked around at the crowd. "Has anyone found blood in the mill?"

A few noes hung in the air.

"Dun mean it didn' happen," the old man grumbled loud enough for everyone to hear.

"I swear to you on my grave it's not me," Reginald blustered. "I'm not trying to get rid of any of you, so calm down. I don't know how we'll get through this, but we can't stop the night shift, even though it's only one man. It's the job to finish off what doesn't get done during the day, and you know that it's important to start the day off with a new load. And not only do we feed the town, but we feed the rest of the state with cotton and wood. It's a growing business that needs to be fulfilled. And we can't fulfil it without the night shift finishing off what you don't."

A few of the men waved their hands in disgust.

"Now, since we supply the rest of the state, everyone get back to work." Reginald watched his men grumble and make rude gestures as they went back to their posts. "If this keeps up, I'm going to be out of men." He sighed and watched his secretary hug and kiss a young girl before they went back to work and wondered who she was. "Ah…Betty…" He stopped by her desk. "Who's that girl?"

Betty glanced at him before continuing to shuffle papers. "You know that's my daughter, Reginald. She cleans the factory floors in the afternoon."

"Ah…right…" Reginald tapped his meaty fingers on his ballooning stomach. "Would…ah…she be up for a night shift this week?"

"Reginald!" Betty's head snapped up and she stared at her overweight, balding boss. "She's thirteen years old and makes two pounds an hour for five hours of cleaning in the afternoons. And now you want her working the night shift when she has school and doesn't even know how to operate the machinery. How dare you!" Of all the people that worked at the mill, it was only Betty who could get away with chastising the boss and putting him in his place. "*And* on top of that, she's not old enough *to* operate the machinery."

"I'll give her five pounds an hour for every hour she works," Reginald persisted. He was desperate to not lose any more men, and figured he'd try a woman. Or girl. "We've lost five men, Betty. All on night shift. All either leaving of their own accord, or something happening to them. What if it's a murderer?"

"And yet you want *my* daughter to be here alone." Betty stared, aghast, at her boss.

"What I meant to say was…" Reginald was sweating bullets, and he didn't like being unfresh in front of women, even married ones. "If it *is* someone taking men and they're not leaving of their own free will, then they're only after men and not women and children."

"So, you think it's perfectly okay to use my thirteen-year-old only child as not only slave labour, but as a guinea pig for your experiment as well." Betty gave him her best evil eye and stared him down. "No, Reginald."

"But—"

"How much would it be? Would I get full wage? How many hours? Will it be every night this week? What are we talking about here?" Marlaine stood in the doorway, broom in hand. She hadn't been eavesdropping, just passing by when she'd heard her name.

Betty's gaze turned from her boss to her daughter. "No, Marlaine. I will not let you work the night shift. You're only thirteen and have no idea how to operate the machinery—"

"Actually, I do, Mama, Mr Sherriff." She leaned the broom against the door and stepped inside the office. "I've been watching everyone operate the machines in both factories since I started. I know how to use them, even though I actually haven't, and if it means more money, then maybe I should try it."

"Marlaine, no. I forbid it," Betty told her. "You're only thirteen and I'm not going to risk losing you when you're all I have."

Marlaine filled with sorrow for her mother, but quickly cast her gaze to their boss. "What night? How long? And how much will I be paid?"

"Well, little lady." Reginald licked his lips. "We could start you on the Friday night shift to see how you go. It's eight until twelve, or two, depending on when you finish. I'll more than double your wage to five pounds an hour."

Marlaine did the sums in her head. "Will I still need to clean every other night?"

"You will. We'll begin with Monday through Thursday cleaning, and then the Friday night night shift. And if you're successful, you could move to the night shift each night."

"No, Reginald!" Betty slammed her hands on her desk and her eyes fired up. "My daughter's schooling will not be affected just because you don't want to risk losing any more men. Just hire more to take their places instead of putting my daughter at risk."

"How much do the men on night shift get now?" Marlaine asked.

"Ah, exactly the same as the men on day shift, five pound an hour, as I said. But they work shorter hours, so it's less money." Reginald could see her considering it.

"Then I will take the same amount for Friday night. And I also won't clean on Fridays. I'll take a nap at home before I come to work."

"Marlaine, I forbid you," Betty said.

"Mama." Marlaine went to her side. "This is more money for us and it's the same hours, just later at night. And a Friday night to start with, so I can have a nap before I come here and sleep in a little on Saturday. I'll be fine."

"No, Marlaine. And I doubt your father would agree, either." Betty grasped her daughter's thin bony hands. "It's too dangerous and I don't want to lose you."

"Then let's discuss it with Daddy and come up

with a plan." Marlaine glanced over her shoulder at Reginald. "If Mr Sherriff contracts me for the same wage on Friday nights as others get, then it's definitely something to consider."

Reginald nodded and tried to hide his smirk. "Oh, absolutely, little lady. Absolutely. Meanwhile, I think you'd better get back to your current job."

"Yes, sir." Marlaine kissed her mother's cheek. "Don't worry, Mama. This will work out. Let's just see how it goes." She picked up her broom and went back to work.

"I don't like this, Reginald," Betty said, sitting at her desk. "And believe me when I say, if anything happens to my daughter, my *only* child, *if* we choose to let her do this, then God help you and the factory's owner because we will sue you for everything you're worth."

*****

The next day at school, Darius tried his luck once more.

"Hey, fun drain." He pulled on her long brown ponytail.

She swung around to face him. "What?" Ice cold water hit her in the face, and she gasped.

Darius cackled evilly. "You're lucky that wasn't something worse—" His voice stopped, and his eyes grew wide. "What...?"

"Serves you right!" Marlaine spat, checking her nails. She'd swung them across his face, leaving four red scratches. "What did you expect, Darius Cormack?" She saw drops of blood forming on the wounds. "You've bullied me for years, more so this year, and just a couple of weeks ago you shoved me so hard I fell over and could have been seriously hurt. And now you pull my hair and throw water in my face. Did you expect me to do nothing forever? To never stand up to you?" Glaring at his friends who all stood around him in shock, she added, "and if *any* of you think you can try it again… Don't!" The heat behind her eyes was blinding her, or maybe that was her fury. Why she was suddenly standing up to her bullies, she didn't know, although it was starting to feel good. "Well?"

The kids looked among themselves and backed off.

She turned to Darius. "Touch me, or assault me, or *in*sult me again, and you *really* won't like what I do." She walked off to the girls' toilets to try and dry her uniform before the school bell rang, and she managed it, only to be accosted by the principal when she walked out.

"Marlaine."

"Mrs Butterworth." She shouldered her bag and stared at the principal.

"I heard you slapped Darius Cormack." While she wasn't happy that it had happened, she was happy that the poor girl had finally defended herself.

"I didn't slap him. I scratched him because he pulled my hair and threw water on me. I defended myself. It's something I should have been doing since I first started being bullied. I've just finished drying my uniform under the hand dryer. I know my mother certainly wouldn't have appreciated it being ruined if it was anything *other* than water." She stood coolly in front of the principal, noting her strange expression. "Is there anything else, Mrs Butterworth? I need to get to class."

"No…Marlaine. But I will be calling your mother, *and* Mrs Cormack, to have a chat about both of your actions. Now…get to class."

"Mrs Butterworth." Marlaine hurried to her homeroom, shaking on the inside about not only standing up to her bully, but talking to the principal eye to eye. For years she'd been shy and walked around with downcast eyes and never stood up for herself. But now she was, and now she held her head high and she hadn't even noticed until now. Now she knew she could defend herself. But what had brought this on, she did not know.

Why is this suddenly happening? she asked herself, catching her breath before walking into class. *Why am I suddenly defending myself? Why am I suddenly standing up to Darius when all I've ever said and done is nothing? Or run away and cry when he's bullied me, punched me, hit me, spat on me. Why?*

Her right forefinger throbbed, and she held up her hand to study it. The bite mark had left a scar, but except for that first feverish night, nothing had happened. She frowned and remembered back to the previous week when Darius had poked her and made fun of her and she'd spun on him, the fire burning in her belly, her skin and her eyes.

It can't be because of a rat? Staring at her finger, she tried to reconcile such ideas, but could not.

"Marlaine, time for class," the teacher called from the door.

Marlaine startled and smiled. She walked into the classroom and over to an empty desk, which meant she would be sitting alone. But she didn't care. Not anymore. She raised a brow at Darius and his friends then turned away. She was done with being bullied and done with not defending herself.

*****

The matter was discussed that night over dinner.

"Marlaine, as much as I'm glad you're finally standing up for yourself, I'm surprised and disappointed that you did so by using physical violence," her mother told her over beef stew. "I've encouraged you for a long time to stand up for yourself, but slapping a boy…" She shook her weary head. "Physical violence is not the way."

"But it's okay for him to physically assault *me* by hitting and pushing, and throwing water in my face?" Marlaine argued. "And that's not all he and his friends have done. You know I spend my lunchtime in the library to keep away from them. Yet *I'm* still bullied and supposed to put up with it. And the first time in my life I finally stand up for myself and defend myself against my bully, *I'm* the one in trouble. And it's not just me they bully, it's all of us mill kids because we're poorer than him and his friends." She paused to eat a spoonful of stew.

"I understand all of that, my darling," Betty replied. "But physical violence is not the answer."

"Well then in that case, it's not the question, either." Marlaine's eyes were wide, but she was determined to defend herself. "But Darius has been allowed to get away with it until a couple of weeks ago when the principal saw him push me. He *never* gets into trouble for what he does. Neither do his friends."

"And I fully understand that," Douglas told her. "I was bullied myself in school and fought back. Got in a few scruffs after that, but my bullies were never bullies again. At least in my case."

"Just because you fought back doesn't mean our daughter needs to," Betty replied and broke her small week-old bread roll into pieces.

"It doesn't mean she shouldn't, either, love. She's thirteen; it's time she stands up for herself, and while I don't agree with physical violence in general, fighting back when you're being bullied is necessary. So, bluebird..." Douglas looked at his daughter across the table. "Defend yourself, but only when absolutely necessary. And Betty..." he interrupted the argument about to come from his wife, "she needs to and it's time she did. As for the other matter we need to discuss, you working night shift, we'll discuss that tomorrow night. It's time for you to go to bed. Off you go."

Marlaine finished her stew and kissed her parents

goodnight. After a hot shower, she climbed into bed and sat looking at her rat-bitten finger. It throbbed a little and the heat from it travelled down her finger to her hand, up her arm, and into the rest of her body. There was no way she was going to continue turning a blind eye to the bullies at school. Not anymore. She was standing up for herself and that's all there was to it. Except for the sweet revenge she was going to wreak.

A sly grin slid across her lips.

CHAPTER FIVE

For the next two days during her shift, Marlaine was shown how to work the wood and cotton machinery and tried it herself. All of this was under the strict supervision and watchful eyes of her parents, with her father leading her. They then discussed it during dinner each night and finally gave their permission for her to try it for one Friday night only to see where things stood. On Friday afternoon, when Marlaine got home from school, she ate the banana she'd taken from the librarian's fruit bowl and lay down for a nap. She had to be at the mill to check in at eight, but since her mother would be home, she knew she'd wake her. Having excited thoughts about her job and the extra money it would bring in, she lay there for a good hour before drifting off to sleep.

She was standing in the mill at the wood cutter feeding through the log of tree to be sliced and diced into smaller pieces. All was quiet, other than the machine. There was no other person, no animal, just her and the wood and the machine. But she had sensed something. Something behind her, beside her, around her. Even though there was nothing there.

She bent to pick up another chunk of log and glanced around to see if someone had sneaked in. Maybe the boss. Maybe another worker, spying on her to see how she did. It could be the guard. He was around somewhere, but she never saw him as he was always as quiet as a mouse. Or rat…

Or rat…

Now where did that come from? Her hearing homed in on other noises and picked up a faint scratching of something connecting with wood. Something flapped against the floor…or a piece of machinery, or wood. She fed through a log and reached down for another and that's when she saw the three-legged, stumpy tailed rat that had bitten her.

He sat near the wood pile sharpening his teeth on the broken bits that had fallen off the logs.

"Ah, there you are," she said to him. "Come to bite me again, have you?" She gently pushed the log towards him. "Shoo, go away. I don't want to be bitten again." Pushing the log, she managed to move the rat back several feet. "Off you go. Shoo. Go somewhere else to bite and wreak havoc. You've already bitten me once, which I *don't* appreciate. Shoo." She picked up the log and fed it through the machine and reached for another. But her hands stopped in mid-air as she saw not one, but *dozens* of rats gathered near the log pile.

"Argh! Where did you guys come from?" came shakily out of her mouth. She didn't know whether to slowly replace the wood, put it through the machine, or whether to shoo the rodents away with it. She watched them standing or sitting on their haunches in rows, watching her back, their eyes glowing red, front legs held up in front of them, noses twitching. Were they sniffing her? Her scent?

"Okaayy…" She slowly lowered the log then rose, hands palm side down in front of her, voice low and even as she backed away. "Okay, I'm just going to go now, and you guys can run the mill. Okay?" Taking a few steps, she backed into something soft. "Mr Sherriff, is that you?" She glanced over her shoulder and caught sight of something that made her body rotate to catch up with the rest of her, her jaw dropped, her eyes closed, and down she went in a dead faint…

"Marlaine…time to wake up." Her mother shook her until she woke, and her eyelids rose to see what was happening. "What?"

"It's time for tea so you can go and work in that godforsaken place for the night." Betty sat on her daughter's bed. "I don't like you being there, bluebird. You'll be alone for hours during the night. All because that blasted Reginald doesn't want to lose another man. Never mind the fact I could lose my only child and he doesn't care."

"Mama, I'll be fine." Marlaine sat beside her. "I'll need to wrap my hair up so it doesn't get caught, and the guard will be there while I'm working, and the doors will be locked except for one. So I'll be fine. Besides, it will mean more money coming in."

"We should all be getting more money coming

in," Betty murmured, distracted by her thoughts. "No one's being paid what they should be except for Reginald. And I have a feeling it's his fault."

"What does that mean?" Marlaine walked over to her chest of drawers and picked up her hairbrush. "Mama?" She whipped her hair into shape while her mother spoke.

"It means that I think Reginald is paying everyone less than their full wage and taking the rest for himself, and not telling the owners. But I can't swear to it and have no facts to prove it. I'm just a woman, and this is the fifties, and no one would believe me over a man." A weary sigh left her. "Plus, that's how he lives so well, and the workers don't. But that's not your concern." Her lips turned into a smile for her daughter. "When you've changed, come out for tea and then Daddy will walk you to the factory."

"Yes, Mama." Marlene watched the door close behind her mother and quickly wrapped her braided hair into a bun. She slipped on a pair of hand-me-down work boots, and pulled long socks over her jeans legs. She didn't want anything crawling up her legs while she worked.

Once she'd freshened up, she met her parents in the kitchen for leftover stew.

"I've made you two sandwiches, added a banana, and a thermos of water in your father's lunch pail in case you get hungry in a couple of hours." Betty set the pail on the table. "Make sure you eat something at some point."

"Yes, Mama." Marlene devoured her food and

gathered the lunch pail and her jacket from the back of her bedroom door. "Time to go, Daddy," she called out.

Douglas came down the hallway and opened the front door. "Are you ready for your first night shift?"

Staring up at her big, strong father, she said, "Not really. I'm a little scared, but the money will be good." She gave him an unsure smile. "It'll be okay, though."

"We hope so, bluebird," he replied and ushered her out, seeing the worried frown on his wife's face as she stood in the hallway.

They walked down the road towards the factory making chit-chat to fill the void.

"How long do you think each job will take?" he asked her. "If you finish early, you'll have to call from the office. Otherwise, I'll be in at one."

"I don't know if I'll take five hours, Daddy. I could take longer. Why don't you get some sleep and I'll just call when I'm done?" Her gait was a half skip, half high step out of nervousness.

"I could do that." He squeezed her hand as they arrived at the door.

"Back again, Douglas?" Stewart, the night guard chuckled. "Can't get enough of the place?"

"Just getting my daughter booked in for the night shift," Douglas replied. "I'll be back out in a few minutes."

Stewart nodded and watched them walk inside.

Marlaine checked in and left her lunch pail and coat in her mother's office then kissed her father goodbye. "Bye, Daddy. See you later."

"Bluebird. I'll be back to pick you up when you call," he said as she walked him to the door. "Stay safe, and let Stewart know if there are any issues. Okay?"

"Yes, Daddy." Marlaine watched her father nod to the guard and set off across the car park.

"Miss Dufrane. Yell out if you need help," Stewart told her.

"Yes, sir." She closed the door and walked through both factories to see which one had the biggest pile of work and found it was the sawmill. "Looks like I'm leaving that until last," she murmured and set to work sorting out the leftover cotton.

An hour into that work she stopped and looked around. She'd been getting tingles on the back of her neck for a while, and they had led to shivers down her spine. Breathing calmly, defying the way her insides were reacting, she slowly gazed around the mill, taking in all the little nooks and crannies. Finding nothing, she heaved a sigh and turned the machine back on to finish the leftovers. When the last of the cotton was done, she turned off the machine, swept up the remnants into a hessian bag and bundled up the cotton into a second, ready for the next round of workers on Monday.

"One down, one to go," she muttered, and walked into the sawmill, turning off the lights behind her.

Stewart popped his head through the door and looked around, seeing her coming towards him. "You all right, miss? Done in the cotton mill?"

"Yes, sir. I'm just going to take a ten-minute break then get on with the wood," Marlaine told him. "I'm okay."

"Good. I'll pop in in another two hours." He closed the door, and all went quiet.

She walked on to the bathroom, where she made sure to get all of the dust and dirt off her hands, and then into her mother's office for her banana and a drink of water. Sitting on the desk, she swung her legs while she ate and remembered the dream she'd had that afternoon. The shiver spread down her spine, and she shuddered at the thought.

That would be very creepy indeed.

A tingle started in her rat-bitten finger, and she stared at it for a few moments before frowning and putting her flask and banana peel in her lunch pail. "That was weird." She looked at it again and heard nails on wooden floorboards. "That's weird too." Her hearing homed in on the sound and she knew it was more than one set of claws, and that freaked her out. Not only did she not know how she knew, but she knew she needed to get out of there.

Hurrying into the main room, she prepared the load and started the wood cutter. Nails on floorboards weren't going to worry her. She'd dealt with worse than that at school for years. Taking a deep breath, she started with the first log, and before long had a rhythm going.

Until she saw a rat…and froze.

It was the rat with the three legs and stumpy tail. The rat that had bitten her. The rat that was just sitting there staring at her in the exact same way as it had in her dream. But she wasn't really scared, or worried. Not even when she pushed the log through and saw more rats when she reached for another. "If you're not going to help me then go away." She pushed another log through and found they'd disappeared when she reached for another one. "Well, there you go, then. You're not going to help me."

Her finger tingled, and the tingle turned into a throb. And that throb pulsated up her arm into her body. Frowning, she pushed another log through and paused. Eyes dead ahead, ears homing in on the breathing behind her. It wasn't human. And that meant the being that was exhaling wasn't either. Her whole body pulsated, but there was no fear, no stress, no need to run. She knew what it was; knew what it could do. She knew in that moment what *she* could do as revelation after revelation bounced through her brain. It was right behind her, she knew it, and she reached her left arm out to switch off the machine.

It was right there. Almost touching her. It might as well have; it was so close. But she knew what it was thinking. How, she did not know. And the heat rising to her face didn't help. Neither did the throbbing in her body.

Something nudged her and a weird growly sound came from it.

Spinning around, Marlaine furiously glared at it just as she had at Darius that day, and she saw the creature back away. It was intimidated, if not scared.

Her right hand rose in front of her, her palm facing the creature, and she slowly moved closer until it was above the creature's snout, wilfully forcing it to bow to her. "You will not harm me. You will do as I say, and I will not hurt you."

The heat burned her eyes and she guessed they were glowing like those of the rat creature before her, and those of some of the rats around them. They all bowed, all told her they would not harm her, and that she was their queen.

"Queen!" She frowned and dropped her hand. "How's that possible?"

Because I bit you, one rat said.

"Wait…you actually speak?" She was incredulous. "How?"

Not verbally, but telepathically. The rat with three legs and a stumpy tail came forth. *I bit you and this is a result we did not expect. But I didn't mean to bite you, so I am sorry.*

Marlaine knelt in front of the rat. "Not the first time I've been bitten, but why is this time different?"

Because I have the strain. That's why I have three legs and a stumpy tail, he said. *Many others have the strain too, that's why our eyes glow, but many also don't have it at all. That is why they look normal.* He waved a front leg out to show off his comrades.

"Mmm…" Marlaine looked up at the creature. "You're not all rat. You look as if you have something else in you. Something that's made my hearing really good now."

I am half bat, as well, it told her telepathically.

Hence my big ears and eyes, and stumpy nose. But I have no idea how I came to be, or how I came to be this big.

She gazed over the black-furred creature with a rat body, webbed arms and legs, and protruding teeth from a snub snout. She could tell which bits came from which animal. "Have you been killing the men?"

The creature glanced away in embarrassment. *There are certain times of our growth where we need to eat substantially, and we could not find local animals. So, humans were it.*

Plus, when they saw us, Stumpy added. *They tried to kill us. So that didn't help.* He held his paws together in front of him. *Not all of us grow so big, like Fatso over there.* He pointed in the creature's direction. *Most of us, no actually the rest of us here, haven't grown like him at all.*

"Either way, stop eating the men that work here," Marlaine chided. "That's how come *I'm* now working here. Because the boss thinks the men are being murdered by a killer only out to kill men. *You're* not helping the situation." Casting her gaze over hundreds of rats, she added, "Which reminds me. I need to get on with it. So, if you want to help, get in a production line and start hauling logs."

The rats looked from each other to the creature. Having never been in this situation before, they had no idea what to do.

"Well?" Marlaine asked, no longer fazed by the situation. "You just told me I am your queen. I have no idea how or why, or what that means, but if that's the case, you do as I say. Right?" She saw the unsure glances before they finally nodded. "Good! Then let's get going and get the rest of the wood done." She directed the rats to pile up the wood at the other end and told the creature to hand her the logs. With him using his teeth to pick them up, the process line was soon underway.

"Tell me how all this came to be," Marlaine said and pushed a log through. "How did you come to be, and come to be here, under the mill? You do live under the mill, don't you? I saw Stumpy run into a hole under the boss's desk."

Yes, the creature replied. *We live under the mill. But we don't know how we came to be, or how I came to be so big, or any of us came to have our powers.* He carefully lifted the last log with his teeth and swung it around to Marlaine. *We just know we exist.*

"And what type of powers are they?" Marlaine fed the last log through and turned off the machine. "Clearly, I can read your minds, and you mine. Our eyes glow red, but that's not a power, and suddenly I have the ability to stand up for myself and defend myself against bullies." Her brow furrowed. "But maybe that's not a power, either."

We don't really know what our powers are, Stumpy told her as he and the other rats gathered around her. *Except for the eyes, and some of us have malformations...* He glanced down at his one back leg and his stumpy tail sticking forward from under his butt looking most unfortunate. He pushed it backwards. *But I was born like this.* He shrugged and glanced up at her. *Didn't you say your hearing was good?*

"Yes," Marlaine murmured, and homed in on footsteps approaching outside. "Quick, hide. The guard's coming." The creature and the rats scurried behind piles of wood or machines while Marlaine casually walked towards the office for the broom.

"You all right, miss?" Stewart asked after seeing her.

"I'm fine. Still have some cleaning to do." She grabbed the broom and walked up to him. "Another hour or so I should think. Maybe two."

"Okay, miss. I'll be back later." He closed the door and left her to it.

"I need to get this place clean before I can leave. Are any of these powers super speed?" she asked the rats as they came out of hiding.

Not that we know of, Stumpy said. *But we're pretty fast, anyway.*

"Right, then. You'd better help out. Think you can help me sweep the wood chips and sawdust up? You go that side; I'll start this side." As she swept her side of the mill floor, the rats got to work on the other creating piles of wood chips and dust for her to sweep up, and she thought about what she'd been told and what all of it meant.

We don't know either, Stumpy replied, racing up her side to sit on her shoulder as she came around to the other side of the factory. *But if we're being honest, Fatso over there will soon need to feed again.* He pointed at the creature who stared back with large soulful eyes.

"Are you sure there are no cows or pigs you can eat?" Marlaine swept the broom towards them. "I can't let you eat anymore humans, and you're certainly not going to eat me, and I won't let you eat the guard, or Daddy when he comes to pick me up. There must be another way. Or something else you can eat."

We've hunted far and wide. Stumpy cast a glance over his friends. *We would have to go miles to get another animal for Fatso to eat. And we can't carry an animal home, and if he came with us, he'd be hungry again by the time we got back.*

"If you live under the mill, can you get to and from other places easily?" Marlaine stopped sweeping and leaned on the broom handle. "Surely there's something?"

No. Stumpy shook his head. *Just the men.*

"Well…there aren't any now." Marlaine shrugged and scooped the piles of wood and dust. "What will you do?" Heaving the dustpan into the bin, she shook the remnants off and piled up the pan again. After finishing the job, she turned to the rats. "Well? What will you do?"

The rats looked amongst themselves and shook their heads or shrugged.

Maybe we could find someone else? the creature suggested. Considering he was the size of the wood cutting machine, it was going to be hard to find him enough food to fill him up.

"Like who?" Marlaine asked and waved everyone towards the offices.

Is there someone who's really hated in town? Or someone who no one will miss if they go missing? Stumpy asked.

Marlaine thought about it while she put the broom in the closet and took out her dust cloths. "Not off the top of my head, but I am only thirteen." She walked into her mother's office and started dusting. As she'd finished the main job early, she figured she'd finish some of her other job as well. "I don't know every person in town, although there are definitely some bullies at school I wish didn't exist."

We know. Stumpy nodded in concern. *We've sensed your power twice, and then sensed a dull throb at other times.*

Marlaine glanced at him from the corner of her eye. "Really? How interesting."

Yes. We know when you're super angry. The creature snorted as he inhaled. *We feel it too.*

"Really..." Marlaine dragged the word out and drifted off into space. "How utterly interesting... yes...I did get angry a couple of times after being bitten. It scared the kids at my school, and they said my eyes were glowing red. I even fought back against my bully after years of never standing up for myself. I have no idea how or why, but it was weird and confusing, and interesting all at once. I have no idea where that power came from. And if you guys don't know..." She looked at each one who had red eyes. It was about half of the group. "Guess you guys have, what did you call it? The strain." She glanced at Stumpy. "Strain of what? The flu, a virus, cold, bad stuff? What *is* the strain?"

Once again, the rats looked at each other and shrugged. *We don't know*, they chorused.

Marlaine sighed and slumped on her mother's desk. "Do I need to go to my doctor? Am I going to grow another leg and a tail? Am I going to grow big and fat and need a lot of food?" When she received blank stares in return, she groaned. "In the meantime, I need to finish cleaning the office. Go and see if Mr Sherriff has any biscuits in his desk drawer and finish them off. Maybe that will tide you over."

They ran off to devour what was left, while Marlaine finished off her mother's office and the creature sat with his head in the doorway watching her. He was too big to fit into the office, so he didn't bother trying in case he got stuck.

"You finished?" she called and entered Reginald's office. She saw them licking their lips and paws. "Make sure there are no crumbs anywhere. We don't want ants and rats…" Laughter exploded out of her, and she realised how ridiculous that sounded. "Ha…that's funny! Quick, get out so I can clean up." She saw their amused expressions and giggled. "Yes, I said it." She was done in five minutes and deposited the biscuit packet in the main rubbish bin out in the factory and put her cloths away. "There." Dusting off her hands, she added, "I'm just going to the bathroom, but don't follow me. It's rude." They twitched as she went to freshen up and when she returned, she glanced at the clock. "Ah…just on two. I better call Daddy. Okay, you lot. Scamper off home so I can get home myself."

When will you be back? Stumpy asked, eagerly standing on his one hind leg.

"Monday afternoon to do the cleaning as I always do. And I'll do that until Thursday, and we'll see about next Friday. It will all depend on what the boss says on Monday. Why?"

Just wondering when we'll see you again, he replied. *We don't come out during daylight hours.*

"Didn't stop you when you bit me." Marlaine waved her finger at him.

Well. He blushed right through his fur. *Technically that was nighttime.* Stumpy tried to look innocent as he grasped his paws in front of him.

"Mmm…very true." Marlaine conceded and went to the office for her lunch pail and coat. "I'm just going to ring Daddy." She called and her mother picked up on the first ring. "Mama, I'm done."

"I'll get your father down there shortly. You wait inside until he gets there."

"Okay." Marlaine hung up and pulled her thermos from her pail. "What do you guys drink?" She listened to them as she chugged back her water.

Water, milk, tea, cola, anything liquid that's around, the creature replied and licked his lips at her.

"Maybe that's part of the problem." Marlaine saw his actions and capped her thermos before opening the sandwich wrappers. "Ooh, two beef sammidges.

Yum." She munched into one and noticed the hungry expressions. "Hey!" she mumbled around the food. "Eyes off! This is mine." She finished the first and reached for the second, pausing long enough to think about whether she wanted it or not. Deciding not, she walked over to the doorway and held it out to the creature. "Here. It's not a whole cow, or even a human, but it might be healthier than what you've *been* eating lately."

The creature bowed his head and carefully bit into the food.

"Got it?" Marlaine removed her hand and watched him throw his head back, so the sandwich went into his mouth. He happily chewed three times before swallowing. "Not much of a chewer, are you?"

Thank you, he said. *That's all I've had all week, besides fruit. But I must feed properly soon, otherwise problems will arise and I can't control what I end up feeding on.*

"I guess I'd better help you find an alternative." Marlaine nodded and donned her coat. "Daddy's going to be here any minute, so you'd better go."

Yes, my queen, Stumpy said and herded up the family. *We will see you next week. Come, everyone, let's go.*

She waved them goodbye and then felt a little ridiculous waving goodbye to rats.

A minute later her father arrived to collect her, and they locked up, said goodbye to the guard, and headed home quickly, where she fell into bed and a deep sleep until late Saturday morning.

CHAPTER SIX

When Marlaine turned up for work on Monday morning, her boss wasn't surprised to see her alive.

"Well, little lady." Reginald accosted her at the utilities closet. "Your parents told me you made it out alive. And you got all the work done, I see."

"Yes, sir." Marlaine removed the broom ready for sweeping and closed the door. "I'd better get on with my work."

"Yes, of course. Do you think you'll be up to do the night shift again on Friday?" His actual plan was to get her to work every night, but he had to ease into that.

Marlaine deflated a little. "Do I have to?"

"Well…no…" Reginald kept his voice calm. "But you do seem to be a better worker than most of my men."

"I'll talk it over with Mama and Daddy," she said. "I've got to get to work, Mr Sherriff." Giving him a small smile, she walked off to the cotton mill to sweep the floor.

Hours later, she was dusting her mother's office

long after everyone except her father had gone home. He was chatting to Stewart when Marlaine spied Stumpy in the doorway of Reginald's office.

"What are you doing here?" she whispered, peering through the doorway to see where her father was.

I came to see you, he replied, racing up her side to sit on her shoulder. *We haven't seen you since forever. And you don't need to speak, remember.*

It's only been three days. She giggled and got on with her job. *Where is everyone?*

Out scavenging for food. Stumpy licked his paw and rubbed it over his face. *Fatso is hungry so we can't hold off any longer. We've all been out every night looking for food, and if it's not scraps, it's the rubbish from peoples' bins.*

What about fruit from all the trees? Marlaine suggested. *We have some fall off every few days. You could come and get those.*

We've been doing that too. Stumpy twitched an ear and sniffed the air. *We raid every fruit tree that we can. Fatso eats a lot of food.*

Why do you call him that? Marlaine moved into Reginald's office to dust.

Stumpy shrugged. *Because he is. He's big and fat and doesn't stop growing or eating. And none of us have names, so he gets called Fatso.*

But how did you know about that name in the first place? Marlaine slid the cloth along the top of the filing cabinet.

We hear workers talk, and other people, when

we're out and about. Some people were calling a rather rotund man that, and he was big and fat and didn't stop eating, so we called him Fatso. He sneezed from the dust and wiped his face. *Why do you call me Stumpy? It's because I have a stumpy tail.*

She giggled. *Pretty much. Do you have a name? I can call you that.*

No. We don't have names, which is why we can't keep ourselves straight. Sometimes, we have numbers. He nodded his head in time with her steps as they walked back to the utility closet for the vacuum cleaner.

Numbers? You have numbers for names? That's funny. She pulled the cleaner from the closet and rolled it into the office. *Is everyone else around? If Mr Sherriff has biscuits left, you may as well have them.*

We already have. Stumpy twitched. *Could barely wait for him to leave to get into them. I think we've become reliant on him feeding us and have become addicted to the yumminess. Does he say anything about his food?*

Marlaine pulled the cord out of the cleaner and directed Stumpy to plug it in. *I don't think so. He probably thinks I eat them, or Stewart, as he's here all night.* Once Stumpy was out of the way she vacuumed the office and removed the empty packet. *Mmm, these are different from his usual ones. I see he likes to change them up every week, but he always picks cream ones.* She dumped the packet into the bin and vacuumed out the drawer before going into her mother's office. *At least I have a good excuse for throwing the wrapper out every night.*

What's that? Stumpy managed to climb onto the desk to watch her.

That if I don't clean out his desk every night, he'll end up with rats. Her brows rose in amusement, and she watched Stumpy shake his head at how bad her joke was.

He's nearly caught us in the act, you know, he said. *Number 42 and I were in the drawer one day when he came into the office. We had to scramble out of the hole at the back of the drawer. That was definitely a close call.*

*****

Tuesday and Wednesday went well for Marlaine, but on Thursday Reginald bore down on her when she arrived for work. It had been a bad day, and no one knew what had set him off that morning. "Marlaine, I want you to stop eating my food that I bring in every day. I know it's you because the biscuits are gone the next morning and *you're* the cleaner."

Scared by the fury in his eyes, Marlaine stepped back. "I don't eat them, Mr Sherriff. I throw the empty packets out and clean up any crumbs, so you don't get rats eating them. That's my job as cleaner. To clean."

Oh, how the conversation with Stumpy was coming true.

"And I understand you cleaning my desk, but it also means you're eating my food and I have to bring a fresh packet every day." Reginald placed his hands on his hips to try and intimidate her.

"Reginald, Marlaine…what's going on?" Betty stood in the doorway to her office. She'd heard her boss and wondered who he was yelling at.

Reginald whirled around. "Your daughter, Betty," he bellowed. "She's been eating my food and throwing out the evidence."

Frowning, Betty glanced from his reddening face to her daughter. "Marlaine?"

"I'm okay, Mama." Marlaine felt the throbbing in her finger. "I can handle this."

"Oh, you can, can you?" Reginald's brows rose in amusement. "Can you now?"

"Yes, I can," she snapped, staring defiantly at him, head held high. "*You* leave at five. *I* don't clean your office until *after* seven-thirty. That leaves almost *all* of the workers here for two hours *after* you, and *before* I even get to your office. By then, the biscuits, and any other food you stash in your desk drawer is gone and I'm left to throw out the wrappers and clean out the drawer so that *you*…" She poked her finger at him, "don't have rats and mice and ants in your office. *You* should be thanking *me* for doing such a good job of cleaning instead of accusing me of stealing, which *I am not doing*." The throb had spread throughout her whole body, and she hoped her eyes weren't glowing. "Instead, *you're* blaming *me* instead of the other five hundred plus suspects that are here when you leave. And considering *I* don't hate you, but many of *them* do, you've got some hide accusing *me*, *Mr* Sherriff." Marlaine breathed deeply and stepped back. "Now, I have a job to do." Grasping her broom, she marched past him and her mother, both of whom were stunned, and into the factory ready to sweep. She saw her father and other workers watching, because they would have seen, but not heard, the confrontation.

Flabbergasted, Reginald didn't know what to say and just stood there. "Ah…da…da…" was all that came out of his stuttering mouth for a good minute until he got himself together. "Marlaine Dufrane, you get back here!" Whirling around, he saw Betty standing in the doorway just as shocked as he was. "And you!" He thrust his fat finger at her. "Come with me." He stormed into the factory with Betty meekly following, and pulled on the alarm to stop work. Once silence rained down and everyone was gathered, Reginald barked, "Who has been eating the food in my desk drawer?" Looking from man to man, he saw no one own up and his gaze landed on Marlaine who glared defiantly back. "As you can see, Marlaine, no one here has."

"That's *not* what their silence means. They just won't admit to it for fear of losing their jobs," she said forcefully. The throbbing pulsated through her, and she hoped the rats could sense it.

"What it *means*, Marlaine, is that *you* are a thief, and a liar," Reginald proclaimed to a stunned crowd. "And because of that, you are now on night shift permanently. And *that* will be your last chance at a job."

With her blood boiling in her veins, she closed her eyes and clenched her hands to try and stop from blowing a gasket.

"Reginald, my daughter is neither a thief nor a liar. She's also not working the night shift permanently," Douglas told him. "No way, she's thirteen."

"I don't care how old she is," Reginald cut him off with a defiant wave of his hand. "I'm not risking any more men, so she can do the night shift as punishment for her crime."

"Crime!" Marlaine cried. "I've done *nothing* wrong except work for two pound an hour cleaning up the mess left by the workers." She pointed to them and saw their shame-filled faces as they shuffled their feet and mumbled. "I clean up *their* mess in the factory, *their* mess in the bathroom, and *your* mess in your office. *That* is what I do. While you what…" Her gaze moved up and down his portly frame. "Get fat on the sugar in the biscuits and the sweat of the men you don't even pay a full wage to. You're a pig with your snout in the trough ripping off your workers. And you don't even care that four men are dead."

She saw his eyes widen in surprise and went in harder, the fury boiling her insides even though she saw and heard her parents trying to stop her. "No, Daddy, Mama. What did *you* do for their wives, *Mr Sherriff*? Their families? Offer money? Help? How do *you* live, Mr Sherriff? *You* certainly don't live like any of us, in worker cottages making ends meet on the paltry sum you pay us. You live high on the hog like a king in his castle and you have the gall to call *me* a liar and a thief when you steal from your workers and do *nothing* for them." Gripping the broom handle tightly, she wished she could stop. "Don't worry, Reginald. I'll do the night shift tonight, but it will be the last one I do." Glaring at him, she sent a silent message. *Rats, I need your help.*

Down below the surface, the rats had been standing to attention for quite some time, having sensed her throb, and then her anger. They had seen and heard everything through her eyes and ears, and knew their queen was in trouble and needed their help. But they also knew they couldn't be seen until after dark.

"No, you won't," Reginald bellowed. "I've changed my mind. *You're* fired!" He thrust a meaty finger at her. "You're not doing the night shift as punishment, you're fired instead."

"Good! That means I get to do other things after school," Marlaine told him. "I'll go and get another job that pays better."

"Ha!" Reginald laughed. "You won't find another job that pays better because I'll see to it that you never find another job. I'll blackball you as a liar and a thief."

"And I'll tell everyone you steal from your workers and don't pay their full wages," Marlaine yelled back. "You've been ripping off everyone and I'll tell everyone about it."

Fuming on the inside, Reginald pursed his lips

and looked from a raging Marlaine who had glowing red eyes that unnerved him, to the workers who stood silent with their heads down, to Douglas and Betty Dufrane who were standing by their daughter. And the anger boiled over. "I've changed my mind again. *All three of you* are fired. Betty, pack your things. Douglas, the cottage is only for factory workers, so you'll need to get out." Seeing another layer of shock roll over their faces, he delighted in it. "And *you*, Marlaine, can put *my* broom back in the utility closet before you go."

"Boss, no…" one of the men yelled.

Douglas Dufrane was not only their supervisor; he was well liked and respected amongst the men as someone they could rely on for a chat, or for help if he could offer it. As was Betty amongst their wives.

"No!" Reginald yelled back. "Get out, all three of you."

"Reginald," Betty cried, distraught, her hand going to her mouth. "Oh…Douglas… What do we do?" She grasped onto her stunned husband's arm. "What do we do?"

"Don't worry, Mama," Marlaine said, an eerie calm in her voice. "Everything will be all right and back to normal soon enough." She linked her arm with her mother's. "Let's go home. Daddy, we're done here, but we'll be back, I promise. Everything will be just fine." Smiling at her mother's worried face; she led them both past Reginald, dropping his broom right in front of him. "*You* can put *your* broom back in the closet along with *your* attitude."

They gathered their things from the office and checked out of work for the last time. In absolute dead silence, they walked past Reginald and the workers and out the door into the sunshine with Marlaine smiling wickedly the whole time.

CHAPTER SEVEN

As soon as they arrived home, Marlaine headed out to the backyard and waited on her swing under her favourite tree. Her father had made the swing out of a wood slat and rope, and she swung lazily until Stumpy ran up the tree, along a branch, and down the rope to her shoulder.

You rang?

She giggled and then turned serious. *Get everyone together and let them know to follow Reginald home, and when it's late and everyone's in bed, let Fatso feed on him.*

Shocked, Stumpy gasped. *My queen, you told Fatso not to eat humans.*

I know. But after what he did today, I don't care. And after what he's been doing, I really don't care. Do you know how to read?

Sort of. Stumpy hid under her ponytail as Douglas came out to call her in.

"In a minute, Daddy," she called. "Go and wait for me."

Confused, Douglas went inside, and she continued.

Reginald Sherriff has been ripping off his workers. Mama knows about it but doesn't think anyone will believe her. We need to find proof and I doubt he'd keep it at the factory. So, if it's not there—

It's at his house, Stumpy finished off the sentence and emerged from under her hair.

Right. Leave it in plain sight for the police to find, but don't leave his body unless you leave a lot of blood. We want people to know he's dead. She paused to think that through. *No. Make that missing. No blood, if possible, and leave no part of him behind. That way, Daddy will be brought back as the manager, and Mama as secretary, and I will never clean those toilets again.*

That must be a dirty job, but someone has to do it. Stumpy stared at his surroundings. It was a small backyard with fruit trees and a small green lawn.

"Unfortunately," Marlaine murmured. "So go now. Follow him home, find those papers and make him go missing. There are a few hundred of you, so there should be enough to make it happen."

Stumpy cocked his head. *A few hundred? Oh no, my queen, we are thousands strong. Most of them were out the other night scavenging when we turned up at the factory.*

"Cripes!" Marlaine exclaimed. "More of you to do the job. You'd better get going and be careful. We don't want you getting run over by a car."

Not a chance. I came via the drain. Stumpy jumped from her shoulder and scuttled off for the backyard drainpipe.

Sighing, Marlaine just had to explain everything to her parents. When she finally walked inside, she found Mrs Brewster from next door.

Word had already spread!

"Bluebird, come and explain to us exactly what happened," Douglas called from the lounge room.

"Yes, Daddy." She said hello to Mrs Brewster and sat in an easy chair.

"Now, Marlaine. From the beginning to the end. What just happened?" Douglas asked.

And from the beginning to the end Marlaine told them and tried to comfort them by telling them they'd have their jobs back soon and everything would be all right. That everything would not only go back to normal, but it would be a thousand times better and everyone would be better off.

When asked by angry yet concerned parents for the fourth time how she knew that, she sighed and lifted herself off the chair. "Mama, Daddy, I just know. I can't explain how, and if I tried, I wouldn't understand it any more than you, so I can't explain it. I just know. I'm off to take a shower. And if you don't want to cook, Mama, I'll make myself something."

"Oh, no, dear, I brought a casserole," Mrs Brewster said. "It's in the fridge."

"Thank you, Mrs Brewster. I'm off to have a shower." Leaving her parents in the capable hands of their neighbour, she took her time in the shower and threw on one of her second-hand dresses to greet more visitors in.

By now the whole street had heard, and all the women were rallying around them, preparing lists of who was going to provide a meal and when, so the family wasn't overrun by food. They were also taking donations of any denomination to help the family out, especially since they had to move.

But Marlaine knew better and glanced at the clock.

Five o'clock. Knock off time!

*****

Stumpy, and a few of his fellow rats, were perched in prime positions to see when Reginald left work. When he finally walked out of the factory and over to his car, they scampered over and made their way underneath to hitch a ride.

There would be others following to perch themselves at intervals along the route, and since they all had the strain, this meant their eyes saw what the others saw, and their ears heard what the others heard. They were one big, connected brain network.

Reginald backed out of the car space and drove through the gates. He wasn't worried about sacking Marlaine and her parents. Nevertheless, he knew he would have to find another secretary and supervisor who were just as good as Douglas and Betty and that would be difficult. He also wasn't worried about Marlaine's threats, but he *was* worried about how she knew, and that meant Betty must know something and had told her daughter. So that was *two* people who had an inkling of what he was doing.

But an inkling was nothing. An inkling was not proof, and he had that proof at home. He just didn't know if his home was a safe enough hiding place anymore. He pulled into his drive, parked under the carport and grabbed his briefcase from the passenger seat. He was ready for a good meal, and an even better glass of whiskey. Going in by the back door, he didn't see the rats come out from under the car.

Stumpy led the way back to the street so the others could see which house they were at and looked at the number on the mailbox so they got it right. He knew the others were waiting in the pre-arranged spots. They'd organised everything when he'd got back to the factory. He raced to the back yard, and they found a dark, out of the way, place to hide until it was time.

*****

Marlaine didn't want to go to bed. In fact, she couldn't, because neighbour after neighbour from the street, the block, the neighbourhood, dropped by to offer their condolences. When questioned why no one had stood up for them that afternoon, the men would glance away, embarrassed, and say the same thing. They feared being fired themselves. Which was understandable.

Marlaine glanced at the clock. Eight p.m. Not dark enough.

The next time she glanced at the clock, it was ten,

and dozens more had come through the door. They were never alone, but it still wasn't late enough.

She quietly wandered off to her room and closed the door. *Stumpy…* She put the thought out there. *Can you hear me?*

Yes, my queen.

Have people gone to bed there yet? There can't be anyone to hear or see you.

There are a few people out and about. Fatso hasn't even arrived yet. He's too big and people will see him, so he needs to be careful.

How far away are you?

Not that far, really. The opposite direction of you. The field behind the factory is between us, and there are lots of underground tunnels for him to use.

Give it another couple of hours. Twelve at the latest, when everyone should have gone to bed and there are no lights in the neighbourhood. Have you been in the house yet?

In there now and have been searching for paperwork. We think it's the pages he's been staring at for the last few hours.

Well don't let him do anything to them. We need them.

Yes, my queen. We'll keep an eye out, and if he does make a move, we'll distract him.

Good. I'll talk to you later. Sighing, Marlaine slowly rose and went back to the lounge room.

*****

She was barely keeping her eyes open two hours later when Stumpy checked in. She slunk out of the room, which was still filled with neighbours, and quietly went to her bedroom. *Stumpy, are you able to do it?*

Fatso is in the backyard and the neighbourhood is asleep. Do we go?

Yes. Do it and save those papers.

Yes, my queen.

She wandered into the kitchen for a drink and chatted with more neighbours. The fact that there were other people in the house provided them with alibis, and when no one was looking, she checked the clock to make sure she knew the time.

Stumpy checked in a half an hour later. *All done. No blood, no mess. The papers are on the coffee table where he left them, and Fatso's finishing him off. He's very happy. I had to tell him to stop making so much noise with his slopping and slurping.*

Marlaine smiled and turned to look out the kitchen window. *Tell him not to leave any evidence behind and get it over with so you can get out of there without being seen.*

There's an old drain tunnel down the end of the street that Fatso came through. He just trundled on down the road, so happy to be finally eating that he didn't care who saw him.

Get out of there as fast as you can without being seen, and then get back to the factory and make a mess of his office. We need a reason for someone to put a call out for him tomorrow, so they find out that he's missing. And don't get caught doing that, either.

Will do, my queen. See you tomorrow.

Still smiling, Marlaine wandered into the lounge room and sat in the corner.

The visits lasted until daylight.

What an alibi that was going to be!

CHAPTER EIGHT

When Reginald didn't arrive for work at nine on the dot, no one worried. But when he didn't arrive at ten on the dot, the guard went into his office and found the mess. He used the phone to call Reginald's home, but received no answer. He decided to wait another hour and called Reginald's home at eleven on the dot when he still hadn't arrived. When the phone wasn't picked up, he called the police who went around to Reginald's house. They found the car in the drive, both back doors wide open, and no one to be seen. What they *did* find was the paperwork from the mill which they collected and took to the police station while some of the men started searching for Reginald Sherriff.

*****

Marlaine was woken by loud banging on the front door. She'd been drifting in and out of sleep for the few hours she'd actually been in bed.

Douglas answered the door to two constables.

"Yes?"

"Mr Dufrane? We need to speak to you about Reginald Sherriff," one of the officers said.

"What about the low down dirty thief?" Douglas had barely had a few hours sleep himself.

The constables eyed one another. "He's missing," one said.

Douglas raised a brow. "Seriously?"

"Yes," the other constable replied. "We need to come in."

Douglas let them in and pointed to the lounge room where Betty was.

Marlaine crept out of bed and opened her door a crack to listen, and heard the whole sordid story of how Reginald Sherriff was missing and it appeared he had been skimming off the top of the workers' wages.

"I knew it!" Betty exclaimed. When the officer stared quizzically at her, she went on to explain how she'd suspected it for a year now, but had no proof.

"We found the proof, and have called the factory owner in to verify it. It will take some time to sort through. Meanwhile..." His gaze flicked back and forth between them. "Where were you two last night?"

"Here." Douglas stared at him point blank. "With every one of our neighbours coming and going all night. They didn't stop and no..." He leaned back in his chair. "We weren't done until around six this morning when the last one finally left and we went to bed."

The officers exchanged a glance and nodded. "As your whole family was fired from the mill last night, we'll need official statements and a list of those neighbours."

"That's going to be a very long list," Betty said. "Will you have the time to check them all out?"

One officer gave her a smile. "We'll have to make time. But for now, we'll go."

Marlaine closed her door, smiled, and went back to bed, only to find Stumpy calling on the telepathic hotline.

How are things?

Just fine. The police came calling. They know he's missing and that we were fired. They also have the paperwork. How's Fatso?

Well-fed and sleeping like a baby. Happy that he finally had a decent meal, and believe me when I say this, there was a lot of Reginald for him to feed on.

Marlaine chuckled. *Good for Fatso. Not sure when I'll see you, but probably next week. Try not to eat any more humans until then.*

Yes, my queen.

*****

All day Saturday and Sunday, the police, the factory owner, and his lawyers, were in and out of the Dufrane cottage. It was so hectic that Betty had to rely on the neighbours to get her shopping done. They also dropped off other things the family might need.

The factory owner was disgusted that Reginald had not been paying his workers and wanted Douglas back at the factory, now in the role of manager. He knew he was a good worker, having been there for over twenty years, and promoted him with full pay. He re-hired Betty as the secretary and listened to her suspicions of Reginald. He also told them to reinstate full pay to everyone, and said that he personally would reimburse all of the back pay out of his own pocket. And if Reginald wasn't found, he'd sell off his house to pay for it because he owned that too.

*****

On Monday morning, Douglas and Betty walked into the factory at eight-forty-five to thunderous applause and cheers.

Douglas put his hands up for them to stop, and when they quietened down, he said, "I guess you've heard what's been happening and all the good news to come from it."

Another cheer went through the five hundred strong crowd.

"Good. Saves me retelling it. You know things will be better. You'll get your full pay, back pay, and holiday pay. But we still need to sort out the night shift. Unless any of you want to work faster so there's no leftovers?" he joked. "But until then, let's get back to work everyone."

*****

On Monday morning, Marlaine walked through the gates of her school with her head held higher than ever before, and a brand new uniform that would give her a couple of years' worth of growth. Her lunch box was filled with lots of yummy food, and she had a plan for the mill kids. If they were willing. She also drew everyone's attention.

Especially Darius's.

She saw him and his group start her way, but flashed her red glowing eyes at him. "Don't even dare! And you can stop it altogether because I'm not tolerating you and your bullying anymore, Darius Cormack. You stay away from me, and the rest of the mill kids. Do you understand? Or *very bad things* will happen to you."

Stunned by the threat, Darius shrank back with an impending surge of doom. "Sure, Dufrane. We'll leave you alone. I promise."

She flashed a wicked grin and kept on moving, sending a thought out on the telepathic hotline. *Stumpy, pay a visit to Darius Cormack and scare the almighty out of him. But don't kill or eat him.*

Yes, my queen.

The grin grew and she headed for class.

At lunchtime, she gathered the mill kids in the library and told them her plan. If anyone was interested in earning some pocket money for themselves, they were to meet her at the mill that afternoon.

And that afternoon, fifty mill kids turned up for work.

"Blimey!" Marlaine exclaimed when she saw

them all. "Okay…let's try and figure this out. Considering there are so many of you, we'll have to come up with a plan to get you all earning." They would be taking over her old jobs so she could just do the Friday night night shift which her parents were reluctantly letting her do, and she'd had some ideas for new jobs to accommodate them all.

After much arguing back and forth, they found a way for each kid to earn some pocket money by taking a one hour shift every two weeks so they had enough to buy themselves something or save up for something better. And by the time they went home, each mill kid had a new purpose in life.

As the weeks passed by, things changed for the better and everyone was happier because Reginald Sherriff would never be their boss again. Betty had her job back, Douglas had been promoted on more pay, the workers had hundreds of pounds coming to their families, and Marlaine didn't have to work if she didn't want to.

She now got to wear some new clothes instead of hand-me-downs and op shop finds, and got to eat the occasional sweet treat. So she was happier, and healthier, as were her parents, and she finally had everything she'd ever wanted.

Marlaine's eyes glowed and a wicked smile turned up her lips. She was also the queen of rats and part of her new life plan was to get Fatso on a diet and scare the bejesus out of Darius Cormack, so taking on the Friday night night shift was just the start of her new life.

*****

Thirteen-year-old Marlaine Dufrane sat back in her chair, dropped her pen onto her school book and smiled. If this story didn't get her an A in English, she didn't know what would. But what she *did* know, was that she was glad she didn't live in the fifties and on struggle street like her character. She had new clothes and shoes in her large closet, a four poster bed in her bedroom, great food to eat, music to listen to on her phone, and a nice two storey house to live in. Unlike her grandmother, for whom she was named and constantly told she looked so much like, she was lucky. So yeah, not much of a fictional story, more of a *retelling* of a story from days gone by as told to her by her grandmother.

"Thanks for the inspo, Grandma." A wicked smile slid across her lips, and her eyes glowed red. She scratched her three-legged, stumpy tailed pet rat under the chin as he sat on her shoulder.

Stumpy snuggled into her neck and his eyes glowed red.

THE BONES OF WRATH: TERRORS

DARK SHADOWS

Thump…

Crash…

Thud!

Sean Gilbert jolted awake, jerking upright on the sofa, his head bobbing on his shoulders like a nodding dog toy. "Was that?"

There were grumbles from his friends as they slowly woke around him. They'd all fallen asleep in the Gilbert's family room while watching late-night horror movies.

"Was what?" Liam Manfred asked, wiping sleep from his eyes and yawning. "Ugh, what time is it? Did we even finish the movie?" He looked at the TV to see an infomercial. "Aw, bum! It's finished."

"Yeah…I think we missed it." Tanner Scott grinned so widely his jaw cracked. "Ow!" His brows furrowed at the pain, and he rubbed the side of his face. "Why are we awake?"

"There was a noise," Sean replied, overcome with a yawn that was contagious as he saw his other friends yawning as well. He'd been having a sleepover with his mates Liam and Tanner, and Zack Coleman and Charlie Hart were there, too. "It had better've not been the cat."

Rusty, the family's tortoiseshell Persian, was sleeping peacefully in his bed of cushions at the side of the couch Sean was on.

"Nope." Charlie nodded at the cat. "Not Rusty."

"Guess we'd better check it out then." Sean yawned a second time and managed to get to his feet. "Ah, God, I'm not even awake yet. Who wants food?" He manoeuvred his way between his friends on the floor and walked into the hallway. Looking left and right, he saw no one and no thing.

The soft yellow glow of the wall sconces illuminated the hallway enough for him to see clearly, so he tiptoed towards the kitchen at the back of the house, flicking on lights in each room as he passed to see what the disturbance might have been. "Nope, nothing in the lounge room. Nope, nothing in the office." He walked into the kitchen and flicked on the light.

Taking a moment for his eyes to adjust, he scanned the room for what might have caused the thud and thump he'd heard. "Nope, nothing…" His gaze landed on the large silver mixing bowl upside down on the floor. "Now, why would that be there?" He bent and scooped it up, spinning it between both hands while he looked around the room. "That doesn't equate to the crash, though."

"Ow!" Tanner lifted his foot and looked at his sole, seeing blood drip from a cut. "This might. Is that glass?" He hobbled to one of the stools at the kitchen bench and hoisted himself onto it, cocking his foot onto the bench to see it better. "Got Band-Aids?"

Sean mumbled, "Yeah", while he leaned down to see how much glass there was and saw a broken drinking glass under the bench. "How'd that get…?" Glancing up, he saw his friends looking at him. "Careful where you walk, I'll get the broom and pan." He carefully made his way to the utility cupboard for the dustpan and swept up the broken glass he could see while Tanner tended to his foot.

"Here's my piece." Tanner dropped it into the dustpan as Sean walked by. "It's not too bad. But how'd the glass break in the first place?"

"That's what I'd like to know," Sean muttered. "If Rusty was in the family room with us, it wasn't him. The window's shut, so it wasn't a breeze, and the doors are securely locked."

Thud…

Crash…

Thump!

Five heads swivelled towards the basement door.

"You sure all the doors are locked?" Tanner whispered. "Someone's down there." He slowly lowered his leg and swivelled the rest of his body to orient with his head. "Can anyone break into the basement?"

"No. The windows are too small and the only way in is through the door."

"So…then…someone's in your basement," Liam

whispered and tiptoed closer to Charlie. "What do we do?"

Sean's gaze darted to the security system on the wall. "There's no motion in the basement, no heat, the alarm's not going off." He thought of what was there. "A shelf could have collapsed. There are some old ones down there."

"Then what made the mixing bowl hit the floor and the glass smash?" Zack asked, inching closer to the others. "Something happens in the kitchen, then something happens in the basement…"

"We'll go down and have a look," Sean replied. "The security alarm says there's no one down there, so it's fine." He nodded confidently, the motion defying his insides which were quaking. "But let's put some shoes on first."

They hurried back to the family room for their shoes before heading for the basement door.

"Do we need anything?" Liam asked. "Torch, baseball bat—"

"Don't be stupid!" Sean rolled his eyes and flicked open the metal lock at the top of the door. "See, even the lock was still in place. No one's down there." He turned the knob and pushed the door open. It creaked on its hinges as he flicked the wall switch. The steps before them were illuminated in bright white light and he started down with more bravado than he felt. "It's probably a shelf," he said loudly, trooping down step by step with the boys behind him. "I hope it was nothing valuable that broke." He reached the bottom of the stairs and looked around, spying a fallen shelf and several broken jars of nails. "See, there you go." He grabbed a dustpan and brush from the cleaning supplies by the wall and hurried over to clean up the mess.

The boys helped lift the shelf and settle it on the work bench.

"Just came out of the wall." Charlie examined the gaps where the shelf had been. "Looks a bit rotted."

"I'll tell Dad when he gets home." Sean finished sweeping up the glass and nails and dumped them into an old tin for his father to deal with.

"Sean…"

Sean glanced around to see Tanner in front of the stairs staring upwards. His face was whiter than Casper the ghost after being sucked dry by Dracula. "What? What is it?"

Tanner's arm slowly extended in front of him, his finger pointing up, his eyes never leaving the spot they were riveted on.

Sean moved over to his friend and glanced up to see black legs swiftly turn and run into the house. "Someone's in the house. *Now* it's time for bats." He grabbed one from the metal drum by the stairs, where the sports bats were kept, and he charged up the stairs to see the dark figure dart into the family room at the front of the house. "Let's go, he's in the family room." Charging down the hallway, his armed friends behind him, he saw the figure dash across the hallway into the lounge room, Rusty the cat hissing and snarling behind it. "Ha! The cat's got him."

Sean flicked on the lounge light and saw Rusty snarling at something in the corner of the room. But there was nothing there. Frowning, he called, "Rusty? Rusty. What's the matter, boy? There's nothing there." He watched the cat slowly back away from the corner, but he didn't stop snarling and hissing and his ears were flat against his head.

Rusty stared at the shadow, watching it slowly inch along the wall towards the door, and he slowly followed it, inching sideways to keep the shadow his master could not see in line, so it didn't hurt anyone.

The boys moved foot by foot in the opposite direction away from the door.

"What's going on?" Tanner asked, favouring his bad foot because the cut ached. "There's nothing there, but I saw a person at the top of the stairs."

"And I saw a person in the hallway," Sean replied. "I have no idea what Rusty's doing, but someone is still in the house."

Rusty was almost at the door, herding the shadow towards it, to get it away from his master. The growl emanated from deep in his throat.

The boys watched the space Rusty was watching and in 0.1 second went from seeing nothing, to seeing a black figure in the doorway as it skedaddled around the corner and down the hall.

"What…the…hell…?" Sean muttered and rubbed his eyes. "Where did that come from? What is that? How did that…?" He heard a loud bang at the end of the hallway.

"Don't know what it is, but that ain't no person."

Zack stared at the doorway. "What the hell was that? It wasn't there, then it was. That's not a person, but a black thing with arms and legs and a head, but no face and no clothes and what the hell was that?"

"A shadow person?" Charlie murmured from the back of the group.

The other boys turned to stare at him. "A what now?"

"A shadow person," he repeated and looked from face to face. "Don't you lot watch *Paranormal Caught on Camera*? They show videos of shadow people all the time. They're normally dead spirits haunting different places."

"How often do you watch this show?" Tanner asked.

"Every Wednesday night." Charlie shrugged. "At least I know what it is and it ain't human."

"Can we catch it?" Sean asked, peeking at the hallway. He was thinking it was a load of bunkum, but the shadow had very clearly appeared before them when just seconds before there had been nothing.

"There's nothing *to* catch," Charlie replied. "It's a spirit."

"Bugger!" Sean swiped his hand through his hair and headed for the hallway. "Come on. Let's deal with this thing." He saw Rusty sitting in front of the basement door staring at it. But he also heard noises coming from behind it and slowed as he approached. "So, what are we supposed to do then?"

"Ask it to leave," Charlie said. "I don't think there's anything else you *can* do. It's a spirit."

Thump…
Crash…
Thud!
Their eyes riveted to the door.

"We gotta go in." Sean said. "Rusty, go back to bed. We don't want to trip over you." Gently moving the cat aside with his foot, he flung open the door, aimed his bat high and yelled, "Whatever you are, I want you out of my house," and stormed down the stairs as loudly as he could, his friends following.

The shadow figure darted into the space under the stairs and snaked a hand through one of the gaps to grab Sean's ankle.

Sean tumbled down the last five steps and landed badly on his wrist. "Bugger! You bloody—"

"You okay?" The boys tried to race down the stairs, but Rusty darted in between them and dashed under the stairs.

The shadow quivered and stepped back from Rusty while also watching the boys gather around Sean. It panicked, materialised through the stairs, and ran back across the room, waving an arm at everything it passed, making those objects fly towards the boys who ducked out of the way.

"After it!" Sean yelled, and cradling his wrist against his chest, took off after the shadow.

The shadow raced around the workbench to make its way back to the stairs, but it had to dash through a shelving unit to avoid the five unruly teenage boys chasing it. Fleeing for the stairs, it dashed around Rusty and fled upstairs.

"Aw, for the love of—" Sean yelled and pounded up the stairs behind it. "Where'd it go?" He saw legs on the stairs to the upper level. "It's gone upstairs, but how do we get rid of it?"

All five boys pounded up the stairs to the first floor to see the shadow disappear up the stairs leading to the attic. "Aw, bum! It's headed for the attic." Sean grimaced at the pain in his wrist. "Give me a minute." He hurried into his room and rummaged in his desk for a wrist brace he sometimes wore after sport. Strapping it on, he rejoined the others in the hallway. "What do we do? How do we get rid of it?"

Four heads turned to Charlie.

"What! I don't know what to do." He shrugged at his friends. "They never say how to get rid of them."

"Maybe it's like an exorcism thing," Liam suggested. "Where the priest comes in and reads from the bible."

"An exorcism!" Tanner raised a brow.

"No one's possessed," Sean scoffed.

"A spiritual cleansing." Zack looked up from his phone to see his friends staring. "What?" He shrugged. "I googled it."

"So...what? We're supposed to call a priest and wave some stinky incense around?" Tanner asked. "My mother uses that rubbish. It's revolting and makes the whole house smell gross."

"We don't need that," Sean butted in. "We just need to get rid of the shadow."

"Well, except for that, I don't know what else,"

Zack said. "And you need sage, not incense. And I doubt you've got any of that."

"No, we don't, but since it seems to hate Rusty, let him go first and we'll close the door behind us to see if we can keep it up there until we destroy it. Come on, let's go." Sean started for the attic door, but soon realised his friends weren't following. "What?"

"We're hardly equipped for it." Charlie limply held up his baseball bat.

"I'll record it on my phone." Zack held it up. "See what we can get."

"And we don't need torches because there's a lot of light up there." Sean urged his friends to follow.

"But what if the bulbs blow? If it does something to them, we'll be in the dark and not know where to go," Tanner argued.

Sean rolled his eyes. "Get mine from my room and arm yourselves, girls. We're off to fight an evil ghost."

"Not really a ghost, I think," Charlie muttered. "More of a manifestation of spiritual energy."

Sean's eyes rolled harder in their sockets. "Isn't that what a ghost is?"

Charlie pondered this a moment. "I suppose. But that still means you can't fight it with physical bats and weapons as they'll go right through and not do any damage. You won't hurt it."

"But it will know who's in charge and it ain't him." Sean struggled to grip the bat he was holding in his right hand. His left was still weak and painful from landing on it.

"Is it a him?" Liam asked. "Are ghosts male or female—"

"And how do you tell?" Tanner finished the sentence.

All heads turned to Charlie.

"What!?" He shrugged. "I'm no expert. Just coz I watch paranormal stuff doesn't make me an expert. I don't know if it's a boy or girl ghost."

"Okay, enough of this!" Sean snapped. "Let's go." He marched up to the attic door and opened it, watching as Rusty bolted ahead of him. "Last one up shuts the door and stands guard at the top of the stairs. Let's go." He led the way up and looked for his cat, finding him in a corner of the room staring up towards the ceiling. "Argh, God, don't tell me it climbs walls, too." He didn't actually see anything, regardless of the intensity of the lighting. It wasn't a typical attic. It had been plastered and laid out to use as a spare room, an office, and a reading room, so the entire area was functional. He also knew after what happened down in the lounge room, the shadow person had the ability to make itself invisible to humans.

"The cat's got it cornered," Liam whispered, bat at the ready. "But we can't see it, so how do we deal with it?"

"Don't know, but let's try this." Sean strode over to stand behind Rusty and looked up at the ceiling. "Whoever you are, *what*ever you are, I want you to leave this house and not come back. If you are a ghost, you're dead. Your body is dead, you're just in spirit form and no longer need to be here. Leave and don't come back." Staring up at the corner, he had no idea if the thing was even there. He only had the cat to go by.

The shadow person materialised so they could see it, and it sprang over all of them, landed on the floor in a slide, and made it to the stairs before the cat could pounce. It flew down the stairs in one leap and was gone before the boys could comprehend what had happened.

"Whoa…what the…?" the boys said in unison.

"After it!" Sean yelled and ran after the shadow, *and* Rusty. They bolted down the stairs to the first floor just as the shadow did a flying leap down the stairs to the ground floor, Rusty hot on its heels. He had nowhere to go because the cat and the kids were after him, and he had long run out of hiding places. But back to the basement he went, hoping to blend in with the dark colours. Maybe he could just fade into the wall. There was a shed outside, maybe he could go there. But no, he was attached to the house and had only turned up because the boys had dug up some of his belongings out in the garden and brought them into the house. He was attached to those, so if *they* were in the house, *he* was in the house. If they were buried in the back garden, *he* would be back in the garden. That could work. Now, how could he get those dreadful kids to figure it out? And where did they put his stuff?

Rusty and the boys pounded down the basement stairs, and while Rusty went straight to where it was, the kids stood back and glanced around.

"Why does it keep coming back to the basement?" Charlie asked. "This is the third time we've been here."

"Don't know." Sean slowly stepped towards Rusty. "Maybe there's something here it's attached to?"

Liam held his phone still, recording all of it. "Did you buy anything recently and store it down here? Find anything and put it here? Dig—"

"Yes…" Sean paused mid-step. "We have."

"Maybe it came with that stuff then. You brought it into the house, it came with it." Tanner stood behind Sean to his right. "What was it?"

Sean thought back to two days ago when he and his kid brother had dug up the items in the backyard. "Just stuff we found. An old tin with some things in it."

"From where?" Charlie hung back, not really wanting to get involved in other-worldly things.

"The back yard…stuff…" Sean's gaze wavered and moved from where Rusty was looking up to the storage container he'd shoved the tin in.

"Yeow." Rusty's head twitched and moved to the right, and he prowled along behind the shadow.

The shadow finally knew where his tin was. The tin was sacred and held only items that were of the utmost importance to him, and so they were priceless.

The boys shifted over to the bench between them and the storage shelf with the container and watched it slide out from the shelf.

Then nothing.

They waited several moments before Sean said anything. "Is that it?"

The shadow turned black so he could be seen and pointed to the container.

"Ah!" The boys jumped back in fright and Rusty hissed.

The shadow rolled the container out until it fell from the shelf, and he saw his tin. Managing the power to pick it up, he held it lovingly to his chest for a moment, before placing it on the bench between him and the boys. The cat no longer mattered. He could sense he was almost home free.

"So…he wants the tin. Is that what you found?" Tanner asked, his eyes never leaving the shadow person.

"That's what I found." Sean nodded. "We found it buried under the oak tree in the back yard and brought it inside."

"What's in it?" Liam held the phone steady despite his shaking hands.

"Um…" Sean thought back. "An old toy car, miniature horses, cowboys and Indians, some jacks and marbles. Really old kids' stuff."

"Maybe he wants it back in the garden." Charlie took a small step back. "You unearthed him when you unearthed his tin."

"Maybe you should rebury it," Tanner suggested. "It might get rid of him."

"Are you the owner of the tin?" Sean asked the shadow.

The shadow visibly moved the tin.

"Would you like me to rebury it under the tree?"

The shadow moved the tin towards Sean.

"Are you here to hurt us?" Sean asked his last question.

The shadow shook his head and fearfully looked down at Rusty. Even as a child, he'd had a fear of cats after one had scratched him badly.

Sean sighed and lowered his bat. "If it means getting you out of my house, then we'll rebury your tin." He walked over to the barrel beside the stairs and dropped his bat into it before selecting a shovel off the wall. "Boys, you'll have to do this for me. My wrist is killing me."

All four were looking at him in surprise, not yet ready to disarm themselves. "You sure?"

Sean nodded at the shadow. "He just said he's not here to hurt us and wants his tin back. Let's rebury it. Where's the torch?" He handed shovels to the boys and picked up the tin. "Okay," he said to the shadow. "Let's go and bury your stuff and get you out of my house." Leading the way upstairs, the other boys were initially reluctant to follow, until they saw the shadow follow Sean, and Rusty follow the shadow. Shaking their heads and exchanging quizzical looks, they followed all three upstairs.

Being attached to the tin, it was easy for the shadow to follow Sean and stand by him while the hole was redug in just a few minutes.

"Here." Sean grabbed Zack's hand and aimed the torch into the hole. "There, under that root is where we pulled it out from." The boys shifted some excess dirt from under the root and pushed the tin back where it had lain for God knows how long.

Memories wandered back for the shadow person to all of the times he played under that tree as a child with his marbles and jacks, played cowboys and Indians, and raced his cars off the above-ground roots. Good memories, happy memories, the only memories he still had. He hovered for a few moments, nodded at the boys, and then disappeared into his tin.

Nodding in return, they filled the hole with dirt, packed it down, then dusted off their hands and trooped back inside to find Rusty sitting inside the door.

"Well, Rust, it's gone." Sean closed and locked the back door.

"Meow!" Rusty licked his lips and headed for his food bowl.

NE-FAIRY-OUS

"Happy birthday, dear Alyssa, happy birthday to you. Hip hip hooray, hip hip hooray, hip hip hooray." The crowd cheered ten-year-old Alyssa Graham as she preened and primped for them.

"Blow out the candles and make a wish first," Kiki Standford, Alyssa's best friend, called as she clapped her hands excitedly.

Alyssa flung her long brown curly hair over her shoulder, leaned towards the large blue castle cake, quickly gazed across the crowd to make sure they were watching, and blew out all ten candles with one breath. Righting herself, she clasped her hands and plastered a sugar-coated smile on her lips. "Thank you so much for coming, everyone. Please enjoy *my* cake that the maid will cut up for you." Turning from her audience, she muttered, barely under her breath, to the maid, "Make sure they only get *one* small piece each. They don't deserve anything else."

The maid waited a moment for Alyssa to walk away before rolling her eyes and picking up the knife from the cake table.

"Oh, Alyssa, what a super cake. I can't wait to taste it. Do you know what it is?" Ten-year-old Brianna Hampton asked her friend. "Do you like my ballgown skirt?" She swivelled side to side, holding out her pink silver star covered tulle skirt to sparkle in the sun.

Alyssa cast a critical eye over Brianna *and* her skirt. "Why on earth did you wear *that* to *my* party? Are you trying to upstage me?"

Shocked, Brianna's eyes widened and she stopped waving her skirt. "Oh, of course not, Alyssa. But your party *is* a princess theme, so I wore a ballgown skirt." She had teamed it with a soft pink tulle top, and silver sequin bolero and matching shoes. Her blonde curls were piled high on her head and set with a small fancy tiara.

"Mmm…" Alyssa's mouth set firmly. "I suppose it will do. Thank yourself lucky I'm not sending you off home to change. But then you could *never* outshine me." She glanced down at her blue ballgown covered in Swarovski crystals. "I *hate* pink, but blue *is* my favourite colour."

Ella Whitman and Nola Prentiss ran up to them.

"Have you tried your cake yet, Alyssa?" Ella asked. "It's *so* delicious and smooth and creamy."

"No, I haven't. Mother bought one for me, so I don't have to share with the peasants." Alyssa's remark scored giggles from the girls.

They all knew that's what Alyssa called everyone else at school as she was the richest student and the daughter of the richest family in town. Not that they had competitors in *those* stakes. *No one* came close to the Graham family where money was concerned, which is why they had their palace at the edge of town. Well, it wasn't *really* a palace, but the three-storey old brick mansion *was* very palatial. It stood on a massive parcel of land that held a considerable acreage of forest. The girls loved to play fairy princesses there any chance they could.

"Well, you better keep it for yourself because Giselle Bodeen is on her third piece already. Everyone else will be lucky if they get any," Nola said rather nastily. The four girls were a clique at school and thought, because they were richer, prettier, and smarter than the rest of the kids, that they could put them down and be rude any time they wanted.

"If she keeps eating three pieces of cake every time she has it, she'll be bigger than she already is," Kiki mocked. "That girl is already a tub of lard. And did you see that *horrendous* dress she's wearing? Who does she think she is wearing a princess dress? She needs to be wearing a servant's outfit. *Why* did you invite her, Alyssa?"

"*Not* because I like her, that's for sure." Alyssa glanced over her shoulder towards the cake table to see Giselle eyeing off the remainder of the cake. "But since it's my *tenth* birthday, I wanted to show the rest of the students what they'll never have. Money, fame, and class." She shook her head and turned back to her friends. "I didn't *want* to invite them, but felt it necessary to lead by example."

"Well, it's not like your parents can't afford it," Kiki told her. "They're the richest parents in town."

"Yes." Alyssa casually flicked her hair over her right shoulder, then her left. "They are."

"Oh, my God," Nola complained. "Giselle just got a fourth piece of cake."

"What!" Alysa spun around and zeroed in on Giselle all but inhaling another piece of cake. "That's it. I've had enough of that fat pig." With clenched fists by her sides, Alyssa stormed through the crowd and over to Giselle who had finished her cake and was licking her fingers. "What do you think you're doing, Giselle? If you keep eating *my* cake there will be none left for everyone else." She eyed the tubby girl in the rainbow party dress that was clearly two sizes too small. "You'll bust out of that Kmart quality frock if you keep eating. You're already fat, and who said you could have *four* pieces of cake? Everyone was only supposed to get one." Alyssa's hands smashed across both of Giselle's, knocking the empty plate from her hands and stunning the crowd into silence. "Who said you could have four pieces?"

The burning heat rising up Giselle's neck and chin reached her cheeks and she knew she was redder than a tomato. She coloured that way when embarrassed, her whole face changing into a fruit she hated. This is why she was often called tomato face at school when the kids teased her.

"Well?" Alyssa demanded, hands on hips and fully aware all eyes were on her. "You peasants were only allowed *one* piece of cake. Who gave you four?" She heard the soft wave of noise filter through the crowd and realised she'd used the wrong word. But she was on a roll and there was no backing down.

"Um…" Giselle clasped her chubby hands in front of her and felt the great balls of tears slide down her burning cheeks. "The-the maid said I could because they were so small and I couldn't get a good taste of it and it was *so* delicious—"

"I don't care!" Alyssa exclaimed. "You were only *allowed one.*"

"Well, then why aren't you picking on everyone else? They had more than one piece. It wasn't just me." Giselle knew she was about to burst into sobs at any moment, but tried to keep up her bravado. She could see the rest of the students, and many adults, standing there watching, listening, and not doing anything to protect her, *or* defend her. She was alone, and she knew it.

"But they're not a tub of lard in a dress two sizes too small and in need of a diet. *Not* four pieces of cake," Alyssa said coldly. "*They* knew when to stop, *you* clearly don't. You're like a pig at a trough, snuffling away for its food. Tub of lard is a pig snuffling at a trough. Tub of lard is a fat little piggy snuffling at her trough." Alyssa repeated the lines and her friends joined in, making grunting noises.

Giselle could see some of the students joining in and the adults just shaking their heads. With a heart exploding in pain, she burst into sobs. "Stop it, just stop it. Why are you so mean?" Covering her face with her hands, she ran from the expansive backyard and into the forest at the back of the property. The children laughed and spent a few more moments grunting like pigs.

Alyssa, Nola, Kiki, Ella and Brianna finished laughing and gave each other secretive glances. They knew there was only one way out of the forest, and that was back the way she'd gone. So, in order to go home, Giselle would have to walk back into the yard and around the front of the house, which would give them another opportunity to bully the school pig.

Giselle ran through the forest, sobbing her heart out, tears blinding her to the path. She stumbled over roots and rocks, dirtied her hands when she pushed herself off the ground, and smeared her face with the soil when she wiped away her tears. She had no idea where she was going, or where she even was, but she had to get away from the bullies who hated her so much.

With her energy nearly spent, she stumbled to the edge of a small clearing with a grassy, sunny circular area, a creek with a small bridge, and a tree root that had grown big enough to use as a bench. Exhausted, Giselle sat on it and wiped her face with the backs of both hands, and took a shuddering breath. She gazed around and heard how tranquil it was. "Nice and quiet," she murmured. "Nice and quiet so I never have to hear those horrible mean bullies ever again."

Smoothing the skirt of her party dress, she smeared dirt on it. "Oh, no, now it's all dirty," she cried and tried rubbing the dirt off, only to make it worse. "Mama's gonna kill me. It's the only party dress that fits me coz I'm so fat." The tears burst forth once more. The rainbow coloured dress had been worn by her older sister who had ripped the bottom of it and never worn it again. Giselle's mother had cut off the bottom, making it just below knee-length on Giselle. But the bodice was straining at the seams and the stitches were unpicking due to Giselle having a little extra weight than her sister had had.

The beings in the clearing watched the girl with interest. They had heard her coming, heard her sobs and her heart breaking, and had seen how pretty as a princess she was. They exchanged glances, excited at the prospect of another being to play with, and one that looked so ethereal in such a pretty rainbow-hued dress. They huddled, converged, and agreed on a plan. Approaching the human, one of the beings gently landed on Giselle's knee. "Hello."

Giselle's head flew up, expecting to see another student. But she saw no one. "Hello?" came out quietly. "Is anyone there?" She didn't want to face another person right now. Not with the emotional state she was in. Especially if they were just going to be mean and bully her.

"I am."

Giselle turned to the voice. It was barely audible, and she barely saw where it was coming from. "Who said that?"

"I did." The being flapped her wings and rose until she was level with Giselle's face. "Hello."

Giselle's jaw dropped and closed, dropped and closed, and she rubbed her eyes and blinked several times until she saw the small dark shape in front of her. "Um…" She gulped and slowly moved her finger towards the shape. "He-hello." Her finger poked the being who grasped her finger and shook it.

"Hello. What's your name?"

"Um…Giselle." She saw the being wave to the forest and more small black beings flew up behind it. She wasn't scared. Well, not a lot. "What are you?"

"We're fairies," the being said. "But we don't look like the fairies in fairy tales. Which is why we look different."

Giselle studied the large swarm. They weren't the usual Tinker Bell fairies, but were small black human shapes with two arms, two legs and a head. Plus wings.

"Are you really fairies? Like, really?"

"Yes," the being said, and settled back on Giselle's knee. "We're really fairies. And you're a girl human."

"Um, yes, yes I am."

"Hello, I'm Mala. You're pretty. Are you a princess? That dress is so pretty and princessy in a rainbow of colours, and your hair is shiny gold."

"Um, thank you…" Giselle wasn't sure what else to say to that. "Um, no. I'm not a princess. I was just attending a birthday party that had a princess theme, but the birthday girl was incredibly mean to me and I ran into the forest." Her voice broke and the tears flowed again.

Mala and the other fairies glanced from Giselle to each other in concern. "Tell us why they were mean. Why would they be mean to a princess?"

Giselle started the story from the beginning, day one of school, and chronicled the last four years' worth of bullying she had suffered.

The fairies oohed and ahhed, comforted her, patted her back as a collective, and agreed that she had indeed been treated unfairly.

"I am so sorry you went through that," Mala told her. "That's not nice, and not a nice thing to do to another human being."

"It sounds as if they need to be stopped," a fairy said.

"It sounds as if they need a good dose of their own medicine," a third fairy added, curling up one hand and smacking it into the palm of the other.

"But Mama taught me that violence begets violence and it's better to not do anything." Giselle took a shuddering breath. "She said to walk away."

"Or in this case, run away," a larger fairy said. "Where's it got you so far? Running into the forest and sobbing like a baby. It clearly isn't working."

"Jerijoh, hush," Mala said. "Princess Giselle is in need of sympathy and friends, not more violence." She studied the human before her. "But we can also help you clean up. Come. Come down to the creek and let us help you clean up. Come." She held on to Giselle's finger and led her down to the creek. "Wash your face and hands and we will clean your dress."

Giselle lifted her skirt and kneeled on the grass beside the creek. She washed her hands and face and then watched as the fairies held up the skirt of her dress, and dipping their wings into the water, flapped them against the dirt on the dress. After a minute or two, the pressure from their wings had washed the dirt away.

"Wow, you cleaned my dress. Now Mama won't be mad. I hope I didn't tear it when I fell." A quick inspection told her she hadn't.

"Can you stay and play with us?" Mala asked when Giselle climbed to her feet. "We can show you where we live, and show you how to get here without going through the mean girl's yard." Mala glanced at her companions. "We have watched her sometimes. We thought she might be our friend, but she was too mean to befriend."

"And she didn't seem to see us," a fairy named Juniper said. "We can't play with people who can't see us."

"Um, I guess." Giselle looked up at the sky to see it was still bright and sunny. "It wasn't lunchtime yet when I ran off. But will I be able to get home?"

"Of course." Mala fluttered in front of her. "We will lead you back if your mama's picking you up."

"No." Giselle sadly shook her head. "Mama made me walk to the party and told me to walk home so I could get some exercise. It was such a long way and I had to carry the present for Alyssa, and I was *so* hot and thirsty and hungry when I got here. That's why I ate four pieces of cake." Her eyes welled with tears. "And I'm still hungry and thirsty."

"Then drink from the creek," Mala suggested. "The water is pure and clean, and we can show you some berries to eat. Will that help?"

Giselle wiped at her tears and sniffed. "I-I suppose so." She kneeled back beside the creek, cupped her hands to collect the water, and raised them to her mouth. When she had quenched her thirst, the fairies showed her berry bushes to eat from, as well as the odd fruit tree that was growing in the forest. After she was sated, they played games in the clearing and enjoyed the rest of the afternoon as the fairies showed Giselle where they lived and played.

*****

At five p.m. Alyssa waved her last guest goodbye and waited until they had walked around the side of the house. "Ugh, thank God that's over and all of the peasants are finally gone. I'm *so* over peasants." Rolling her eyes, she collapsed onto a lounge chair on the back patio.

"Not *all* of the guests are gone," Kiki replied. "Giselle didn't come back. Which means she's still in the forest."

"What!" Alyssa bolted upright. "Who said that little pig could hide in *my* forest? Did anyone see which way she went? Ugh, I *so* don't want to go after her. Maybe I can send one of the maids instead." She flopped back on the chair. "Someone *really* ought to teach that little pig a lesson. How *dare she* eat four pieces of *my* cake."

"She wasn't the only one," Brianna said. "As much as it *pains* me to say this, she *was* right when she said others were eating more than one piece."

"I know!" Alyssa exclaimed. "The self-serving peasants thought they could eat *all* of my cake. Well, I'm *done* with the peasants at school, and I'm *done* with pigs. Let's go and teach the little piggy a lesson." She marched towards the entrance to the forest with her friends following.

*****

"Mala, Mala, they're coming. Humans are coming." Jerijoh rushed at the group in the clearing. "I went to be nosy and they're coming after Giselle."

"Oh, Jerijoh, you know we don't spy on humans," Mala chastised.

"That's rubbish," Sundida chortled. "We spy all the time. But I say we teach these humans a lesson they'll never forget, so they leave Princess Giselle alone."

"Yeah," chorused through the herd of fairies.

"I don't want to see them." Giselle's head shook stubbornly. "I don't want to deal with them again. The party must be over."

"Yes." Jerijoh fluttered closer. "Everyone left except for five girl humans."

"That's probably Alyssa and her friends. No one likes them and they don't like anyone else except themselves," Giselle told them.

"Well then, I say we fight and teach those girls to stay out of our forest." Saturnly punched a fist into her hand. "They can't see us, so they won't know what hit 'em."

Mala sighed. "Everyone, we're supposed to be nice fairies, not mean ones."

"We are," Juniper agreed. "Until our friends are bullied, then we fight back."

"Yeah," the group chorused again.

"Gis-e-elle…"

All heads turned in the direction of Alyssa's voice.

"She's coming. That's Alyssa." Giselle clenched her hands together. "She's the meanest."

"Here, little piggy, where are you…?" Grunts and snorts followed.

Mala's hands clenched by her side as she floated up beside Giselle's face. "Oohh, that makes me so damn mad." Her hands slapped over her mouth and her eyes widened. "Oops," she mumbled.

Giselle giggled. "Aren't you allowed to swear, either?"

"Normally not," Jerijoh told her. "But I say this occasion calls for it. What's the plan and let's get going."

The fairies huddled around Giselle and quickly whispered through plan after plan until they came up with a good one.

"Okay, everyone, break." Mala pulled back. "I suppose it's a good thing they can't see us because then they won't see us coming."

"Gis-e-elle…here piggy, piggy…"

"Oohh, that makes me so mad," Mala growled. "Let's go."

Giselle watched the fairies fly off into the forest towards Alyssa and then turned and ran behind a wide tree to hide.

"Where is she?" Kiki whined. "My feet are hurting and I'm tired of holding my skirt up." She glanced down to see her shoes covered in dirt. "You'd better be cleaning my shoes, Alyssa. *You* made us do this."

"I didn't make you do anything," Alyssa retorted and powered on. "And my shoes are getting dirty too, you know. It's not all about *you*, Kiki. It's *my* birthday."

"Ow." Brianna slapped her neck. "I think I was bitten by something."

"Ow, my hair." Ella was pulled backwards. "Help me, it's attacking me."

Nola laughed and broke off the branch caught in Ella's hair. "It's not attacking you, it's just a branch. Hey!" She slapped at her ankle. "Something bit me."

"Would you lot stop whining and come on." Alyssa stomped her foot. "You're all acting like idiots and we need to find that pig, Giselle. Come on, hey—" Her hand flew to her face. "Who hit me with that branch?"

"Not me," came fourfold.

"Besides, you're ahead of us, how could one of us hit you?" Brianna asked just as her ear was pulled. "Knock it off, Ella."

"What'd I do!" Ella exclaimed. "I'm over here. Hey!" Her nostril was pulled on. "Something's up my nose. Argh! Something's up my nose. Get it off me, get it off me."

"There's nothing there," Kiki told her. "You're fine. Where's the queen bee?" They turned to find Alyssa stomping through the forest and sighed. "Let's go."

Hurrying after her, the girls kept slapping their necks, arms, and ankles.

"Ow," Brianna growled, pulling a tendril of hair. "Stop it."

"There's something on your dress, Kiki," Ella said.

"Ah, is it a spider, get it off me, get it off me." Kiki slapped at her back and spun around in circles. "Get it off me, get it off me."

"It's gone." Ella brushed the back of her dress. "It's gone."

"Oh, thank God." Kiki shuddered. "You know I hate spiders."

"I'm not even sure it *was* a spider," Ella said as they all stopped behind Alyssa. "What now? I'm tired, hungry, and I want to go back. We can't even find Giselle."

"That little piggy's here somewhere and we're gonna find her." Alyssa stood, hands on hips, staring around them. "Come out, little piggy. We know you're here…ow—" Her hand flew to her face. "Who slapped me? Ow."

The slap came from the other side, and the other, and then the other. "Ow, stop it. What's going on?" She covered her face with both hands. "What's slapping me?"

"Don't know, but maybe it's what's attacking us." Kiki slapped her neck.

"Hey!" Ella grabbed at her ear. "Something's tugging on my ear. Ow, now my nose."

"Stop pulling my hair," Brianna screeched. "Ow, my ankles." Slapping at them, she thought she saw mosquitos. *Large* mosquitos. "Oh, we're being attacked by blood suckers. Get away from me."

"Hey! It's under my dress." Nola grabbed her ball skirt and ruffled it around her legs. "Ow, my ear, hey, my nose. What's going on? We're under attack."

The fairies had herded the girls into a circle so their backs were to each other, and now the full force of their anger made them visible to the girls. "Keep away from Giselle," they said as one. Their wings flapping furiously, the hum of them grew louder and louder. "Keep away from Giselle."

"Oh, my God, what are they?" Alyssa stared at the black mass before her, around her and her friends, disturbed at the sound. "Are they saying to keep away from Giselle? Is this a joke, little piggy? Did you set this up?"

"Keep away from Giselle, you bully." The fairies' full-blown anger emanated from them, showing their full figures to the girls who shrank back in fright. "Keep away from Giselle, you bullies, and never say bad things *to her*, or *about her*, ever again." They advanced on the screaming girls, and, as a collective, grabbed onto their clothing and hair, lifting the girls enough to move them.

"Oh, my God, what's happening?" Alyssa flailed her arms like a pinwheel and her feet scuttled across the ground. "Where are you taking me? What's going on? What are you? Are you aliens? What's happening? Mother, Mother, help me."

"Help you, what about us?" Kiki screamed as something chomped on her ear.

The fairies carried the girls to the clearing, over to the creek, and threw them in on top of each other.

The girls screamed and stumbled around in their soppy ballgowns, trying to keep their heads above water so they didn't drown.

"Help, help," Brianna screamed. "Help us, somebody."

The fairies circled the sopping girls and watched them climb to their feet, soaked and bedraggled. They showed themselves once more. "Leave Giselle alone. Stop bullying her and stop being mean. It's not nice, and we will find you if you don't."

Seeing the dark, tiny winged beings around them, the girls screamed, stumbled out of the creek, and ran back through the forest.

The fairies watched them go and waited until the girls could not be heard any longer before finding Giselle hiding behind the tree.

"There you go, Princess Giselle. They will never bully you again," Mala said, fluttering at eye level. "We can take you home now. Will you come and play with us again? We had so much fun."

Giselle's head bounced up and down. "Absolutely. I've had so much fun today. But I'm hungry and thirsty. How do I get home?"

"Where do you live?" Mala asked.

"The other side of the forest, that way." Giselle pointed in the opposite direction of Alyssa's house.

"Then we can take you that way." Mala and the others led her through the other side of the forest to the path that led to her own house. They were happy they had a new friend to play with, especially a human, and a nice one at that.

A RAKE IS NOT JUST A GARDEN TOOL

"So…what are we going to do today?" Quinn Kingsley asked his friends. They were sitting on his front porch trying to come up with something to fill their Saturday.

"Movies?" Gibson Everly asked.

"Nah!" Judd Harriman was lying back on the porch steps, hands behind his head. "We did that last week. What about the BMX bike track?"

"We did *that* the week before," Gibson replied.

"What about the game arcade?" Emmett Tyson asked from his spot in a chair, one leg cocked over an arm. "Or did we do that the week *before* the BMX track?"

"Yep," Quinn confirmed. "We've pretty much done everything in the neighbourhood that there is to do, and now I'm bored." He flopped back on the bench seat cushions and heaved a sigh. "There *has* to be *something* we can do."

"That depends," Armand Thierry replied, waiting

for his friends to look his way.

All five boys were in year eight at high school and had come up through primary school together. Even Armand, whose parents had moved to Australia from France the year before they'd started school, enrolling him in year one at the age of six. He'd taken to his new land and culture the moment the boys had asked him to join their football game at lunchtime. Now they were all turning thirteen and in the same classes.

Four heads turned to Armand, and four mouths opened to say something. But Quinn got in first. "Depends on what?"

"Depends on whether you want to do something boring, or something exciting, or something that will scare your pants off." Armand watched his friends' curious expressions.

"Depends on what you mean by scare our pants off," Quinn said. "We did a horrorfest of movies last month at the cinema."

Armand shook his head. "Not talking about movies."

The other boys frowned in thought, trying to figure out what Armand was referring to.

"It's not Halloween…" Gibson murmured.

"What about that theme park in town…doesn't that have some horror thing going on?" Judd asked. "Do you mean that?"

Armand rolled his eyes. "Not even close."

"Then what the bloody hell *do you* mean?" Emmett asked. "Spit it out."

The grin flew from ear to ear on Armand's face. "We go and explore the old hospital ruins."

"What!" came four voices. "Why the hell would we do that?"

"Why not?" Armand grinned at each friend. "We've never done it before, but a bunch of kids from school have all said they have."

"And they're a bunch of liars," Quinn argued. "Anytime any of them said they did it, it wasn't too hard to figure out they hadn't by their social media. If they'd gone, why wouldn't they post it? They *didn't* because they didn't go."

"Then let's be the first and document it." Armand's grin grew wider. "We'll go in with cameras and phones and lights."

"Baseball bats, cricket bats, hockey sticks," Emmett quipped.

"What do you want those for?" Armand frowned, puzzled by the remark.

"In case some loony attacks us." Emmett scowled. "Do you *really* think we'd go without weapons to defend ourselves? Geez, Armand."

Armand chuckled. "Do you *really* think loonies live there? The place has been abandoned for twenty years and the government hasn't bothered to knock it down yet."

"Which is why loonies live there," Emmett retorted. "It's a free for all and I'm not playing without weapons to defend myself."

"That sounds like you're going." Quinn nudged Emmett with his foot. "Who *you* goin' with?"

"What?" Emmett's puzzled expression gave way to a grin, and he casually shrugged a shoulder. "I's just sayin' in case we actually do it. I ain't goin' without somethin' to keep myself safe."

"I suppose we could," Judd piped up from his spot on the steps. "We haven't done it before, and it would be a new experience."

"Isn't it haunted?" Gibson asked. "I ain't goin' if it's haunted."

"All rumours," Armand said confidently. "Just because some people hear noises and howling at night, or during the day, and see lights bobbing around at night, doesn't mean the place is haunted."

"What!" Gibson exclaimed. "If that ain't haunted I don't know what is and why the hell would I want to go with wailing noises and bobbing lights?"

"I didn't say there was wailing." Armand's grin was back. "Just noises and howling."

Gibson scowled. "As if that's not bad enough."

"Look, do we have anything else to do?" Quinn looked pointedly at each friend. "We've done everything else. We can arm ourselves to the teeth, but I say why not, for something different. All those in favour?" He raised his hand and watched Armand excitedly wave his in the air. Gibson, Emmett and Judd reluctantly raised their hands after seeing who put theirs up first. "Okay, so we do it. Let's go get our stuff."

The boys raided the shed for sports bats, grabbed their phones and cameras, and armed themselves with backpacks full of food and water. The old hospital was about five kilometres away and they were riding their bikes there. They set off, arriving an hour later, and parking outside the gate for a drink and snacks.

"You do realise the signs say keep out, right?" Gibson pointed his water bottle at the signs and read them to the others. "Enter at your own peril. You will be charged with trespassing."

"Gotta catch us first." Quinn stared at the signs and then beyond. "Doesn't look like there's a guard around, so who's going to arrest us? And the brush has grown around the buildings, so nobody's going to see us."

The dilapidated building was a fair way back from the road. The car park had given way to bushes, and the old buildings were covered in vines and moss. The trees had overgrown, windows had been smashed, paint had peeled, and doors were hanging from hinges. You couldn't see much of it from the road, but up close it was an absolute wreck.

"Yeah…" Emmett shifted uneasily on his bike. "I'm not sure I want to go in after all. What if we're caught? Or what if there are squatters in there and they're bat excrement crazy."

The other boys laughed at Emmett's use of the word excrement. Since his mother had forbidden Emmett to swear, he'd been creative in coming up with other words to use.

"There could be," Quinn agreed. "But we'll just wave our bats at them."

"Or, if we see any, we'll run the other way." Judd

got off his bike and kicked the stand down. "Are we leaving the bikes here?"

"No, we'd better hide them in case a patrol car, or security guard, does come by." Armand rolled his bike towards the gates, which opened easily since there was no lock on them. "There are some bushes near the entrance that we can hide them behind."

"But what if some loony sees them and steals them? They won't be there when we come out," Gibson complained. "My olds will *kill me* if someone nicks my bike."

Armand stopped and gazed across the landscape until his eyes rested upon some trees with high grass around them. "Okay. What about back there? It's out of the way, away from the door, and the grass will cover the bikes."

The boys agreed and rolled their bikes over to the trees, laying them on their sides in the high grass.

Maniacal laughter wafted on the breeze followed by a loud, echoing screech.

"What the hell was that?" Judd instinctively crouched down, spinning left and right to look for the person, animal, or thing that had made the demonic sounds.

"Calm down," Armand commanded. "It's just a bird. There are probably hundreds of nests around here and we'll come across them as we go."

"How do you know?" Emmett demanded. "That could be some loony on the brink of madness." The others burst out laughing, making Emmett scowl. "It's not funny."

"Yeah, it is." Quinn slid his backpack off and rummaged for his camera. "Come on, let's get our stuff ready and go in while it's still daylight. Wouldn't want Emmett to wet himself by waiting until dark."

"*So* not funny, you drongo." Emmett's scowl deepened and he hung his GoPro around his neck.

"How about we lighten things up a little and pretend we're making a documentary on the place?" Judd suggested. "We could be David Attenborough. Who's got the best Attenbro voice?"

All five boys put on their fanciest English accents to sound like the great wilderness expert, and it was Quinn who won out.

"Cool. Me and Armand will film, and Emmett and Gibson can wield weapons. We got everything in our backpacks?" Judd asked them.

All of the boys made sure they had their storm lamps, flashlights, and weapons handy. Each one had two bats sticking out of their bags, so they could be grabbed easily.

"And we've got the GoPros and cameras," Quinn added. "How many?"

Each boy had one around his forehead, and one strapped to his chest. They weren't taking any chances of missing footage. Armand and Judd also had video cameras around their necks for recording.

"Okay, let's get started." Quinn clapped his hands for attention. "Lights…camera…action!" He went into a David Attenborough spiel. "Behind me, is the Abandonedous Hospitalis. A fairly common creature on the planet, one that is left behind when humans decide it is no longer needed. It's taken over by Weedous Interruptus, and Oversizous Treeous, two native plants that grow wildly when left untamed."

The boys giggled and kept on filming.

"We're here to find out what creatures now inhabit the Abandonedous Hospitalis, and whether we can find a new species of animal, mammammal, or mineral. Or if even human lifeforms exist in the Hospitalis ruins."

Armand snickered. "You said mammammal. Were you meant to say mammal?"

Quinn frowned. "I was, but who cares. I'll leave it in and cut this out."

An animal screeched, making the boys jump. Quinn took the opportunity to talk into the camera. "And there you have the Screechous Hideous, a bird-like creature who sounds as if it's being strangled to death, or it's excreting in its pants."

Laughter burst from the boys, and they kept going, with Quinn walking backwards towards the entrance.

"And now we're about to enter the Hospitalis." Quinn carefully stepped backwards through the doorway and lowered his voice. "We must now be as quiet as possible to not disturb any other beings that may be in these ruins." He paused in what was the main lobby and looked into the camera. "We have entered the inner sanctum of the Abandonedous Hospitalis, and, as you can see, the main desk still stands, the signs on the wall are still intact, and there are clear signs of Horribleous Graffitious where humans and creatures alike have excreted their signs of ownerships all over."

More giggling escaped the boys, but they kept it low.

Quinn spread his arms out and slowly turned in a circle. "As you can see, the inner sanctum is like a spider. Many legs extend from the main body. You have the left leg which leads to longer legs lined with rooms. To the right you have more legs leading to offices and waiting rooms, and to the back, we have what was once the outdoor green space for humans to sit and bake in the sunshine. It also has Liftous Operatis, an electronic device that lifted humans to the multitude of floors above us."

Quinn played up for the camera. "And now we're going to explore the inner sanctum some more with a look into the outdoor space that once gave humans a place to bathe in the sun." He led the boys towards the outdoor garden that was once enclosed in glass, and which sat in the middle of the four walls of the building. It was overgrown and littered with twenty years of rubbish and graffiti.

"As you can see, what was once a beautiful green garden has now turned into a cesspool of excrement, left by humans *and* animals. Which is a shame because it was once so beautiful. Come, let us explore the rest of the Hospitalis."

He led them through the right downstairs branch of the hospital where waiting areas and exam rooms were once filled with doctors and patients. They didn't go further than the corner of the hallway on the right side before turning back, not wanting to disturb whatever was down there, and not knowing if you could walk right around the hospital, or whether it would be too difficult.

They made it back to the lobby and crossed over to the other corridor that led past offices. They saw a few squatters sleeping in the rooms and kept on going, exchanging glances with each other to be silent and move on. They made it halfway down the side corridor before turning back.

Arriving back in the lobby, Quinn spoke up. "As you can see, the Hospitalis may have been abandoned by regular humans, but a sub-human known as Nowhere-To-Go-Ous Squatterous has grown in those subterraneous sections of the Hospitalis. While few and far between, they have come to exist out of need and necessity. And so we move on…" Quinn slowly walked towards the main staircase. "Now proceeding to the second floor to see what we can find elsewhere. This staircase seems to still be in good condition, and it doesn't require electricity as the Liftous Operatis that died a long time ago does." He carefully took step for step up the concrete and metal stairs that led up to the first floor. "And so we come to the upstairs, the next flight up from the ground floor which contains the wings for mothers and newborns, and the wing for infants and the Childrenous Terribleous Two-ous where small humans would come when they were sick."

A sound came from Quinn's left, the boys' right, and they all turned towards it.

With pounding hearts and wide eyes, Quinn

whispered, "And so it seems that the residue of these small humans is still present. And if it's not, then maybe it's the Nowhere-To-Go-Ous Squatterous making a racket. Shall we go and find out?" He glanced at the boys who just stared back. "We shall go and have a look, then." Another brief glance and Quinn slowly moved into the corridor leading to the children's ward.

Stopping to look in each room, but not entering, he glanced over his shoulder at the boys every time he did so.

Judd had his back to Armand's so the two of them filmed from front and back which meant no one could come up behind them with a surprise attack. Emmett and Gibson were on either side and had their baseball bats raised ready to strike.

Armand nodded to Quinn and kept walking behind him, feeling Judd's back against his. He was grateful they had weapons because this was even starting to freak him out.

The sun had risen and slowly lowered, making it close to four in the afternoon. They had been there for over four hours, and it was time to finish. Reaching the end of the corridor, they found the hall to the right blocked by a roof collapse. The rubble was chest to head high and Armand held his camera up to film over the blockade. "Can't see much," he whispered. "Time to head back. It's getting late and will be dark soon. Let's wrap things up."

Quinn nodded and moved around so he was walking backwards, back the way they'd come. "And so we come to conclude this tour of the Abandonedous Hospitalis. As you can see, it has become a refuge for the wild and untamed, and will no doubt stay that way until humans once again take control of it."

They reached the halfway mark of the hallway and Quinn saw Armand's eyes widen as he ground to a halt. Then he saw Gibson and Emmett look past him. Their eyes widened and they stopped short.

"What?" The hair prickled on the back of his neck and every fibre of his being told him not to turn around.

"Why'd everyone stop?" Judd turned around and peered between Armand and Emmett, seeing the creature in the distance. "Wha-wha-what is that?"

"Back the way we just came," Armand replied softly as his hand snaked out to grab Quinn's. He saw the creature lower itself to the floor, so it was on its hands and feet, its back level to the ground. Its body was white, almost translucent, and hairless. "Run," he shouted, and turned on his heels.

Quinn was spun around by the movement and finally saw what had stopped his friends in their tracks; a being so ugly and terrifying it was like an alien running on all fours. The loudest screech came from its throat.

"Come on." Armand grabbed Quinn's shirt and pulled him back the way they'd come. "Into that room at the end of the hall. Get ready to shut the doors behind us and jam it with something." He saw the others reach the room ahead of them and grab the doors.

"Come on," Gibson screamed, waving them on frantically. "Come on."

Armand and Quinn pelted through the doors and Emmett and Judd slammed them shut and shoved a table in front of it.

The creature pounded against the door, and it almost rattled off its hinges. The table had bounced away from it, but the boys quickly shoved it back.

"Get everything you can and pile it on the table," Armand told Quinn and Gibson. "Emmett, you and Judd keep the table in place." A quick look at the room told him there were only chairs and a few old metal filing cabinets. "Help me push those over."

He, Quinn, and Gibson pushed the empty cabinets over to the door and lifted all three onto the table.

The creature wailed and shrieked and battered itself against the door.

"Ugh, make it stop." Emmett covered both ears and squeezed his eyes closed. "Make it stop, make it stop, make it stop."

"What the hell is that thing?" Quinn sputtered in fear.

"Probably what people have been hearing when reporting shrieks and wails," Armand said, looking around for a way out. He rushed to the windows and noticed the high drop. "We could jump, but if one of us is injured—"

"Or if we're *all* injured, like broken ankles or heads, injured, we're screwed." Quinn joined him to see how high was high. "We can't make that, regardless of how fit we are. And we'd break our ankles on all the rubble. There's no dirt, no grass, nothing soft, just bricks and rubbish." He looked up at the sky and then at his watch. "It's nearly five for freak's sake. We have to get out of here." He turned to the door which the creature was still trying to get through. "That's the only door. The only way in, the only way out, except for the window we can't actually get out of without killing ourselves."

"But if we go out the door, we'll be killed anyway," Emmett managed as he held fast to the table.

Whatever that creature was, it still had the strength to move the table and three filing cabinets a couple of inches every time it banged against the door.

"Maybe, maybe not." Gibson looked up from his phone. "I've been googling monsters and it looks like what's known in monster legend as a rake. But it's supposed to be a made-up monster and not real. Even though it looked pretty damn real to me."

The rake rammed the door and screeched.

"*Sounds* pretty damn real to me," Judd quipped, knowing full well he'd excreted in his pants. "What do we do to get the hell out of here?"

"Does it say how to kill it?" Armand rushed over to them. "Or hurt it if you have to. Does it have a vulnerable spot?"

Gibson shook his head. "There's nothing. And I *mean nothing.*"

"Damn it! What do we do?" Quinn jumped back as the cabinets rattled.

"Um…" Armand tried to rack his brain, but even he had no idea.

"You got us into this, Armand, you better get us out of it," Quinn warned.

Sighing, Armand quickly went through all the tricks he'd learned in martial arts and self-defence classes. "Well…"

"Well, what?" Quinn demanded, with his hands firmly planted on his hips. "What?"

Armand sheepishly stared at his friend. "We could beat it at its own game. Literally."

Quinn's brows furrowed. "And what does that mean?"

"It means we beat it. *Literally.*" Armand slid off his backpack and rummaged around before pulling out two cans and holding them up.

"What are they?" Emmett asked as he bounced against the moving cabinets.

"Mace. Well, technically pepper spray, which is still illegal, but homemade," Armand told them. "Don't tell anyone I have these."

"Why in God's name do you have that, let alone two, and how is that going to help?" Quinn demanded.

"What do you think it's used for?" Armand rolled his eyes at his friends. "Now, here's the plan." He quickly told them what he had come up with, and as they hadn't come up with plans themselves, they agreed it was the only way.

"Okay, let's do this." Quinn tightened his backpack around him and helped the others to do the same. They armed themselves with their bats and stood five abreast with Armand in the middle. "Okay, moving the table and cabinets will be noisy, so we'll have to be quick. Line up and get ready…and in, one, two, three… Go."

Quinn and Gibson pushed the cabinets off the table while the others kept it firmly pushed against the door. The creature had stopped, obviously tired, yet curious about the noises.

"Table next. Lean against the door, everyone."

Four of them held the door fast while Judd pushed the table out of the way.

"In five, four, three, two one, step back," Quinn shouted and readied his bat to swing.

The rake rammed against the door, and it swung open. Armand hit it with both pepper sprays in the face. It was ugly, translucent, and hairless with large black eyes and distorted features. Armand emptied both cans and holstered them into his pants pockets while the rake shrieked, pawing at its face as its eyes burned.

"Now," Quinn yelled, and all five boys gave a loud rebel yell as they beat the creature into retreat.

The rake took off down the hallway, with the boys running behind and yelling as loudly as they could. They saw the creature skid into the upstairs lobby and head for the stairs.

The boys continued with another yell and watched the rake tumble down the first flight of stairs and over the railing into the lobby below. The boys pounded down the second flight of stairs, bats raised, and around the stairs to see the rake disappear into the outdoor garden and through the back section of the hospital.

Another yell, bats still raised, and the boys turned on their heels and ran out the front door, over to their bikes where they finally stopped yelling, and ran their bikes past the gates and jumped on.

Pedalling as fast as they could, they headed for home, knowing they'd never be back, and would more than likely have nightmares for the rest of their lives. But by God, they had better have got all of that on film.

WELL, WELL, WELL...

"What are we treasure hunting for again?" Samara Lane asked her friends as she wiped the sweat from her brow and took a drink from her canteen.

"Gold," Wynn Ellery replied from his crouched position by the river. It was his twelfth birthday and the only thing he'd wanted to do was pan for gold. And luckily, there happened to be a company in town who specialised in panning tours.

He gently shook his pan, which was full of dirt, and lightly dipped it in the water, hoping it would reveal the shining yellow metal he was after. "Why? Aren't you having fun?"

"Meh, sort of." Samara fanned herself with both hands. "It's something new to do, but my knees and back are hurting and I'm hot and hungry."

"So am I," Kobe Connelly replied, standing up and stretching his back. "Isn't lunch supposed to be supplied with this shindig?"

"It is and we're just setting up now," Tristan called from the nearby campground's table. The tour company was putting on a spread of hot dogs and hamburgers with a variety of toppings and salads, ice-cold sodas, and ice cream for dessert.

"Cool!" Wynn settled his pan on the riverbank so it wouldn't float away and stood up and wiped his hands on his cargo pants before hurrying over to the table where his friends were gathering. "Let's eat."

As they munched on hot dogs and hamburgers, they talked about the gold they'd already found.

"I found about five bits," Elias Finnegan managed around a mouthful of both hotdog and hamburger. "They reckon it's about fifty bucks."

"Well, I haven't found anything," Marissa Perriman complained, and tasted a bite of tangy coleslaw. "Maybe you can give a couple of pieces to me."

"Hell to the no!" Elias exclaimed and promptly choked. "Why would I give you what I worked hard to find?" He coughed loudly and swallowed the food.

"Because it would be the right thing to do." Marissa smiled sweetly at him.

"Then get your bloody own." Elias picked up another hamburger from the tray on the table. "I did all the work. Those five pieces are mine. Go find your own."

The six of them were sitting at the table in the Perrigrove National Park outside of the town they lived in. It had long been held as a state treasure based off the tales of the gold rush days with tall, lush trees, a gently flowing river, and plenty of spots to picnic. It was made better by the warm spring day.

"You're a nasty little pasty," Marissa spat back. "You'll get yours."

Wynn rolled his eyes. "Quit your arguing. It's *my*

birthday and I don't want no arguments."

"It was your birthday during the week," Shelby reminded him. "Not today. So it doesn't matter if the five-year-olds argue."

Wynn snickered. "Yeah, defo five-year-olds."

"How *dare you* call me a five-year-old, Shelby Harper," Marissa scolded. "*We're* supposed to be best friends."

"We are." Shelby shrugged at the others. "But you and Elias *are* acting like five-year-olds. He found those five bits of gold; you didn't, so you don't get any."

Marissa huffed and turned her back on them. "So much for *you* being my best friend."

"Now you really *are* acting like a five-year-old." Shelby reached for a hot dog and smeared on butter and fried onions. "Mmm, yum."

"Look, regardless of how many bits Elias found, you should be finding your own, Marissa," Wynn told her. "I've only found three pieces, and Kobe was lucky enough to find a small nugget. Today's about doing something different and doing something *I* wanted to do for *my* birthday. *Not yours.*"

"Maybe if you'd actually *bothered* panning for gold, Marissa, instead of just watching everyone else, you would have found some for yourself." Samara had been lucky enough to find several small blobs of gold a little way upstream. But she was keeping it to herself for now. "Why did you come if you weren't going to bother doing anything?"

"Because it *sounded* like fun," Marissa retorted. "But it's just too hot and too much hard work, so I've been scrolling through social media and posting photos instead."

All of them had been posting to their socials, excitedly talking about their gold finds or just about the adventure in general.

"Yeah, we have too." Kobe grinned. "Bet they're all jealous."

They finished up lunch and stood facing the river, taking in the quiet, scenic views and smog-free air.

"Are we going to do this all afternoon?" Marissa asked. "I'll need to reapply my sunscreen, which I see you boys didn't bother applying at all." She eyed their red necks and arms.

"Who needs sunscreen?" Wynn grinned. "Let's wrap this up so we can go and explore the forest across the river."

They hurried to their pans and went for one last dig in the river where Marissa *finally* found a speck of gold.

"Oh, I found some," she shrieked and rushed over to one of the guides for help. Soon she had that speck of gold in a small clear tube which she capped securely.

Within a half hour, everyone else wrapped up their panning and had their gold put into small tubes for safe keeping.

"Cool." Samara held up hers and showed off her full tube. "Looks like I got the most today. Suck on that, suckers." She gently shook it in the sun to make the gold glint before putting it in an inner pocket of her bumbag.

"How'd you get more than the rest of us?" Wynn

glanced from Samara's full tube to his barely a quarter full tube. "How'd you get more than me? That sucks." He looked at everyone else's.

Samara shrugged. "I found it upstream. Not my fault you're a sore loser. So, are we going on that hike, or are you going to cry like a baby?" She flung her blonde ponytail over her shoulder and put her hands on her hips.

"Meh!" Wynn stomped his foot and stared at her. "You cheated." Shoving the tube into a pocket in his cargo pants, he made sure to zip it up tight. "Let's go." He walked over to one of the guides. "We're ready for the second half of the adventure now."

Tristan looked up from packing the equipment into the trailer. "Okay, then. Jess and I will be leading you on the tour for the next hour or so. We'll be exploring the old shacks across the river and seeing how the miners used to live. Stock up on water, fruit, and nuts, and we'll head off. Jess will help you." He finished packing the panning equipment while the other guides finished packing away the food into the second four-wheel drive.

Tristan had started the company only a year ago after receiving permission from the council to pan in the river and explore the old shacks. And the business had taken off. There were always four guides or more in two four-wheel drives per party; two to deal with the food and set up, and two or more to help with customers and lead tours.

Jess helped the six kids stock up on water and supplies and flung her backpack over her shoulders.

"Ready to go? Don't forget your hats and sunnies."

Tristan led the small group over to the footbridge, where they lined up in single file and walked across the hundred-foot-wide river.

The council had carefully put the bridge in place two years previously so as not to disturb the environment, and regularly checked the area for rubbish and graffiti. You also needed permits to camp or to set up tours.

They made their way up a small incline to the plateau where the small huts sat. With stone walls and wood floors, the buildings had seen better days, but provided a showcase of what the area had once stood for. Prospecting.

"Okay, here we have the residence of Captain Harvey Fleiger, who retired from the army to a small house in town. But he also had this small hut. He mainly did his fishing in the river and that's how he stumbled across the gold he found. He knew he had hit a literal gold mine and very quickly snapped up a hefty length of river for himself. He built the other cabins from trees he cut down and kept all the gold he found in what could be considered underfloor safes. The very early beta versions." Tristan carefully led them into a cabin and over to a section of floor that had a Perspex cover and shone his torch into it. Burrowed deep in the ground was a ten-foot by ten-foot hole with two wooden doors. "Most people didn't trust banks back then and kept their money and riches buried in walls or floors until needed. Captain Fleiger was one of them."

Wynn glanced around the old stone cabin with its creaking camp bed, small kitchen cupboard that held a sink and stove top, dirty windows with tattered check curtains, and a small table and chairs. "Why would he stay here in this dingy dump if he had a nice house in town?"

Tristan switched off his torch and led them back outside. "It's rumoured he kept all of the gold he found in that hole. Never proved, mind you, and when he died, his wife and son inherited everything. There are no records to say they found it, or that it was hidden at their house, *but*," he paused for dramatic effect, "the wife and son *did* upgrade their house and lived very well after Fleiger died. They took grand holidays every year, and had lavish parties. So, who knows, maybe they found it after all." He grinned and swiped his brown wavy hair back under his cap, making the three girls swoon and the boys roll their eyes.

"Let's check out the other buildings before going deeper into the woods." Tristan led the way to the two other cabins, explaining their heritage before leading them to a small structure a little deeper in the woods. He opened the door. "Anyone know what this is?"

The kids huddled around the entrance, peered inside at the hole in the ground, and promptly screwed up their noses. "No."

"It's an outdoor toilet." Tristan's grin grew larger as the horror fled over their faces. "Yep, knew you'd like it."

"Ew, that's disgusting." Marissa spun on her heels and stomped away. "Dis-gus-ting. Why would you show us that?"

"To show you how good you have it these days." Tristan closed the door and ushered them away. "That's the way it was then. There was no running water to have a shower, or do the dishes and washing, or flush the toilet. You can see this part of the country has no electricity. It's essentially off the grid. If you wanted water, you got it from the river, the stream that runs into the river, or the well. It essentially all runs into one, but it isn't as clean as it used to be. But then again," he added as he watched the six of them about to take a swig of water from their bottles, "it probably wasn't all that clean back then, either. By the time everyone bathed in it, the animals frolicked in and drank from it, and probably went to the toilet in it, it wouldn't have been *that* clean."

"Ugh, don't." Marissa turned to barf, but only dry retched.

Tristan chuckled and watched their repulsed expressions. "Just a little something to remind you of how lucky you are these days to have clean running water in your taps and in those bottles. Do *not* leave them behind. If you don't take them home we'll recycle them. Okay, let's wander up to the stream." He walked off through the thick greenery with native trees bowing overhead in all their green glory. The sunlight filtered down into magical rays of soft light, and the birdlife twitched in unison at the presence of intruders.

"It's so peaceful here." Samara glanced around her as they walked further up the hill. "So green, so lush, so private."

"No one to hear you scream," Kobe joked. "Better not hurt yourselves, girls."

"Why would *we* hurt ourselves?" Shelby carefully stepped over a small log. "We're not the clumsy ones."

"Who's clumsy?" Elias asked and promptly tripped on a rock. He righted himself and blushed as the others snickered.

"Yeah, right, who's clumsy?" Wynn nudged his friend and continued after Tristan who'd stopped at a small pile of stones.

"Here we are." Tristan cupped his hands in the water trickling from the stones and drank from them. "Mmm, still fresh after all these years. From an artesian basin apparently. All natural, all fresh." He stood up and turned to his charges. "Try it."

All six stared from him to the water and back to him.

"It's clean, I promise," he said, knowing they'd been put off by his jokes about the water supply. "It's been tested several times and is cleaner than the water in your bottles." He watched their expressions change to horror. "Just kidding. *Again.* You guys fall for it so easily. Seriously, have a taste." Stepping aside, he waved the kids toward the spring. "It won't hurt you."

The boys, trying not to be outdone by the good-looking tour guide, stepped up and sampled the water.

"Not bad," Wynn declared, wiping his hands on

his pants. "Refreshing. Tastes clean. Quite cool."

Marissa screwed her nose up, but Samara and Shelby crowded around the pile of rocks and cupped their hands. The water was cool on their skin and slid down their warm throats.

"Mmm, it is nice and refreshing." Shelby nodded and glanced at Tristan. "It tastes clean, and it's definitely different from the bottled water."

"Exactly. And so this is where Captain Fleiger would get his drinking water, whereas, he'd get his other water from the river. Or, he'd just bath in the river fully clothed and clean himself *and* his clothes at the same time."

"Two birds, one stone." Wynn nodded. "Economical given the circumstances."

Tristan grinned at him before glancing at his watch. "We have enough time to check the well. It's on the way down the hill, so it's not too far. It's usually empty, but there have been some noises heard echoing from the depths of its bowels by trespassers who have camped here at night." He set off away from the stream. "Since this is a national park we're not permitted to stay the night, to protect the area. But, as you know, some people don't listen and don't care, and break the rules anyway." A scowl fled across his handsome face. "I guess they get their just desserts when they get the fright of their life."

"Has anyone figured out what's causing the sound?" Shelby asked, bringing up the rear with Marissa and Samara. "Has anyone bothered looking?"

"A few people have come out every now and then

when campers would bolt into town as if a ghost was after them and end up in the local pub drowning their fears in alcohol. A couple of search parties came out after reports that some of the trespassers had disappeared. But nothing was ever found. No bodies, no packs, no proof that those people were even here. And no search party has ever found what causes the sounds they'd heard." He stepped into a small circular clearing about twenty-by-twenty-foot round with an old stone well in the centre and stopped at the tree line, waiting for the kids to catch up. "There she is," he whispered and slowly gazed around.

The sun bypassed the tree line, so didn't reach the well, but there was still enough light to see clearly. However, an eerie chill tickled the back of his neck and caused him to shiver. "It's a bit creepy without decent sunlight."

Samara shivered. "It certainly is." Looking over her shoulder into the brush they'd just passed, she sensed someone watching.

"Nah, don't be a bunch of wusses." Wynn grinned. "It's just a well. Hey, Elias, still got your phone on? Let's check it out." The two boys walked straight over to the stone circle and peered over the edge.

"Hellooo-ohhhh," Wynn called down and heard this echo reverberate. When the noise stopped, he looked back at the others. "See. Nothing down there."

"Ah-oh-ooooohhhh…"

"Ah!" Wynn and Elias jumped back. "What the

hell was that?" Wynn gasped, beating a hasty retreat away from the well. "What *was* that?"

"Probably just the echo of your voice," Kobe said, the hairs standing up on the back of his neck.

"That was creepy." Marissa shuddered and linked her arm with Shelby's.

"Here." Elias shoved his phone at Wynn to hold and pulled out a small video camera from his backpack. "I'll keep recording while you check that footage." He aimed the camera at the well and kept recording. "Okay, check the phone footage."

Wynn quickly hit play on the video. They all heard them talking, Wynn calling out hello, and then not ten seconds later a reply came back.

"Ugh." Shelby shuddered and clung to Marissa. "That's even creepier."

Elias's eyes darted from the video camera to his phone. "What was that? Rewind it."

"To where?" Wynn touched the screen.

"To where I lean over the well. Watch for after you yell into it and it answers. Watch closely." His gaze darted back and forth between the well and the phone. "There."

Wynn zoomed in. "What the hell…?"

Two bright blue eyes stared up at them in the video.

"Are they…?"

"They can't be…"

"Just not possible…"

"What would live down a well?"

"I don't know, but I don't like it." Kobe stared dead

straight at the well in the middle of the clearing. If there was something in there, he didn't want to see it.

A soulless wail came up from the bottom of the well.

"Clearly not a human." Shelby inched towards the left. "Is it an animal? Maybe an animal is trapped down there, and those blue lights are its eyes." She slowly dragged Marissa with her as their arms were still linked.

"I just had a weird thought." Wynn stared at the well. "It's like a portal to another place and time. Maybe it's an alien. How deep is that thing?"

"No one's actually sure," Tristan murmured, his eyes never leaving the well. He certainly hadn't been expecting this today. "Some have said it's only twenty feet, others fifty, some have said there is no bottom."

"Ah-oh-ooooohhhh…" drifted into the late afternoon air.

"Ugh." Jess shivered and looked at Tristan. "Let's just go."

He nodded. "But…what if it *is* an animal, or person? They could be injured and hurt, unable to get out. Maybe have a broken leg."

"Can't they speak English?" Marissa asked.

"Not if it's an animal." Wynn rolled his eyes.

"What sort of animal could it be?" Shelby pulled the back of her polo t-shirt tight around her neck. The prickle on the back of her neck hadn't stopped the whole time they'd been standing there. The place was creepy to the next level and nowhere like she'd ever been before. She wanted to leave. Desperately.

"If it's an animal, then that could be what all of those campers and trespassers heard," Kobe suggested.

"But that's been over quite a time, not now," Elias reminded him. "Weeks, maybe years ago. Right, Tristan?"

Tristan nodded. "Very true. Those rumours were started years ago, and any animal trapped would have died by now."

"What about if an animal keeps getting stuck?" Samara suggested. "Birds, uh, foxes, whatever might be on this side of the river. Bears—"

"There are no bears here," Jess told her. "But small ground animals and birds could definitely get caught. And if one of the campers or trespassers put a cat or dog down there…"

Tristan's brow furrowed. "I hardly think it's a dog or cat given that it's been a few years since the last rumours circulated."

"We don't know who's been here," Jess replied. "We've only just started coming in the last year and this is the first time we're dealing with this."

Tristan thought about what she'd said. "That's very true. And each time we've been here we've led kids *and* adults to this very spot and never heard these noises before. We've looked in the well and there's been nothing. It must be an animal that's got stuck. Maybe an injured bird or something, attacked by a wild dog, or another bird, and it just fell in. We should check it out. Right?"

He turned to the others for support, but only got wide eyes in return. Breathing deeply, he set up a plan. "Okay, it's not an alien, it's just an animal. We need light, so we need torches." He slid his backpack off his shoulder and rummaged. "Jess, got yours?"

"Here." She handed it over. "What are you going to do?"

"We're going over there and looking in." He held up the two torches. "Is this it?"

"We all have our phones," Shelby said. "Use those lights."

"Great idea, Shelby. Boys, use your phones, two each. I'll use both torches. Elias, you keep filming. We'll approach the well and aim the light and camera down and have a look. Ready?"

"I need another phone." Kobe glanced at the girls.

"No way, no how, uh-ah," all three said.

"Here, use mine, but don't drop it." Tristan pulled his phone from his pocket. "Turn on the lights now so we're prepared."

The boys set up the four phones and Tristan tried both the torches.

The wail rose into the chill of the air.

"Let's make this quick; it's getting late." Tristan nodded at the three boys. "Ready?"

Wynn, Elias and Kobe exchanged glances before looking at Tristan and nodding.

Taking a deep breath, Tristan marched over to the well with the boys right behind him. Jess held the girls back at the tree line and all four of them watched with bated breath.

Tristan tried *not* to shake in his twenty-four-year-old boots. He'd never experienced this before, but he couldn't have planned an adventure day out better if he'd tried. In the last year of the tours, nothing had come close to being this weird, creepy, *or* exciting.

They reached the well and circled it.

"Ready?"

The boys nodded.

"Okay, shine your lights, and Elias, record it."

Leaning over the edge, they peered down into the well as far as the lights would let them. And what they saw blinked back at them with its big blue eyes.

"Argh," the boys screamed and ran back to the girls with Tristan hot on their heels. "What was that?"

"That wasn't an animal!"

"No bird looks like that!"

"That was a freak of nature!"

"Freakin' alien!"

All three boys were as white as ghosts and their eyes were wide and very scared.

"What was it?" Jess asked a pale-faced Tristan. "Was it an animal?"

Tristan stared at her with glazed-over eyes. "No. But I think we'd better get out of here now, fast."

A thudding sound of nails in stone came from behind them and they turned to stare as the clawed hand landed on the top of the well. A second hand landed beside it and a head rose behind them. Big blue eyes, small triangular shaped ears on a round head, translucent skin, and a bony sinewy body rose.

The girls screamed. The pitch was so high birds took flight. "What is that?"

"I don't know, but we go now. Run," Tristan

yelled, and herded Jess and the children ahead of him and away from the well, watching the beast crawl over the edge, throwing his torch at it, hearing the terrified screams of everyone, himself included, watching his torch fly through the air and hit the beast on the head and knock it back into the well, his torch flying down after it.

All eight of them ran pell-mell through the forest to the river, single file across the bridge, and to the vehicles on the other side which now consisted of the company's vehicles, and the cars belonging to the parents come to take them home.

And the first things out of their mouths when they came to a stop at the cars were met with laughter and applause, for their parents thought it was part of the adventure. But the kids and two guides knew better, and it made Tristan seriously rethink his future business plans.

Meanwhile, the beast sat in his home playing with his new toy. He marvelled at how it radiated light, and how by waving it behind his hand he could make shadows dance on the well walls. Oh, how he was going to enjoy having something to play with, since all the other animals avoided him, and the humans didn't come near him. He was so lonely and only wanted to make friends with everyone. He had thought the last group could be his friends, but, sadly, that wasn't to be either. And so he sat, all alone and lonely in his home, playing with his new toy, not knowing, that one day soon, that too would disappear.

ELIZABETH WANTS TO PLAY

"Isn't there some joke about going off to grandma's house?" Gage Allen asked his friends as they walked down the street.

"Nah, that's Red Riding Hood, not a joke," Rupert Edwin replied and punched his friend in the arm. "What? Scared she'll turn into a werewolf?"

"Grandma's hardly a werewolf." Harlan Glenn scowled. "What's wrong with you yobbos? It's Grandma!" Along with his cousin, Levi Madden, and their other friend Zeb Roland, they were walking three streets over to house sit for his grandmother while she spent most of the day getting some tests done at the local hospital.

"Hey, no offence to your grandma," Gage replied. "Just seemed a bit weird that we're all going to babysit your grandma's house. Why can't you two do it on your own?"

They turned the corner and headed left.

"Well, we could…" Harlan glanced at his cousin

and grinned. "But considering all the cool things Grandma has in her house, we thought you might like to come along and check it out."

Their grandmother was an avid collector of all things bizarre and they had figured they'd get a laugh out of scaring their friends.

"Meh." Zeb shrugged. "It gets me out of the house for the day."

They hurried along the street, crossed over, and walked down Annabelle Lane. Their grandmother lived at number 13.

"Seriously!" Zeb exclaimed, standing stock still on the path outside of the house, staring up at it. "She lives in house number *13*? Dude, that's creepy. *And* bad luck. *And* on Annabelle Lane. Don't you know what that means?"

Harlan and Levi grinned at their dumbfounded friends. "Yeah. Fun!"

"Come on, let's go." Harlan hurried up the driveway and around to the back door, which he knew his grandmother always left by. Using his key, he let his friends and himself in. "Wait till you see all the cool stuff she's got." After locking the door securely behind them, he and Levi hurried down the hall and into the lounge room that was filled with paraphernalia from all decades.

Gage, Rupert and Zeb followed, staring agape at the artefacts on floor-to-ceiling shelves, pictures on leftover wall space, with full side tables, and every inch of free carpet space taken up with something.

"Whoa." Their friends stood, gobsmacked at the room.

"Is that a skull?" Rupert pointed to a small object. "What is that?"

"A monkey skull, mummified, so the flesh and teeth are still on it." Harlan picked it up and extended his arm. "Wanna see?"

"Ew!" Rupert screwed his face up and backed away. "No, thanks."

Harlan chuckled and replaced the skull. "Sorry, Mr Chuckles, Rupert doesn't want to play."

The boys carefully studied the collection, not getting too close, and definitely not touching anything. Voodoo dolls with pins in them, mummified remains, small carved statues of ancient gods, and creatures adorned every surface, and while the three boys found it fascinating, they also found it macabre.

"Ugh." Gage shivered in the cool of the room. "It's weird in here. Let's go to another room."

"We can…" Harlan exchanged a glance with Levi. "How about the dining room?" He led the way across the hall into a room that was just as packed as the lounge room. "What about here?"

"Is *every* room full of stuff?" Rupert asked, frowning at the full-figured suit of armour in the corner next to the door. "Wear this a lot, does she?"

"Funny." Levi grinned. "No, Grandma loves collecting oddities and weird bits and pieces from around the world."

Suits of armour stood in each corner like sentinels guarding a treasure. The wall opposite the door had a fully lined buffet of knick-knacks, and decorations of teeth, tusks, and what looked to be eyeballs, hung between the two lights above the dining table.

"Wouldn't want them falling in your soup." Gage pointed them out. "Could be a cool party trick, though."

"It is on Halloween," Harlan replied. "You should see the place then." A knock on the door interrupted the conversation and he went to answer it. "Hello? Oh…" No one was there. "That's weird." He closed and locked the door and walked into the dining room. "No one there."

"Happen a lot, does it?" Zeb asked. "Knocking on doors and no one there." He was more than a little rattled being in that house.

"Could be neighbourhood kids." Harlan shrugged and put his hands in his pockets. "Let's go into the kitchen and grab a snack. Grandma always has great snacks for us."

Levi led the way into the kitchen and opened the fridge door. "Ooh, chocolate cake." He pulled the platter out and kicked the door shut with his foot. "She even iced a note on it. *For my boys.*" A grin spread ear to ear. "She knows how to feed us."

He set it on the kitchen island and grabbed a knife and forks from the drawer while Harlan collected five glasses and the jug of homemade lemonade from the fridge.

"That she does," he said.

They enjoyed slices of the decadent three-layered concoction, although Gage, Zeb and Rupert kept gazing at the paraphernalia in the room. Small mummified skulls sat in a line across the top of one set of cabinets, while one-foot high warrior figures lined the other. Tribal masks hung on walls, and there was even a black metal umbrella stand full of deadly looking swords.

Gage gulped down a mouthful of cake and followed it with a chaser of lemonade, his gaze never leaving the swords. "Come in handy, do they?"

Levi chuckled. "They do. Especially for cutting up food."

Gage's eyes darted from the swords to Levi. "Not funny."

"But it is." Levi's amused expression made his blue eyes twinkle. "Grandma collected this stuff long before we were born. Even before our mums were born. She took over from her dad who lived in India and helped out during the British handover in 1947. She inherited a lot of his stuff and added to it over the years. She likes unusual things."

"Haunted…things…?" Zeb's voice broke. "Are they um…?"

"No, *they're* not haunted, but I can see how you'd think that." Harlan nodded and heard a knock at the door. "I'll get that." He hurried down the hallway, where he unlocked and flung open the door to find no one there. "Again," he groaned. "That's the second time that's happened. Must be pranksters." After locking the door, he rushed back to the kitchen and told the others.

"They must know Grandma's out." Levi scraped

up the last of his second slice of cake and licked his fork clean. "They think they can prank us."

A knock sounded three times on the back door, startling the boys.

"And there you go." Levi nodded, and collected the plates and cutlery.

Harlan went to the back door off the hallway and peered out the small glass panel that sat at eye height. "No one's there."

"That you can see." Gage finished his lemonade and placed his glass on the sink. He looked out the window into the backyard and saw nothing but green grass and fruit trees.

The knock sounded again.

Harlan unlocked the back door and opened it about twelve inches, keeping his foot behind it so no one could push it open and surprise them. But he was surprised anyway, as no one was there. "Hello?" He stuck his head out through the gap and looked around. "Hello? Anyone there? Please stop knocking on the door if you're just going to run away. It's not funny and not helpful." Retracting his head, he closed and locked the door. "That's the third time that's happened," he said, walking into the kitchen. "It's either a prankster, or something's going on." Staring his cousin in the eyes, he wondered if there was more happening than just ghostly knocks on the doors.

"It can't be anything other than the neighbourhood kids, right?" Zeb asked. He'd had a sense of foreboding the moment he'd set foot in the house.

No offence to his friends' grandma, but there was a lot of weird stuff in that house.

"Don't know." Levi stepped in front of his cousin, not breaking eye contact. "Maybe Grandma should have warned us there was funny stuff going on."

There was a knock at the front door and their heads swivelled in that direction.

There was a knock at the back door and their heads swivelled back.

The knocking sounded on the front door, while the back door was still knocking, and both boys frowned.

"Get the front door and I'll get the back," Harlan told Levi. "Hurry, we'll open them at the same time." He reached for the handle and quickly unlocked the door while his cousin did the same thing with the front. He held up three fingers and counted down. On zero they opened the doors simultaneously and found no one. But the knocking did stop.

Puzzled, they glanced at each other, standing at opposite ends of the hall, with a door in hand, shaking their heads at the ridiculous situation. They closed and locked both doors before walking back to their friends who stood in the kitchen doorway.

"What's going on?" Zeb asked. "Is this place haunted, or what? Coz it's freaking me out." He crossed his arms over his chest, almost hugging himself. "This is getting creepy and you didn't tell us your grandma's house was like a freak show museum."

"Yeah," Gage agreed. "I'm freaked out a bit, too.

How long do we have to be here? And is there anything we can do to keep our minds off all of this?"

"There's the TV room," Levi suggested. "But that's not fun. Let's show you the rest of the house. There's better stuff upstairs where Grandma's turned all of the bedrooms into museums. Come on." He had started leading the way to the front landing stairs when a sound rattled against the basement door that was under the stairs. He stopped and stared down at it. "*Now* what's going on?"

"What is it?" Harlan came to his side. "Someone in the basement? What was it?"

"Sounded like something small fell…against it, or hit it," Levi answered and reached for the door.

"Do you *really* want to do that?" Rupert took a step back. "With all of the other freaky stuff in this house, and the knocking, do you *really* want to open that door?"

"It's only toys in the basement." Levi shook his head in amusement and opened the door. It swung open and Harlan flicked the light switch on the inside wall.

There was a doll lying on the second step down.

The cousins traded a glance with each other, puzzled as to how it got there, but not as to what usually happened in the house.

"She's new." Harlan gently picked her up under her armpits. "Hello, new doll, what are you doing all the way up here. Grandma would have put you on a shelf with all of the other dolls." He studied the blonde shoulder-length bob, and the updated clothes. "Definitely not an old doll. Clothes are new and current. So's the hair."

"You do know you're talking to a doll, right?" Gage snickered. "And you're holding it."

Harlan glanced over his shoulder to his friends. "*You* obviously don't know how to respect other people's belongings." His gaze turned to his cousin. They knew full well they had to treat these items with respect. Their grandmother had taught them well. She believed that these items more than likely held some residual effect of the previous owners who'd passed and would always treat such objects as dolls as if they were people. The boys were more alike than just in their five-eight, brown curly-haired, blue-eyed looks. At fifteen, they had been taught from birth to respect others' belongings. *And* the afterlife.

"Well, miss," Harlan said to the doll. "Let's get you back downstairs. I'm sure Grandma set a place for you to play with the other dolls." He carried her downstairs into the well-lit basement that had been turned into a toy room. Levi and the other boys followed, keeping an eye out for toys underfoot. "Well, look here. Looks like everyone's been having a party." He side-stepped teddy bears, dolls, toys of all vintages on the floor, and several tea party sets, to place the doll on a small chair. "I'm not sure *where* Grandma put you since so many toys are off their shelves, but I'll let her know you're all having a tea party and she can put you back."

The bright fluorescent light bounced off the white

roof. Floor-to-ceiling shelving units lined three walls and children's tables and chairs sat filled with dolls and bears. "We'll let you guys get back to your party. Boys, come along." He led the way upstairs and waited until they filed out one by one before he shut and locked the door. "Come and see the upstairs rooms. You'll get a kick out of one of them."

When they reached the bottom of the stairs and started heading up, they heard a thump against the basement door.

"Oh…you *are* kidding," Harlan muttered and looked at his cousin. "She can't be?" He stepped down and looked along the hall to the basement door and saw it shudder slightly as another thump happened.

"Persistent little thing, isn't she." Levi walked around him to stare down the hallway. "Guess she wants to play."

Exchanging a curious glance with his cousin, Harlan approached the basement door, unlocked it, and swung it open to reveal the same doll lying on the second step. With a little trepidation, Harlan picked her up as he had before and carefully carried her downstairs. "Now, you know Grandma's not going to be happy about this. I'm sure she wanted you to stay down here and play with the other dolls." As he crossed the floor towards the chair he'd left her in the first time, he felt a warmth radiate from her torso and he nearly dropped her into the chair. "Ah, you are a little firecracker, aren't you. Please stay down here this time. You have everyone to play with, and I'm sure Grandma doesn't want anyone getting out in case they get hurt. She'll be back later to see you all."

He observed the rest of the toys as he turned and walked towards the stairs, but a rustling behind him pricked up his ears and made the hairs on the back of his neck stand on end. He kept walking, but he turned his head and looked over his shoulder. He didn't see anything different. But he felt it.

"Hey!" He stopped, his arms flying out to steady himself, and he stared down at his right calf. There was the doll, attached to his right leg, her arms and legs wrapped around it. And…she was biting him. "Oi, you little!" Having *never* experienced something so ridiculously evil, or hilarious, such as this before, he didn't know whether to laugh or freak out. He wrestled with it, hopping on his left leg while trying to get the doll off his right leg.

"Hey! Stop that." He managed to pull both of its arms off only for the doll to bite him again. Not wanting to violate his grandmother's rules, but not knowing what else to do, he karate chopped the back of its neck and stunned it into releasing him. Holding her up, he saw its eyes fire up red. "Uh-oh." He drop-kicked her to the other side of the basement and bolted up the stairs, slamming the door behind him. He locked it just in time as the doll pounded against it, making it tremble.

"What the hell?" Levi saw his cousin's whiter than white face and glassy eyes. "Is that thing possessed, or what?"

"Oh, it's possessed all right," Harlan panted. "Its body heated up, then it grabbed onto my leg and bit me." He pulled up his right jean leg and saw red marks on his skin. "And when I got it off, its eyes turned red, so I kicked it across the room and raced up here."

The door thudded and he quickly moved away. "It's possessed all right."

"I wonder if Grandma knows it." Levi jumped and stared in horror at the small frosted glass window in the door.

The doll's hands were flat against the glass, her face pressed into it before she slid down to the step below.

"What the hell was that?" Gage's high pitched voice squeaked out. "We need to get out of here. This shit's freaky."

"We can't leave until Grandma gets home," Levi reminded him.

"She's *your* grandma, *not ours.*" Zeb violently shook his head back and forth. "We can leave. You can stay."

Harlan called out loudly, "I don't know your name, but Grandma's going to be very angry at you when she gets home. She doesn't mind you having parties in the basement, but attacking people is a no-no." He waited in the silence, the others staring at him, knowing the doll was contemplating its next move.

Until it moved.

She threw herself against the glass. "I just want you to play with me," she said.

The boys jumped back, hearts pounding, blood racing.

"Which is fine, but your behaviour is not appropriate, and Grandma won't tolerate it." Harlan checked his watch for the time. His grandmother wasn't due home for another half hour.

"I just want you to play with me." The doll smashed through the glass, and after a moment of getting caught on the broken piece, tumbled to the floor.

The boys jumped back in shock, staring at the doll who carefully righted itself onto its feet.

"I just want you to play with me." Its eyes glowed red and it raised an arm. A shard of glass was clenched in its fist.

"What the bloody hell!" Zeb screeched and turned on his heels, racing for the front door. Rupert and Gage followed close behind.

"Don't open the door," Levi yelled, racing after them. "Get upstairs and lock yourselves in Grandma's room. It's protected." He grabbed his friends by the arms and swung them around towards the stairs. "It's the only room overlooking the street. Go, and lock the door." He watched his friends race up the stairs while also seeing the doll racing down the hallway.

"Levi, shut the lounge room, so she can't hide in there. We'll head her off back this way."

Levi slammed the lounge door shut and grabbed an umbrella from the rack beside the front door. It was the only weapon he had.

A chilling laugh came from the doll, and her face screwed up into a sneer as she grabbed hold of a banister leg and swung around and up the stairs. She ran up to the landing.

"Hey!" Levi followed, determined to get her away from his friends and back downstairs. He found the doll trying to break into his grandmother's room. "Oh, no you don't. Harlan, get ready." He grabbed the doll with both hands and dumped her over the banister down to the ground floor where Harlan kicked her down the hall.

"Get down here and keep an eye out. I'll shut the doors," he yelled to his cousin and ran through the dining room, shutting the door behind him. Into the breakfast nook and into the kitchen, he ran, closing all the doors behind him. He skidded to a halt in front of the doll. "Aye, aye, aye."

The doll had managed to pick up one of the swords from the umbrella stand and was holding it above her head. But considering the height to weight ratio, the sword made the doll unsteady on her feet.

Harlan used that to his advantage, and when she swayed, he grabbed the sword and swatted her into the hallway, quickly following and pinning her down with the tip of the sword. "Shut the door behind me," he told Levi, and he heard a car pull into the driveway. "Oh, you're so gonna get it now," he muttered to the doll.

The doll's eyes glowed red and she struggled with the blade to free herself.

They waited until their grandmother was inside

and the door safely locked behind her.

"What on earth…" she muttered, seeing the broken basement window, the doll struggling with the sword, and her red-faced, panting grandsons. "What happened?"

They told her and she shook her head in disappointment.

"Elizabeth Blakefield, what did I tell you when I brought you into this house? If you misbehaved you'd get a warning." She pulled the cross on a chain from under her top and held it out to the doll as she picked it up. The doll became subdued as she examined it. "But, instead, you decide to break out and cause damage."

"I just wanted them to play with me," Elizabeth said.

"Biting my leg, chasing us around the house, and trying to kill us is not playing," Harlan told it.

"No, it isn't. And so you must be punished, Elizabeth. Open the basement door for me boys."

Waiting until they cleared her way, she descended the stairs to chaos. "I see you all decided to misbehave. You all know what's going to happen." She walked around to the small door on the wall under the stairs, and holding the doll against her chest, she unlocked and opened the door to reveal a large lockable metal box. She lifted the lid and removed the wire mesh that attached halfway down. "You'll have to stay here for forty-eight hours. I warned you when I brought you home. I told you if you misbehaved you'd get one warning. But in this case, you chose to hurt my grandsons and that means you go straight into the box." She laid the doll inside, and set the mesh in place.

"But I just wanted them to play with me," the doll cried, tears running from its eyes.

"That may be so, Elizabeth. But you have plenty of friends here to play with, and hurting people is a no-no, so now you will do your punishment. Forty-eight hours in the box." She closed and locked the box lid and then closed and locked the door. Turning, she saw the toys in a semi-circle in front of her. "Oh, don't you lot start. You were all warned when you came here. So unless you want to spend time in the box with Elizabeth, go back to playing nicely."

The toys didn't move. They just sat or stood there staring up at her.

"Go, *now*." She waved them on and ascended the stairs. Once the door was locked, and the window boarded over, she stopped to check on the boys. "You two okay?"

"What the hell was that?" Harlan rubbed his calf. "To say it has bite is an understatement."

"It's the spirit of a young girl who wasn't meant to be. Her mother was having her and her sister, but she died in utero and her fetus attached itself to her sister who started having mental disturbances when she was fifteen. They found the twin's fetus and removed it, but the young girl, Jessica, was very disturbed for some time. They believed she was talking to her twin on a daily basis, and after some disturbing things happened, they sought help for

Jessica, but it didn't work. After a year of treatment, they spoke to a priest who spoke to me, and we devised an exorcism for the dead twin. We managed to move her spirit into a doll, and now I have her to deal with." She cupped their faces. "I'm so sorry you had to deal with that. We only did it last week, so she's still settling in."

"Weird question," Levi held up his forefinger. "Does the doll ask for her sister?"

"She has done, so far, but that will fade. That's why all of the toys are downstairs, so they have each other. Now, have you boys eaten your cake and had some lemonade yet?"

"Yeah, yeah, we have," Harlan murmured. "Grandma, what happened to the other girl?" At fifteen he couldn't imagine going through what the poor girl had suffered.

"As far as I know, the young lady is fine, so far, physically she's well, but it will take some time for her to heal mentally. But from what happened after the exorcism, I'd say she'll be fine. Now…" She clasped her hands. "Did you bring your friends with you and what do they think of my house?"

ABOUT THE AUTHOR

T.K. is a children's TV show veteran who loves watching disaster and creature/zombie movies and TV shows, but not at night.

T.K. started writing many a year ago back in primary school, but only started her author career in 2015 with the release of her first three stories and anthology. She will write and release stories until there are twelve *Bones* books and a special edition numbered 13...

T.K. lives in Australia, loves extra cheesy cheeseburgers and chocolate, and gets a kick out of watching funny dog and cat videos.

T.K. Wrathbone is the kid's/tween pen name for author Tiara King. You can find more about Tiara on her website; follow her on social media, or visit her publishing house, Royal Star Publishing.

SOCIALS

tkwrathbone.com

tiaraking.com.au

royalstarpublishing.com.au

Sign up for *Tiara's* Newsletter…

Make sure you're always in the know and never miss free exclusives, the latest news, book updates, and so much more with newsletters from…

tiaraking.com.au

HAVE YOU READ THESE?

Next Top Mannequin
Cinderfella and Princess Charming: Witch Hunters
www.badluck-youredead.com
The Bones of Wrath: Changes
One Bone: Anthology 1

The Orphanage
Hantel and Gresel: Food Critics
Mirror, Mirror On The Wall
The Bones of Wrath: Haunted
Two Bone: Anthology 2

The Howler
Shadow Walkers
Faded
The Bones of Wrath: Ghosts
Three Bone: Anthology 3

I Spy With My Little Eye
Knock, Knock…Who's Dead?
It Creeped At Midnight
The Bones of Wrath: Monsters
Four: Anthology 4

Trick Or Treat
All Hallows Possession
They Rise On A Blood Moon
The Bones of Wrath: Horrors
Five Bone: Anthology 5

All Clowns Must Die!
The Demon Resides
Infestation
The Bones of Wrath: Terrors
Six Bone: Anthology 6

www.ingramcontent.com/pod-product-compliance
Lightning Source LLC
Chambersburg PA
CBHW060737190726
48285CB00001B/252